John Beveridge Gladwyn Jebb

A Strange Career

Life and Adventures of John Gladwyn Jebb

John Beveridge Gladwyn Jebb

A Strange Career
Life and Adventures of John Gladwyn Jebb

ISBN/EAN: 9783337073879

Printed in Europe, USA, Canada, Australia, Japan

Cover: Foto ©Raphael Reischuk / pixelio.de

More available books at **www.hansebooks.com**

A Strange Career

LIFE AND ADVENTURES

OF

JOHN GLADWYN JEBB

BY HIS WIDOW

WITH

AN INTRODUCTION BY H. RIDER HAGGARD

With Portrait

BOSTON
ROBERTS BROTHERS
1895

THE compiler of this history wishes to state that its production has been materially aided by several sketches of the more striking among his adventures, which from time to time were set down by Mr. Jebb himself.

The story which he contributed to ‘Blackwood’s Magazine’ for January 1872, entitled “The Haunted Enghenio,” has been here reproduced in the slightly altered form in which it actually occurred.

CONTENTS.

CHAPTER IV.

COFFEE-PLANTING IN BRAZIL.

CHAPTER V.

IN THE FAR WEST.

CHAPTER VI.

AN ADVENTURE ON THE PLAINS.

CHAPTER VII.

SPORT IN COLORADO.

CHAPTER VIII.

FURTHER PURSUIT OF GOLD.

CHAPTER IX.

THE ROCKY MOUNTAINS DURING WINTER.

CHAPTER X.

AFFAIRS AT DENVER.

CHAPTER XI.

LAST EFFORTS AS A PIONEER.

CHAPTER XII.

THE LAND OF MONTEZUMA.

CHAPTER XIII.

A BRUSH WITH BANDITTI.

CHAPTER XIV.

MEXICAN HISTORY AND LEGEND.

INTRODUCTION.

It is a matter of common experience that among the many acquaintances we make from year to year, we chance now and again to find one whose personality has for us a singular attraction. Such was the fortune of the writer of this preface in the instance of his late friend John Gladwyn Jebb.

I think it was in the year 1889 that I was introduced to Mr Jebb, one night at a London dinner-party, and I remember being impressed at first sight by his powerful build, his kindly face, and the peculiar gentleness of his brown eyes. Before the evening was over I found in him a person different from the generality of men — a man rich in a rare quaintness and originality of mind, and withal one of the most agreeable and interesting companions whom I had met for many a day.

At that time Mr Jebb was at home on a visit from Mexico, where he was engaged in business affairs, and it was of Mexico that he talked — its history, its legends, and many strange adventures which had befallen him there. This meeting led to others, and resulted at length in an invitation, that I accepted, to visit Mr Jebb in Mexico, when we proposed to explore some of the ruined cities in the Palenque district, and also to make an attempt to recover Montezuma's, or rather Guatemoc's, treasure, whereof the story is told in these pages. To the hiding-place of this hoard he had a key — now, as I believe, lost for ever.

Accordingly, at the beginning of the year 1891 I journeyed to Mexico, where I was warmly welcomed by Mr Jebb, and from that time I date my intimate acquaintance with him. All the things which we were to have done together we did not do, seeing that we were stayed by a sudden and terrible domestic calamity, whereof it is needless to write. Therefore it was that the ruined cities for which we were about to start remained unvisited and Guatemoc's treasure unsought.

Still, we made several expeditions together, and among them a month's trip into the interior of the State of Chiapas — on the whole the roughest piece of journeying that has come within my experience in any part of the world.

It was as a travelling companion that Mr. Jebb showed at his very best ; for not until discomfort and even danger had been endured in his company, was it possible to measure his complete, his collossal unselfishness. When the nerves are shattered by sorrow and anxiety, and the body is worn out with petty vexations and weariness ; when the stomach turns at the nastiness that in the wilder parts of Mexico passes for food, and every square inch of skin is smarting from the stings of insect pests,— then it is, perhaps unconsciously, that the most patient and considerate of us are apt to revert to the primitive principle of "every man for himself."

Not so Mr Jebb, however. If there were not enough hammocks, or a lack of room to swing them in the shed, it was he who insisted upon sleeping outside in the rain and on the ground; if there was a choice of places in the coach, it was he who sped to secure the worst one, and so forth.

Indeed he carried this principle to extremes, as the following story will show.

Among our baggage on the occasion of this journey into the depths of Chiapas was a mule-load of silver — some 3000 dollars of it, which we were conveying to the Santa Fé mine. One night we reached a certain inland town, and were hospitably entertained in one of the larg-est houses; still, as such a thing as robbery, highway and wholesale, has been heard of in the more remote districts of Mexico, Mr Jebb thought it safer to take to his bedroom the bullion which we were known to have in our charge. Now, as he learned afterwards from native sources, the possibility of possessing themselves of so much cash proved too much for the feeble honesty of sundry of the inhabitants of this town, who entered into an agreement to steal the dollars that night, and should we interfere in the matter, incidentally to cut our throats.

About midnight these worthies began to attempt the execution of their plan. As it chanced, Mr Jebb and myself occupied different sleeping-places, separated by the length of a large eating-room. The house stood upon the edge of a very steep slope, at the foot of which ran a river, and immediately beneath the rickety and latchless French windows of Mr Jebb's room rose a supporting wall built of loose stones.

In the middle of the night I was awakened two or three times by the furious barking of some curs belonging to the establishment as they rushed through the gardens on the slope; but the noise ceasing after a while, having ascertained that my revolver was at hand, I went to sleep again, thinking no more of the matter.

In the morning Mr Jebb, who had risen early to make inquiry and investigations, asked me if I had been disturbed in the night. Then he told me this story. It seems that he had some suspicion that an attempt would be made to steal the silver, and therefore he slept very lightly. In due course the barking of the dogs roused him, and he crept from his bed to the French windows, which it was impossible to secure, and listened. Hearing the robbers whispering below at the foot of the wall, he retreated to the bed again and seated himself on the edge of it, holding a wax match in one hand and .his long-barrelled Colt cocked in the other.

This was his plan: to wait till he heard the thieves push open the French windows, then to strike the match (for the night was pitch-dark), and by its light to fire at them over it before they could attack him.

For a long while he sat thus, and twice he heard the loose stones dropping as his assailants began to climb up the wall beneath the window; but on each occasion they were frightened by the clamour of the dogs, which at length grew so loud that, thinking our Indian servants, who slept at a distance from the house, would be aroused, the thieves took to flight without the dollars, leaving nothing but some footprints behind them.

"And why did you not come and wake me?" I asked, when he had finished his tale.

"Oh," he answered, "I nearly did so, but I knew that you were very tired; also there was no use in both of us handing in our checks, for there were a dozen of those devils, and had they got into the room, for their own sakes they would have made a clean sweep of us."

I did not make any reply; but I remember thinking, and I still think, that this conduct showed great courage and great unselfishness on the part of Mr Jebb. Most people would have retreated at the first alarm; but this, with the utter fearlessness which was one of his characteristics, he did not do, since the dollars in his charge were too heavy to carry; and before men could be found to assist him, they would have been secured by the robbers, who knew well where to look for them. In the rare event, however, of the supply of personal pluck proving equal to such an occasion, how many of us, for the reasons given, having a well-armed white companion at hand, would have neglected to summon him to take his part in the fray? A man must be very brave and very unselfish indeed to choose to face a band of Mexican cut-throats alone when a word would bring a comrade to his side.

I have told the story of this particular little adventure at length, although it is trivial compared to many others which are to be read of in this book, because I happen to be personally acquainted with the details, which serve to illustrate one side of my late friend's character.

Into Mr Jebb's history I do not propose to enter, for it is set out hereafter by his biographer. Rarely if ever in this nineteenth century has a man lived so strange and varied an existence. "Adventures are to the adventurous," the saying tells us, and certainly they were to Mr Jebb. From the time that he came to manhood he was a wanderer; and how it chanced that he survived the many perils of his daily life is nothing less than a mystery. In the end, however, they brought his fate upon him prematurely; for the diseases of which he died resulted from neglected illnesses and continual exposure that would have sufficed again and again to kill any one of a less perfect constitution.

When I returned to England in 1891 he came also, and for a while took up his abode in London. Soon, however, his old restlessness and his love of sunshine got the better of him, and he journeyed back to Mexico armed with an invention for extracting metals from refractory ores by a new process which, he was convinced, would bring in thousands. As might be expected, it did nothing of the sort; indeed it broke down utterly when put to the proof, and Mr Jebb's health with it. For the last of many times, a mere wreck of his former self, he crossed the Atlantic homewards, to die in London, after much suffering most patiently endured, on the 18th March 1893.

On next page is reproduced a fragment of a letter which he wrote to me, dated shortly before his death. I believe that these are the very last words he was able to pen, and it will be seen that his strength failed him before he could complete them.

It only remains for me, if I may venture to do so, to say a few words as to Mr Jebb's character, which in many ways strikes me as one of the most attractive that ever came under my observation.

24 Redcliffe Square
March. 2. 91

My dear Haggard.

I may make another rally but I confess my own view nothing is the other way — as apart from the regular illness I am getting day by day awfully weak — so much so that I can't dress without help and can hardly keep out of bed longer than from 11 till 4 or something of that kind.

Of all friends he was the gentlest and truest; of all men the most trustful. Indeed it was this childlike guilelessness that ruined him, for throughout his life he was the prey of his own sanguine temperament. He worked hard for many years, worked as few men work, and yet I believe I am right in saying that he never once got the best of a bargain, or had to do with an enterprise which proved successful — at any rate, so far as his own interests were concerned.

It is not wonderful, therefore, beginning life as a rich man, that he ended it as a poor one. Yet so perfectly upright was his nature, that never did the slightest blame or suspicion attach to him among so many failures; and every time that he discovered afresh the imperfections of commercial humanity, it seemed to come upon him as a surprise.

In the city of Mexico, where business men are — business men, he was respected universally, and by the Indians he was adored. "He is a good man, Jebb," said an honourable old Jewish trader of that city to me, — "a man among a thousand, whom I would trust anywhere. See, I will prove it to you, *Amigo ;* he has lived in this town doing business for years, yet, with all his opportunities, he leaves it *poorer than he came here.* Did you ever hear the like of that, *Amigo ?"*

And so it came about that John Gladwyn Jebb left both Mexico and this land, where we have "no abiding city," almost as naked of the world's goods as when he entered it. He was not suited to the life that fell to his lot, at least not to the commercial side of it, for an adventurer — using the term in its best sense — he must always have been.   He was too sanguine, too romantic, too easily deluded by others, and too mystical — a curious vein of mysticism was one of his most striking characteristics — for this nineteenth century.   As a crusader, or as a knight-errant, doubtless he would have been a brilliant success, but as a manager of companies and a director of business matters it must be confessed that he was a failure.

Would that there existed more of such noble failures — the ignoble are sufficiently abundant — for then the world might be cleaner than it is.   It matters little now: his day is done, and he has journeyed to that wonderful Hereafter of which during life he had so clear a vision, and that was so often the subject of his delightful and suggestive talk.   But his record remains, the record of a brave and generous man who, as I firmly believe, never did, never even contemplated, a mean or a doubtful act.

To those who knew him and have lost sight of him there remain also a bright and chivalrous example and the memory of a most perfect gentleman.

H. RIDER HAGGARD.

Ditchingham, *21st August,* 1894.

A STRANGE CAREER.

CHAPTER I.

BOYHOOD, AND ENTRANCE INTO THE ARMY.

JACK JEBB'S PARENTAGE — EARLY LIFE AT WALTON — EDUCA-
TION AT BONN AND AT CHESTERFIELD — HOLIDAYS AT FIR-
BECK — HIS DARING AND LOVE OF MISCHIEF — AT SCHOOL
AT CHELTENHAM — FAVOURITE STUDIES — AN ADVENTURE
AT LECKHAMPTON — SENT TO AN ARMY COACH — ENTERS
WOOLWICH — GAZETTED TO THE 88TH REGIMENT — HIS
MOTHER'S DEATH — HAS A PREMONITION OF THE EVENT —
THE LAST TIE GONE — SAILS TO JOIN HIS REGIMENT IN
INDIA.

IN telling the life story of a real or a fictitious
personage, it is usual to start at the beginning
and plod on more or less steadily, until at the
last " Finis " can be added to the adventures or
the days of the hero. But there are times when
the chronicler feels that it would be easier to
begin at the end — when the character has attained to all that it ever will of good and of
evil, and when we can see by what strange
chances and weary paths it came to its maturity.

As this book is intended, however, to be a sketch of many adventures in distant lands rather than of the manly and loyal nature of him who underwent them, it shall follow the orthodox course.

There are many disadvantages about being an only child; and if there are any corresponding benefits to be derived from that fact, the subject of this memoir, John Beveridge Gladwyn Jebb, never profited by them. Born in 1841, when both his parents had passed their first youth, he was naturally regarded by them as a sort of Koh-i-noor, a roc's egg, or something equally rare and priceless. They agreed in doing their best to spoil him; but unfortunately they held diametrically opposite views as to the best way of performing the operation.

There is no need to go further back in the annals of the Jebb family history than to the time of John's grandfather, himself an only son, who at one time possessed considerable property both in England and in the West Indies, but who, through various mischances, died a comparatively poor man. The small estate of Walton, Derbyshire, was entailed on his eldest son, Sir Joshua Jebb, K.C.B., Director-General of Prisons, who, not wishing to live there, sold it to his third brother, the Rev. John Beveridge Jebb, who, since his marriage in 1839 with Charlotte, eldest daughter of Mr Richard Dann of Watermouth, Devon, had lived at Walton with his father until the death of the latter in 1845. The Rev. J. B. Jebb, who held the living of Walton together with that of Brampton, Chesterfield, was a person decidedly above the average in ability. The same may be said of his wife. Moreover, the couple had this in common, that they both held strong and settled opinions on life, religion, and other leading questions.

For the first few years of marriage they were strongly attached to each other, though there arose between them the usual amount of occasional " jars "; but unfortunately the " jars " multiplied and the affection diminished as time went by. It was a case of misunderstanding; for there was no deep root of bitterness in either. The fortune was chiefly on the side of Mrs Jebb, who had given her husband absolute power over it, and he was not sufficiently mindful of the generosity she had shown. This circumstance is only touched upon because of its effect upon the training and character of the son.

The one thing in which there was perfect accord between husband and wife was their intense love for the lad, who very early showed signs of a strong and original character. Cousins much older than himself, who remember " Jack " (as from boyhood he insisted on being called) in the arms of his tall, gaunt, faithful nurse, talk of his dark eyes, even then intent and searching. At that early age they say his powers of observation were remarkable, and that he would ask questions and make remarks with an intelligence beyond his years. They tell a story of his escaping from the faithful one into the farmyard, when he was two years old, and being shortly discovered holding on with both hands to the throat of a half-strangled gander which had flown at him. As he had no companions, it was fortunate for him that he was not at all a gregarious child; indeed, from the time he could run alone, his chief joy was to get away from every one, and hiding in the woods, to play at being a solitary Red Indian by his camp fire.

In 1850, at the early age of nine, he was sent to a private school at Bonn, where he picked up the German language and the noble art of fisticuffs at one and the same time. He had the misfortune to be the youngest pupil in the school, and therefore never got a boy of his own size to fight; but probably that was good training, for before he left he could " lick " half the school. Everything had to be fought for, and the weakest, as usual, went to the wall ; so for the first few months poor little Jack Jebb had a very rough time. All letters were read by the master before being sent, so he could not complain to those at home of the insufficient food and bed-clothing, which the tenderly-cared-for boy suffered from greatly. The school had been highly recommended to his parents, who believed they were doing the best thing possible for their son, while they travelled about the Continent for the benefit of his father's health, which was never good.

However, in spite of occasional hunger and continuous black eyes, Jack fought his way to the top of the school and to the mature age of eleven, when he was taken home and delivered over to a clergyman at Chesterfield — a clever man and a very good fellow — for the continuance of his education. He was glad enough of the change, for in time fighting will pall even upon a boy if he only gets enough of it, and that had been the one thing of which there was a plentiful supply at the German school.

Moreover, he now spent a good part of his holidays with his aunt, Mrs Miles, a wealthy widow, then living at Clifton, but who shortly afterwards bought a lovely old place in Yorkshire, where the harum-scarum boy was allowed to run as wild as he liked. Usually there were a dozen or more young cousins all stopping there together. Their ages ranged from twelve to eighteen, and they were ripe for any sort of mischief into which Jack — generally the ruling spirit — would lead them. Those who were not admitted to late dinner used to hang about the dining-room door, coaxing the old butler out of such dishes as looked tempting and he could be induced to give to them. They also coaxed him out of a good deal of "language" once. It happened this way. A large dinner-party was to take place — a typical county solemnity — and the old butler, of course, felt himself to be the pivot on which everything turned; so until about five minutes before the first arrival was expected, he fussed and fidgeted, ordered and reproved, in the dining-room, and then betook himself to his bedroom for a last review of his own irreproachable appearance. No sooner was he inside the room than the key was turned in the lock by his natural enemies, the "young gentlemen," who adjured him (through the keyhole) to keep calm! But when he heard the first carriage drive up the strength

of his feelings became too much for his respect-
ability, and his language was " frequent and pain-
ful and free." They kept him there until he
began to show signs of being about to break
down the door, with some of the family plate as a
battering-ram, when they hastily unlocked it and
fled. He had not time to settle matters with his
persecutors then, but he got even eventually by
means of some peculiarly cheap and nasty sherry,
which he ever afterwards declared was the only
wine he was allowed to give them! Another
delight in Jack's frequent visits to Firbeck was
the capital hunting to be got with Lord Galway's
pack; and probably some of the happiest moments of his life were when, " well up " on his
little brown mare, there was a good scent, and he
could follow the hounds over fences and ditches
through some of the loveliest country to be found
in England. When at home at Walton his life
was much quieter and duller, which may account
for the fact that, with all his hardihood and sense
of humour, there was throughout his career an
under-current of melancholy and fatalism.

At about fourteen he was thought to be ready
for a public school, and after a few months on the
Continent with, his father and tutor, he was sent
to Cheltenham. His own desire, like that of most

boys at some period of their lives, was to go to sea. With Jack Jebb the wish was no light o' love, but the passion of his life; and long years afterwards, whether lying on a moonlit deck half the night listening to the swish of the waves and watching the tropical stars, or helping to throw cargo overboard to lighten a labouring ship in an angry sea, he had the misery of feeling that here was his vocation and he had missed it! At Cheltenham he distinguished himself chiefly by his drawing and painting, which were so much above the average that it was said of him later by an authority on the subject, that if he did not make his fortune on the operatic stage by means of his beautiful voice, he ought to make it as an artist.

I regret to say that while at Cheltenham he was also distinguished for being the head and front of any mischief that might be on foot, as when once he went off to Leckhampton with a couple more boys, for the purpose of pistol-practice, well knowing that the owner of Leckhampton Hill strongly objected to his lands being made the happy hunting-ground of a lot of schoolboys, and that he had ordered his workmen to capture and consign to the authorities any college youth who might be found upon them. Of course this gave a charm to the proceedings, and the lads shot gaily all one afternoon, smoking the while — they didn't like it, but thought it the thing to do — and never noticed that they were being "stalked" by a party of workmen, who had divided themselves into groups and were surrounding the boys on three sides of the hill, the fourth being occupied by a stone quarry, almost impassable, and therefore considered safe. When the boys first caught sight of the men, they were not more than 200 yards off, and there was very little time left for reflection. "I have it," said Jack. "Let us divide and fire the gorse in a line. The wind is blowing away from the quarry and towards the men. They won't be able to follow us through the smoke, and we must scramble down the quarry somehow." This brilliant idea was acted upon, and they got out of the quarry in safety, dodging a gamekeeper by the way, and lighting a fire along the foot of the hill, which effectually kept the pursuers in check for an hour — long enough for the incendiaries to walk calmly home, glowing with the consciousness of a well-spent afternoon.

Tricks of this sort at school, and similar proceedings at home, soon gave Jack the reputation of being about as reckless and unmanageable as even a schoolboy could be. Therefore, when on his sixteenth birthday his father invited a party of friends and relations, and semi-publicly presented him with a gun, saying in the course of his speech that his son had never caused him a moment's anxiety in his life, a subdued titter ran through the audience, who knew well that there were very few moments of the reverend speaker's existence which were *un*troubled by anxiety as to what his young scapegrace might be doing next! However, when Jack left Cheltenham, he did so with the assurance of his house-master that he was a " noble and truthful boy "; and well knowing that to be the fact, his parents could afford to forgive him a few " mistakes of youth."

After leaving Cheltenham he was sent to an army coach at Putney, to be crammed for Woolwich, in spite of his decided preference for the sister service. As may be imagined, a healthy active boy, with a hatred of town life and no love for his future profession, did not take very kindly to the coach and his methods, especially as the latter were very autocratic. But a little incident soon occurred which had the effect of causing the tutor to relax his rules considerably. At that time Cremorne was in full swing, and Leotard was drawing crowds nightly. Of course the half-dozen lads engaged in cramming at Putney were wild to see him, though they had little hope of obtaining leave to do so. However, there was no harm in trying; so one day, with young Jebb as spokesman, they went in a body to their master and begged for the embargo to be taken off Cremorne, if only for one night. They were met by a stern refusal, and the assurance that the master himself would not dream of visiting such a sink of iniquity.

Having been refused leave, naturally their next idea was how to get there without it; and they adopted the simple and obvious plan, to a boy, of climbing out of a bedroom window, sliding down the drain-pipe, and trusting to a rope and each other's shoulders for getting back again. This was all very well as far as it went; but a *contre-temps* they had not counted on was that, just inside the gates of Cremorne, they almost ran into the arms of their tutor himself! But Providence was kind to them even at that awful moment, for before they could begin to stammer out excuses the coach said hurriedly, " You had better not mention to my wife that we met here, as she does not approve of Cremorne, and I only came to see Leotard."

" That's all we came for, sir," replied the boys,

departing promptly before their master recovered sufficient presence of mind to send them home.

Whether the memory of his previous diatribe or the fear of his better-half lay heaviest on his soul I don't know, but the boys never heard another word of their adventure. They loyally held their peace to the lady, and her lord made their yoke a little lighter.

After about a year of fortifications, mathematics, and similar joys at Putney, Jack went to Woolwich. When the examinations came off, he passed well in most subjects, but was plucked for mixed mathematics, and had gone home to perfect himself in this science, when he received a notice from the War Office informing him that, as he was proficient in the other branches, and had only failed in one, he might be gazetted at once for service in India, if he chose.

At that time so many officers had been killed and wounded in the terrible retribution which followed the Mutiny, that the War Office decided on sending out all cadets who had gained a certain number of marks. Jack Jebb caught eagerly at the chance. With his adventurous roving spirit, the one thing which could content him with the profession he had been obliged to adopt was the hope of active service. He was gazetted to the 88th Regiment, then under orders to sail almost immediately; and but for the anxiety which his mother's health was causing, he would have been very glad to start.

Mrs Jebb had been ailing for some time, and had been moved to London in order to be within reach of the best advice. The natures of father and son were too diametrically opposed for them to find much in common with each other as the lad grew to manhood, but between his mother and himself there always existed the strongest sympathy and devotion, so that they both felt that when the parting came it would be very bitter. But it was not to be as they expected. Shortly before sailing Jack was dining with some cousins, when in the middle of dinner he started up suddenly from the table with a white face, saying, " My mother is dying ! " Of course his cousins tried to persuade him that if his mother were worse he would certainly have heard of it; but he persisted that he was right, and with a heavy heart started home immediately, only to be met on the threshold with the news of Mrs Jebb's death. She had been seized quite suddenly, and had died with her eyes fixed in a long last look on that portrait of her only son, which stood always by her bedside. In what strange fashion her latest thought and yearning had communicated itself to him, who shall say ?   If it be true that a man's last thought and cry, when his life is going out, is for her who cared for his earliest years, how much more likely is it that the supreme enduring mother-love should be able to conquer space and circumstance that it may take farewell of its beloved !

Jack's grief was silent and deep.   He felt that now he had little to regret in leaving the empty home; and when the time came for him to sail to join his regiment, he probably left fewer living memories behind than most of those with whom he voyaged to distant lands.

CHAPTER II.

INDIAN SERVICE.

IN those days a voyage *was* a voyage, and took
time. Thirty years ago people were not so much
given to " running across " a few thousand miles
of land and ocean on the smallest possible excuse. They did their travelling slowly and with
much forethought, and if any of them suffered
from the restlessness of this generation, they
usually concealed it in a shamefaced way, as
they might have hidden a tendency to shirk
afternoon church in the dog-days. There is no
need to describe the journey to India, because
most people have taken it, and know all about
the heat and the gossip, the cliques and the flir-

tations, on every P. and O. that sails the seas. Sometimes those same flirtations end in love and a cottage for two, but more often the result is unpleasantness for somebody.

There was once a girl who was going out to be married, and who confided to about ten people (by moonlight) that she adored the man she was engaged to. Unfortunately for him, her adoration was unable to stand the test of a shadowy deck-corner in the tropics, and the insidious advances of the ship's doctor, who appeared to consider that the most important of his duties was to make· love to the prettiest girl aboard, and who had a nice little wife at home who understood his weaknesses and did not mind them in the least. Well, this particular girl, not understanding the rules of the game, took it all in dead earnest, and when land and her *fiancé* appeared, his entreaties and arguments notwithstanding, she refused to quit the ship without the doctor, who meanwhile had fled to his cabin, from which sanctuary he refused to emerge until his would-be abductress had gone. Eventually the girl was taken below and matters were explained to her by several matrons (assisted by a damp towel), so that she finally consented to be led away by the unhappy being who was to

have charge of her affections for the rest of his
life.   One wonders how they settled it, and
whether in their matrimonial bickerings the
mention of that voyage ever failed to reduce
her to a pulpy silence!

On the ship which was bearing Jack Jebb to his
new duties only one incident occurred to break the
monotony of the voyage. There was a pretty but
rather " loud " looking woman on board, who gave
herself out to be the wife of a high official " up
country." Several passengers knew of the man,
but had never heard that he had a wife; and this
fact, together with her manner and appearance,
surrounded her with a slight air of mystery,
though, as she was decidedly amusing, no one
hesitated about making acquaintance with her,
until a curious event brought about a change.
Late one evening conversation in the reading-
room turned on mesmerism, and Mrs B. remarked that she made a capital subject, although
she had no power over other people. Whereupon
Jack, knowing a little of the art, and being greatly
interested in it, offered to try to send her into a
trance. The lady was quite willing to be experimented upon, and a group of spectators gathered
round to watch the " passes," which soon had the
effect of sending her into a deep sleep.

Directly she became unconscious she began to talk, and it was soon evident that she was embarking on a narrative of her past history, which seemed to have been varied, to say the least of it ! " We must wake her before she goes any further," said Jack; but this was not easy, for nothing that any of them could do had the slightest effect upon her, and her even, monotonous voice went on ceaselessly. And the tale that she told was such, that first the chaperons sent their young people off to bed, and next they themselves fled before that terrible truthful voice, until only a few men were left in the room. They also got tired of it at last, as hour after hour went past and there seemed to be no chance of Mrs B.'s awaking, and one by one they dropped off, until only Jack and another man were left. Towards 2 A. M. the latter showed signs of departure also, but Jack put his back against the door and said, " No; you have got to stop with me in this room until she wakes, in order to see fair-play, and we must each give our word of honour never to repeat what this woman is unconsciously revealing."

The man, a young civilian, agreed, and they both sat down again, while that changeless voice continued its tale. It told them some things which they knew and many which they did not. It also made them acquainted with a little plot against the peace (and purse) of the high official whose wife the sleeping lady was supposed to be. It went on until about 3 A.M., when she moved, yawned, and remarked, " I declare, I must have had a doze! everybody seems to be gone to bed. What time is it, gentlemen?" Then the two men lied, as they were bound to do, and she went off to her cabin quite happy, never to the end of the voyage having the least glimmering as to why the dowagers picked up their skirts and fled before her as from a plague! She probably attributed it to jealousy. How her plot against the high official fared no one ever discovered; but Mrs B. would certainly not have been mesmerised again had she known the effect of hypnotism on a tongue which perhaps never spoke the truth, and the whole truth, on any other occasion.

The rest of the voyage was uneventful enough. Immediately on landing Jack went up country to join his regiment at a small town with an unpronounceable name, which was suspected of being a hotbed of mutiny, and was therefore closely watched and guarded. Of course by this time, 1861, the mutiny proper was over and the ter-

rible punishment had been meted out. But so
many officers had been killed, or sent home
broken down in body and mind by the awful
suffering they had witnessed and endured, that
those who were left had to perform double duty.
Guard and " sentry go " were incessant, and for
months at a time the officers of the 88th thought
themselves lucky if they got three clear hours in
the twenty-four for necessary rest. Actual fighting would have been bliss compared with the long
dark nights spent in creeping stealthily round
from sentry to sentry, with the idea strongly
developed in the mind that unseen eyes were
watching, and that treacherous hands might be
waiting to do murder at any moment! Now
Jack Jebb was a broad-shouldered active youth
who had never known fear in his life (though
once afterwards he made acquaintance with it
when out driving with a talkative friend in the
Rocky Mountains, who *would* gesticulate wildly
with the reins in her hands, while the hind wheel
of the dog-cart was half over the precipice!).
Still, a few months of sleeplessness, overwork,
and anxiety in a hot climate reduced his nerves
to such a state of irritability and irresponsibility
that he always rather doubted whether he had
not committed a murder during that time — or
at least, justifiable homicide.

Going quietly into his tent one evening, he caught a native in the act of stealing a pistol. Of course the man should have been handed over to the authorities for punishment; but Jack preferred to settle the matter himself, and devoted the whole of his Hindustanee, together with his very powerful fists, to instilling a knowledge of the eighth commandment into the thief. When he considered that he had accomplished this, he gave the man a parting kick and sent him off. He then turned into bed, to meditate on the regulation which says, " On no account shall an officer strike a native."

After a wakeful hour or so, he was just dropping off to sleep, when he was roused in an instant by the uncanny sensation which most of us have experienced, of some unseen presence being in the room. He had sufficient self-control to open his eyes without moving in bed, and to his horror he saw something long and black and shiny within half a yard of his face. He immediately jumped to the conclusion that the disturber of his slumbers must be a snake, and that his only chance lay in being able to draw the pistol from under his pillow, and fire, before the creature was upon him. He held his breath in the dead silence of the night, and groped noiselessly for his weapon, the stealthy movements meanwhile coming ever nearer. Directly his hand touched the pistol, he raised himself on his elbow and fired simultaneously. The shot was followed by a heavy groan, which certainly never issued from the throat of a snake; and realising instantly that the object he had seen must have been the long black arm of a native, Jack sprang up, pushed his feet into slippers, and was soon outside. The shot had roused a few weary sleepers, who were readily satisfied with the assurance that it was a false alarm, — for, to Jack's surprise, instead of a defunct native, there was absolutely no sign of his midnight visitor, though, to judge from his groans, the man must have been severely wounded. A further inspection, however, showed a large pool of blood just outside the tent, which testified to the fact that something *had* been there recently. Jack now felt pretty certain that his assailant was the native who had first tried to rob him, and who had now made a futile attempt to revenge himself for the pommelling he had received.

Another moment's drowsiness, and in all probability this history would never have been written.

As soon as he caught sight of the blood, Jack began to follow the trail, anxious both to make sure of the identity of his enemy and to discover if he was seriously hurt. The track was easily followed to the edge of the jungle, about half a mile distant; but to try to explore a jungle in the darkness of an Indian night, while lightly and tastefully clad in pyjamas and slippers, was a task to which even the depths of his anxiety did not seriously incline him. So he went back to his tent, feeling rather chilly, and narrowly escaping a bullet, from a sentry unaccustomed to see his officers taking constitutionals in the dead of night in that sort of attire.

Of course next day Jack made inquiries about the suspected native, who turned out to be well known as a petty thief; but no one had seen him since the preceding afternoon. And strange to say, no one ever did see him! Whether he was exhausted by loss of blood and exertion in running so fast and far, and crawled into the jungle to die; whether in his wounded condition he was set upon by wild beasts and killed; or whether, thinking the camp an unhealthy place, he simply decided not to return to it, — are things which no man knows. And his family said it was a pity; but of course he was a bad man, and would the sahib give them rupees? which, naturally, the sahib did.

There is little that is interesting to be told of the rest of Jack Jebb's life in India. He spent three years there — dreary years, when fever and overwork alternated with each other, and the only scraps of enjoyment to be got out of existence were occasional shooting-parties, where he first tasted the delight of bagging " big game." He had shot ever since he knew which was the killing end of a gun, so he was not far behind even the old hands, and secured several good heads and skins in the course of these expeditions. But eventually these delights were put a stop to by repeated attacks of fever developing what is euphoniously called " hobnailed liver," whereby he was so pulled down that the doctor insisted on his going to the hills at once.

Leave for him meant extra work for the others, so for some time he refused to apply for it; but when it became evident that he could no longer fulfil his duty if he stayed, he at last consented to go. It happened that at the station from which he was to start there ruled a native station-master, who, though never actively engaged in the mutiny, was strongly suspected of having done a good deal in a quiet way towards keeping it going in his locality. Nothing definite could be proved against him. Still it was quite certain that this official loathed the English and never missed an opportunity of covertly insulting any sick officer leaving from his depot for the hills; while, in view of the tremendous " race " feeling engendered by the mutiny, the regulations most stringently forbade any Englishman, no matter what the provocation, to take the law into his own hands in the chastisement of a native. Jack, of course, knew the man's reputation, and consequently was prepared to stand some " cheek " from him.

By clinging to his post long after he was unfit to do his work, the invalid was so reduced that he had to be carried to the station in a litter, and doubtless he looked so ill that this native bully thought him a perfectly safe victim. Accordingly he began to make unpleasant remarks about the sick officer to his subordinates, speaking in a voice intended to reach the ear of the sufferer as he lay in his litter waiting for the train to be signalled. Jack set his teeth hard and besought his gods to lend him patience. As he made no sign, the station-master felt quite secure, and ventured a little further than he had ever gone before — just a shade *too* far for his own health; for rage giving him back his lost strength, Jack sprang from the litter and " went for " the surprised native in a thoroughly practical, scientific manner. Every blow was followed by a corresponding bulge on the station-master's fat body, as he doubled up on all-fours and abjectly entreated the sahib not to kill him!

The sahib graciously consented not to do so, especially as he felt on the verge of fainting himself. So he gave the man leave to get up, and crawled back to his litter more dead than alive, but with the joy of a virtuous action animating his soul. The station-master began to collect his own remains, wondering meanwhile how to be revenged. He soon thought of a plan, and going over to the litter, informed his enemy that he would not be allowed to proceed by the train then due, but would be sent to the station-house, there to await his trial next day for assaulting a native. Now Jack was anxious to get off to the hills, and felt, moreover, that the native had had the worst of it so far; so he offered him Rs. 20 as a salve for his bruises, if he would say no more about the matter, and keep a civil tongue in his head for the future.

" I will take Rs. 200 and not an anna less," said the man.

"Then you may go and be hanged," replied Jack, " for you won't get it from me."

Well, the police arrived, and, sure enough, he was marched off to durance vile. Now it may be imagined that a night in a close, hot cell, with no sort of refreshment for his body, and a cheerful prospect of being " broke " occupying his mind, had anything but a good effect on the health and appearance of a man already down with fever.

So it came about that when he was carried into court next morning, the presiding magistrate smiled visibly on being told that it was the emaciated invalid in the litter who had overnight produced the awful wreck of humanity to be seen in the witness-box. For in order to produce a better effect, the station-master had allowed the blood to dry on his cheeks, and with one eye closed and dirty scraps of sticking-plaster artistically arranged over the other, he looked a very ill-used native indeed. He said, and had twenty witnesses to prove, that the sahib had flown at him like a tiger while he was simply doing his duty and trying to make his passengers comfortable, and that, not content with nearly shaking the breath out of his body, he had deprived him of his eyesight, as my lord, the judge, could see.

The judge listened to this moving tale, and he also listened to the witnesses. Then he heard what Jack had to say for himself, and also some details added by several Europeans who knew.

Then he said, " You can pay this native Rs. 5 for a doctor's bill, also you can pay costs, and then I should recommend you to take the next train for the hills." Jack fully expected to have to pay about Rs. 500 and get cashiered into the bargain, so his joy on hearing these words of wisdom may be imagined. As for the station-master! He had refused Rs. 20 down in the hope of getting 200, and now he was to have Rs. 5 and his enemy was to go free! He went home, washed off his war-paint, and made himself look like a human being again, the while he talked to himself softly and fluently. He ceased to talk aloud, though, from that day forth, and never again insulted an invalid officer. It didn't seem so safe as he had thought! Jack Jebb got to the hills at last, picked up health and strength rapidly, and was soon ready for duty again. But the oddest part of the story is, that years afterwards in Honduras he met a stray Englishman, who in the course of conversation began to tell him the foregoing story, but stopped abruptly when he saw his companion shaking with laughter.

" Why, have you heard it before? " he asked.

" I am the man! " was the reply.

CHAPTER III.

BUSINESS DISASTERS.

To return from Honduras to India, nothing interesting enough to write about occurred to Mr Jebb for some time after his return convalescent from the hills. But something of great importance to him was taking place at home — namely, his father's re-marriage. It was a suitable marriage enough, and nothing was more likely than that a man in the Rev. Mr Jebb's position — virtually bereft of wife and son, and in bad health — *would* contract a second marriage, if only for the sake of mitigating his loneliness.

No hint of the event was given to Jack until it had taken place; and this omission, aggravated as it was in his mind by the short time which had elapsed since his mother's death, did a great deal towards lessening the small store of affection which he had ever felt for his father. The natures of the two men were too utterly opposite from each other for them ever to have got on well, once the son had arrived at maturity and become entitled to opinions of his own.

As things turned out, there was never any chance either for recrimination or reconciliation, since within two years of his marriage Mr Jebb died at Nice, whither he had gone in search of health. A posthumous child was expected, and all his affairs were left in great confusion. He had enjoyed a life interest in his first wife's property, but upon his death it went at once to her son, and there was little for the widow and her child except Walton, which accordingly was left to them. Jack, who had been brought up to consider the place his own, and who loved every foot of land upon it, naturally felt very sore at his loss, whilst acknowledging that, owing to his father's inability to provide otherwise for a second family, it was inevitable.

Owing to this complication and other things,

there was so much business to be settled that it became absolutely necessary for Jack to go home. Now this was exactly what most of his brother officers had been desirous of doing for a long time; and as many of them had been abroad far longer than himself, it seemed unfair that he should be the first to get leave, particularly as, if it exceeded six months, his absence would prevent their getting away at all. Quite seeing the force of this, he promised that if on his arrival he found that his business would take longer than six months to settle, he would send in his papers and retire from the Service, rather than deprive any of them of a well-earned holiday. He was then senior subaltern, with a prospect of soon getting his company but for this rather quixotic piece of generosity.

The plea of " urgent private affairs " obtained the necessary leave, and after an uneventful voyage Jack landed in England, young, rich, good-looking, and talented, but about as solitary a human being as could well be imagined. He soon discovered that it would be impossible to straighten his complicated affairs and be back in India within six months, so he sent in his papers, as he had agreed to do; and though there was much that he regretted, he was not

altogether sorry to be free from a profession
which had not been his own choice, and of which
he had only seen the dullest side. It is, perhaps,
superfluous to mention that he had fallen in and
out of love a few times prior to this stage of his
career, as that is a thing which happens so
regularly and methodically to most men under
five-and-twenty that it scarcely seems worth
chronicling. Besides, love-stories always read
better in works of fiction, where they can be
rounded off to suit the requirements of the tale.
So this being — for a biography — a truthful
history, such periodical attacks of love-sickness
may be left to the imagination of the reader.

The great question now agitating Jack's mind
was where to settle down for as long as his restless spirit would allow him to stop in one place.
Home he had none; and his relations were
limited to two aunts, and a few cousins, mostly
older than himself, who were already plodding
steadily along their appointed paths in life.
What his soul really inclined to was travel, and
the shooting of more big game; but the family
lawyer had marked him for his own, and refused
to let him go under two years. So he had to
decide on some place wherein to bestow himself
and his Indian spoils of rare chased weapons,

gorgeous state shields, little ugly Burmese gods, and his own hunting trophies.

It suddenly occurred to him, " Why not go to Oxford ? " The originality of entering college after leaving the army rather pleased him ; so he became a gentleman commoner, put his name down for lectures on the subjects which most interested him, decorated his rooms, took with him a couple of hunters and a groom, and prepared to have a " good time." He quite succeeded in this ambition, for he made some lasting friendships, got some capital hunting, rowed in his college eight, won a match at billiards, carefully refrained from overworking himself, and altogether spent three happy years.

If there is such a gift as second-sight, it seems probable that Jack Jebb possessed it ; at all events, if anything of a supernatural nature happened, he was sure to witness the occurrence. Shortly before leaving Oxford, he awoke from a sound sleep one night with an impression that some one was looking at him. Sitting up quickly, with a sudden wakefulness born of his Indian experiences, he distinctly saw the figure of a man standing at the foot of his bed ! He was just about to ask the reason of this midnight visitation, when to his horror he recognised the figure as *himself!* There he seemed to stand, in trousers and shirt-sleeves, gazing into his own eyes, while his real self lay wondering in the bed! The fire had not quite gone out, and by its subdued light he could take in every detail of his strange visitor's appearance. However, to make sure that he was not dreaming, he prepared to strike a match. As he did so, his double walked over to the fireplace and literally and completely vanished! Jack by this time was feeling rather queer, but he got out of bed and began to search the rooms, hoping to find concealed in them some undergraduate trying to give him a fright. The quest proved vain, for no human being was to be found: moreover, the doors were locked on the inside, so no ordinary visitant could have escaped.

Jack was going to hunt next day, and as he went slowly back to bed he reflected that by all ghostly laws this apparition must mean that he would break his neck. It would, however, have been quite contrary to his principles to take warning and stop at home on that account. On the contrary, he went off in the morning full of eagerness to see what would come of his vision; and the oddest part of the story is, that absolutely nothing happened either then or afterwards! The run was good and they killed their fox, but never a sign was there of the reason for that strange sight. It would have made a capital ghost-story, if only the event had come off! Anybody less hard-headed might have attributed the whole circumstance to " looking on the wine when it was red " overnight, but it was well known among the men of his set that it was " impossible to make Jebb see double! " Several of his friends had frequently done their best to that end, but the result was always that after three or four hours of " mixed drinks," he saw such of them to their rooms as were able to walk, and laid out the rest comfortably on the floor, before retiring in excellent order himself.

On leaving Oxford, Jack went off with a party of friends for a yachting and shooting tour round about Skye. They met with plenty of sport and had a thoroughly good time, stopping, when belated at night, at quaint little country inns, where they ate the freshest of herrings and drank the purest of Highland " dew," with appetites strengthened by the long day's tramp through the sharp sea-air.

At this time Jack was in receipt of about £2000 a-year, all invested in those good old-fashioned securities which give low interest but

an easy mind; and had he been contented with
" the sweet security of the Three Per Cents," his
history might have been a very different one. As
it was, partly from a frail desire for high interest,
and partly from sheer lack of employment, he
began to cast about him for an investment which
would give him something to do, while yielding
more for his money. So, when on the conclusion of the yachting expedition the friends all
separated and went their respective ways, he
accepted an invitation from an acquaintance, who
was just starting the first steel gun-barrel factory
near Glasgow, and who wanted him to go and
see the works, with a view to putting in more
capital.

The young and optimistic investor went, was
charmed with the new invention, and, certain of
its success, he put £23,000 into the concern, besides throwing all his energy into the work of
organising and helping it forward. It gave him
a year's congenial employment, and it cost him
— half his fortune!

All was going well, and orders were pouring
in, when the men in a neighbouring factory went
out on strike, owing to some trifling dispute with
their masters. The employés of the new factory
entirely disapproved of the strike, and were

most unwilling to join in it; but they were compelled to do so by the trades-union to which they and the malcontents alike belonged. An old steady-going firm would probably have weathered the storm, but in this case a very few weeks of unfulfilled orders tired out their customers, who withdrew their commissions and cancelled their obligations, with the result that within two years from its opening the new venture closed its doors.

Up to the last Jack Jebb and his friend hoped against hope that a large order which had been half promised by the Government might come in in time to save them. Eventually it came, but a little too late for the purpose.

Twenty years afterwards Jack met a War Office official of his acquaintance in Piccadilly, who said to him, " By the way, aren't you interested in a steel gun-barrel factory near Glasgow? Because we are just sending it a large order."

" I *was* deeply interested in it," answered Jack, " before it ceased to exist, a score of years ago, and I should have been fervently grateful for the order then; but owing to the slight delay, it isn't of much use to me now."

This affair, besides considerably damping

young Jebb's ardour for speculation, cast him on the world again at rather a loose end. Not quite knowing what to do with himself, and being of a nature that could not endure inactivity long, when a friend suggested his joining in an expedition to explore some of the less known parts of Nicaragua, he was delighted with the chance of adventure. Their idea was to penetrate into that part of the country where tradition tells of a wonderful white race which has kept to its native jungles for generations, and which has permitted very few, if any, of the people who have penetrated its recesses to live to tell the tale.

Unfortunately for themselves, Jack and his friend arrived at Nicaragua in the rainy season; moreover, they soon found that no native guide would take the first step into the impenetrable forests which were supposed to shelter the strange and savage people of whom they were in search. Awesome tales were told them by frightened peons of party after party of " mad Englishmen " who had passed away out of sight beneath those dark and heavy trees, never more to be seen of mortal eye. Tales, too, of ghastly bodies placed by unknown hands at the verge of the mysterious woods, in whose denuded bones were found arrows fashioned and poisoned in a manner unknown to all the Indian tribes who saw them. However, these difficulties did not in the least detract from the eagerness of the friends to pursue their investigations, although their failure to induce any natives to accompany them as servants and guides was a great drawback, as it precluded their carrying with them anything like a sufficient outfit.

Consequently, exposure during the hot days, and wet cold nights, shelterless as the travellers were, soon brought on attacks of " shakes," and put an end to their progress before they had time to make any discoveries. The wonder is that both did not leave their fever-stricken remains in that unhealthy spot, for it frequently happened that in a pouring rain, which promptly extinguished their fire, they were obliged to sit on the ground all night, back to back, in order to leave as little surface as possible for the rain to penetrate. But nothing short of patent-roofing can withstand a tropical downpour when it is really doing its best, and by daylight the two men were chilled through, feverish, and miserable. The rain usually ceased at dawn; and then how eagerly they coaxed damp sticks to burn, and comforted their wet and weary souls with pannikins of hot coffee. After they had quite given up any hope of being able to attain the object of their journey, they still went on travelling about in the interior, picking up odds and ends of curiosities here and there in the shape of arrow-heads, idols, and various relics.

In order that none of the joys of a tropical climate might be lost to them, they one night arrived at an Indian village simultaneously with an earthquake — with several earthquakes, in fact; for no sooner did one shock die away into a gentle tremor than a fresh one would begin to make itself felt, and straightway along came another and a worse shaking of the " solid " world, until at last the frightened peons forsook their huts and encamped in the streets and fields, taking with them as much of their portable property as they could carry. Our Englishmen, not having any valuables to protect, strolled about in the intervals between the shocks, trying to administer comfort to the frightened people, until they came across an old lady, who delighted them so much that they spent the rest of the night by her side. She had, with difficulty, carried a large picture of her patron saint out into the street with her, and

was now kneeling before it with much piety.
She evidently did not regard it solely as an
ornamental possession, for every time the deep
low thunder of a coming shock was heard, she
blessed and invoked the pictured saint vigorously, entreating him with every term of endear-
ment in the Spanish language to avert the
threatened danger. When, however, the earth
trembled and the houses fell without any inter-
ference from the peccant saint, the aged believer
invariably changed the tone of her adjurations,
and heaped every abusive term she could think
of upon his useless, indifferent head! Her
vocabulary being copious, and her power of
speech remarkable, the two travellers got more
insight during that one night into the true
inwardness of the Spanish language than they
could have obtained in a year of every-day life.

Towards morning the earthquakes grew
fainter, and by daylight had entirely ceased;
so the natives began to collect confidence and
their belongings together, and soon the village
presented a normal appearance, though a pretty
general " up all night " look about it testified to
the previous alarm.

It was, I believe, on this journey that the
friends made an expedition into Guatemala.

While staying in an Indian village in the interior they heard that the annual native dance — a sort of half-religious gathering — was about to take place, and they made up their minds to see what it was like, in spite of a warning from the landlord of the little *tienda* where they lodged, who told them that the presence of strangers was apt to be resented.

When the night came they were allowed without any difficulty to pass into the room where the dance was held, and for a time all went well, notwithstanding a good many suspicious looks at the foreigners on the part of the native gilded youth. Unfortunately for the former, the female portion of the community took to them at once, and when the belle of the ball — a pretty, soft-eyed " muchacha," whose white garments seemed to be constructed out of starch alone, so stiff were they — began to show a preference for the visitors' society over that of her more legitimate admirers, the glances became more and more lowering. At last, after a hasty consultation in a corner, about half-a-dozen young bloods drew their knives and made a sudden ugly rush for the Englishmen. Meanwhile the cause of the disturbance, together with the rest of the women, had fled, and realising that they were in for a bad quarter of an hour, the friends placed themselves back to back and prepared to fight their way out of the room.

Fortunately for themselves, they were close to the door, which happened to be so placed as to partly shelter them from their assailants. Moreover, thinking that the young men who first began the attack would be able to bring it to a satisfactory conclusion without any extraneous aid, the rest of the Indians in the room carefully abstained from joining in the fray. The odds were, of course, overwhelming so far as numbers were concerned; but then no Indian ever dreams that his fists were given to him to use, and the besieged managed to keep such a circle round themselves that it was not easy to get a knife scientifically placed. Still, the affair could have had but one ending eventually, had not the women in their flight from danger found the presence of mind to go and explain the situation to the gendarmes. As it was, an armed detachment arrived only just in time, for Jack and his friend found their strength rapidly failing. Weakened by loss of blood from several slight flesh-wounds, they began to despair of ever getting out of the place alive. But at the first glimpse of the soldiery every knife was sheathed, and every harmless native tried to look as if he had merely been indulging in a little horse-play. Several of them, however, were marched off in custody, in spite of their protestations; while the enemy were sufficiently grateful for the escort of a troop to their domicile. They shortly received a message from the captain of the guard that the villagers seemed to have conceived a prejudice against them, and that he thought it would be well for them to seek fresh quarters. They were rather of that opinion themselves; so as soon as their cuts had been strapped and their bruises anointed, they went on their way, feeling thankful that the matter had ended no worse.

Although they had been disappointed in the primary object of their journey, the travellers managed on the whole to spend a very interesting six months before they began to think of returning. They succeeded in collecting a good many antiquities, some of the best of which they afterwards presented to the British Museum; but among those that they retained were several interesting specimens dug up before their eyes by native archæologists, who, having previously placed these treasures in their hiding-places, naturally knew exactly where to look for them!

Jack Jebb's *compagnon de voyage* was a fervent orchid worshipper, and as Nicaragua abounded with what, in those days, were rare specimens, he returned to England laden with joy and with flowers.

Jack himself had a much less satisfactory home-coming. For one thing, during his absence there had been a further drain on his resources by the now quite defunct steel gun-barrel company, and of course the loss of so much money had been rather a blow to him. Still, there was enough left to live upon, safely placed in good old-fashioned banks. But the fates seemed to have conspired to make him a pauper, and worse was yet to come. He had scarcely landed when the almost national calamity known at the time as " Black Monday" occurred. Overend & Gurney's stopped payment, dragging down in their fall many smaller concerns, to the disaster and •ruin of thousands of confiding depositors. Mr Jebb had invested nearly all the rest of his fortune in these very banks; and within four years, through no fault of his own, he found himself reduced from something like affluence to a condition nearly approaching pennilessness. His relations now entreated him to put the very few thousands saved from the wreck into something absolutely safe and reliable. He promised to do so, and chose for his remaining capital an investment thought to be as safe as Consols. Within a year, to the surprise and consternation of half England, that too failed, and at the age of twenty-six Jack found himself destitute of means or the knowledge of how to provide himself with them. He had been brought up to feel secure of always having as much money as he required, and had been put into the very profession least likely to be of the smallest practical use to him in his present strait.

It was now necessary that he should find employment in real earnest, but, varied though his acquirements were, there seemed few openings for a man of his age and with his abhorrence of routine, or sedentary pursuits. He drew and painted far beyond the average, sang beautifully, could ride anything that went on four legs, and had at odd times picked up enough knowledge of engineering to be frequently mistaken for a civil engineer. Moreover, he could sail his own yacht, and give his orders in five languages, had a quick intelligence, a strong inventive bent, and with his broad shoulders and athletic frame could stand hardships which would have killed a weaker man.

But with all these advantages, congenial work was hard to find. Finally, he decided on spend-ing a few months with a sheep-farmer in the Highlands, in order to learn sheep-farming, thinking that if he went " out West," as he was strongly inclined to do, the more knowledge of this sort he could acquire the better chance he would have of being able to make his way in a new country.

CHAPTER IV.

COFFEE-PLANTING IN BRAZIL.

ACCORDINGLY Jack agreed with the owner of a farm in a remote Highland district to spend six months upon it, taking his share of whatever work might be in progress. And a very rough life he found it too: up before dawn, and to bed at dusk, tired out by the heavy labour of the day. Little but Gaelic was spoken, and in those lonely regions speech of any sort was rare, for the men who spent their lives alone with dumb animals on those wide and silent moors soon ceased to have much use or wish for words. Sometimes at night, over a hot glass of whisky — their one luxury — the old farmer would unlock his lips and tell strange stories of unquiet spirits said still to haunt the secret glens in which they had once lain hidden from their persecutors.

It is certain that there was one road along which no native of those parts could be induced to walk after nightfall. The few who had dared to do so declared, in hushed and fearful voices, that ever in front of them walked a soldierly figure, clad in a general's uniform of the time of George II.; and no matter how fast the spectator ran, the upright military shape always kept exactly the same distance in front, while apparently never going out of its measured pace. The story went, that after a rebellion, so large a price was put by the Government on the rebel general's head, that one of the few who knew of his secret hiding-place had been tempted to reveal it, and that when dying from the wounds inflicted in a last desperate struggle with his captors, the betrayed man had sworn that his spirit should for ever haunt the spot from whence treachery had driven him to his death.

The strange mystic vein — strange in a man so adventurous and practical — which was largely developed in Jack Jebb's character, was stimulated by tales such as this; and it is easy to understand that in those snowy solitudes a man would feel nearer to the unseen world than to that lower one which seemed never to have penetrated through the dim Highland mists.

Between days of hard reality and evenings of weird stories, Jack passed his probation, and at the end of six months left the old farmer, with a practical knowledge of his trade, and a greater aptitude than ever for " roughing it," fostered by the long hours, the bitter cold, and the scant food of his Highland sojourn. The plan of his life, however, seemed to be that, having mastered one thing, he was to be called upon to work at another! For when he got back to town he fell in with the people who were then trying to arrange a scheme for a fresh line of steamers across the Atlantic. The new ships were to be chiefly for passenger traffic, and were to be built entirely with a view to speed — a desideratum little cared for up to that time. A business of this sort, appealing to both his love of the sea and his power of organisation, was after Jack's own heart. So he threw himself vigorously into it, and had the satisfaction of becoming one of the founders of the White Star Line. Anybody else would have made a fortune out of an undertaking so successful, but Jack Jebb's *métier* was rather to lose fortunes than make them; so, true to his vocation, nearly all he got out of a year's work was a good deal of enjoyment and about twenty trips across the Atlantic. It was a proud day for all concerned when the first ship was launched, and performed her journey at what was then thought the acme of speed, but would now be considered very slow sailing indeed.

Once the White Star Line was " floated " in both senses of the word, it soon became a steady-going concern in which Jack ceased to take much interest. He went over to America and made a tour in some of the distant States, appointing agents, and expatiating, as he passed through small towns and villages, on the speed and comfort of the new line of steamers. Of course at first no one believed that they would be able to perform all they promised, and their pioneer was generally regarded with admiration by the 'cute Yankees as an unusually expert liar!

However, he secured a good deal of business for the company in this way; and when he had done all that he could, he began to look about for some other opening for himself — the office

work, which was all that remained to be completed in the White Star Company, being too
uncongenial for him to do more than give it
a trial. So, having long wished to visit Brazil,
he thought that this would be a favourable
opportunity to see something of the country,
and at the same time to find out if he could
do anything in the way of coffee-planting
there.

Accordingly he started for that land of natural
beauty and acquired nastiness. His sensations
when he first caught sight of the surpassing
loveliness of 'Rio need not be described, because
probably to most people its charms are as well
known as those of the Thames below Marlow.

Before he had been many days in the city,
Jack chanced to hear from a stray Englishman
of a coffee and sugar plantation some distance
in the interior, whose Portuguese owner was
looking for a manager willing to put a little
capital into the concern. The district in which
it was situated had a bad name for swamp fever;
but as there seemed to be nothing else against
it and a good deal in its favour, Jack resolved
to go and reconnoitre.

When, after a few days on mule-back through
the wild scenery of the Sierras, he reached his

destination and put up at the village *tienda*, he found that the owner of the plantation — a Visconde de B. — had received notice of his coming, and was only too willing to arrange any terms by which he could secure a reliable manager — " Inglese " for preference — and be off himself to the Mecca of every South American — Paris ! The Visconde told Jack that — for that part of the world — the estate had been under cultivation a great many years, as it had belonged to his grandfather, but that the district now being worked was formerly virgin forest, while the part cultivated during his grandfather's lifetime was at the present time almost deserted, being quite ten miles away from the new plantation. He added, however, that there was still a small yearly yield of coffee at the old *fazenda*, and that it was customary to send over a party of blacks to get as much as they could. The Visconde offered no explanation of the change of *locale;* nor did Jack feel very curious on the subject, as the new plantation was evidently doing well, — and if anything more were to be got from the old one, well, so much the better ! As the owner and he were both equally anxious to come to terms, they quickly succeeded in doing so; and as soon as the necessary deeds could be drawn up by the village notary, Jack entered on his new duties.

He soon found that the unassisted supervision of a couple of hundred blacks did not exactly promise a life of " lilies and roses," but he got on fairly well with them; though, probably, if his views on the subject of slavery had been proclaimed, they would not have been well received at Exeter Hall. But the people who have *lived* with negroes, and the excellent persons who are only acquainted with them through missionary sermons, usually *do* hold entirely conflicting views as to their treatment.

Jack had not been long in the neighbourhood before he heard the reason of the desertion and decay of the old *fazenda*. It seemed that the late Visconde had been one of the old cruel masters that one reads about as having existed in the dark ages. On his vast estates he was as absolute as a Czar. And he used his power with little mercy. There were grim tales told of the tortured, writhing blacks he had caused to be flogged to death — strong men some, ay, and women among them. He had owned 500 field hands, and had ruled them with a rod of iron. It was said of him that should he see a slave touch with the handle of his hoe one coffee-tree whilst clearing the roots of another, the unfortunate wretch was sure of a hundred lashes. Some he murdered outright; some fled to the woods and lived like wild beasts; while others, more happy, died of misery and ill-usage. But suddenly a strange complaint appeared among them, and by twos and threes they began to die off, week after week, month after month, year after year. And no man could say what this new scourge might be.

The old Visconde was frantic. Bribes, medicines, and floggings were alike powerless to check the new disease — if disease that could be called which none doubted was *poison*. Yes, poison! No one was certain of the reason of the strange killing that went on for years among the poor people at the *fazenda* of Boa Vista. Whether it was owing to the awful wretchedness of their lives, or to the thought that only by dying could they be revenged on the tyrant who tortured them, or whether it was a sort of contagious, murderous mania, which spread through the whole mass of slaves, no man ever discovered; but the fact remained that in a few years the muster-roll dwindled from five to three hundred, and do what he would, the Visconde found the work getting beyond the power of the over-taxed slaves. Then two Portuguese factors disappeared. Murdered, no doubt! Also, partly owing to the dykes being neglected, a portion of the river-bank was swept away one rainy season and never replaced, so that soon hundreds of acres of level land (on part of which sugar had been successfully grown) were flooded, quickly degenerating into marsh.

The natural consequence, of course, was that fever soon bred malaria of the most malignant type, and the blacks died off faster than ever. Finally, the old Visconde abandoned the *fazenda* in despair, sold off such of his slaves as remained, dispersing them in small gangs to different districts, bought 150 new ones, and planted the hill ground where the new *fazenda* now stands.

Such was the cruel story of the old plantation, of which Jack soon was to see a good deal more than he had bargained for. The yield of coffee at the neglected place became less and less every year, until at this time there were not more than 800 *arrobas* to be gathered. There would have been more, but that the fever suddenly appeared, in spite of Jack having taken all such precautions as giving the people extra rations, including spirits, and frequently changing the gang that was employed there. It was all in vain, however, for in three days there were a dozen on the sick-list. So they gave up work and retreated to the hills, where one poor fellow sank and died.

Unfortunately, the drying-grounds were so close to the river that there was every chance of the coffee already picked being stolen, as nothing could have been easier than to fetch it away in canoes during the night. Therefore it was necessary for some one to stay at the old *Enghenio*, in order to watch it. Now there was not a soul on the plantation who could be trusted to do this except an Englishman who had just arrived with his wife and family, and it was like Jack Jebb to reflect that the new-comer would be more liable to fever than an old stager like himself, and that the other man had ties, while he had none. So the matter was arranged by his taking the night-work on his own shoulders.

Accordingly, after a hard day's work, ploughing, draining, sugar-planting, or clearing forest-land, he used to lie down in his clothes for a couple of hours, be called at 9 P.M., and then ride over to spend the night at the deserted *fazenda*. The house was close to the drying-grounds, so he got into the habit of estab-

lishing himself inside, with a bundle of cigars, a
dose of mixed spirits and quinine, and the useful, necessary revolver. If only the mosquitoes
had been less painstaking, he might have been
fairly comfortable as he sat and watched the
white mist, reeking with poisonous miasma,
seethe up from the great marshes. The brightest moonlight could but dimly struggle through
it on to the desolate ruins of the *Enghenio*. No
sound ever broke the silence of those long and
dreary nights, save the hum of the mosquitoes
and the chattering of the bats. Even a thief
would have been a welcome change ! But none
ever came ; for, little though Jack knew it, not a
black in the country would have ventured near
the place after nightfall. Great as was its tropical beauty, the old plantation looked as the
Garden of Eden might have looked if, after
Adam's expulsion, a joint stock company had
taken it up, gone bankrupt, and fallen into
Chancery.

Well, one night Jack rode over as usual,
although he was dead tired and sleepy, after a
long day's work in a rice-swamp under a grill-
ing sun. The last half-mile or so of the road
ran through an avenue of magnificent bamboos,
fifty feet high at least, and which met overhead

in an arch. It was a shady ride by daylight,
but at night was almost pitch-dark, when of
course it was necessary to ride at a footpace.
The avenue was quite straight, so that, as in
walking through a tunnel, you could see an
arch of light in front of you long before you
reached it. Beyond the end of the bamboos
the road swept sharp round to the right for a
hundred yards or so, through scattered clumps
of orange-trees and guava scrub. Farther still
to the right was the half-ruined *Enghenio*, and
directly fronting it the drying-grounds, now
scraped clean of the six months' accumulation
of weeds, and covered with heaps of half-dried
coffee.

On this particular night Jack had ridden
slowly through the avenue, and was within a
few yards of where the white moon streamed
across the road at its termination, when his
mule started aside, and suddenly stopped short.
No doubt, thought her rider, a snake was crossing her path, or she had scented a skulking
puma. He was feeling thoroughly fagged out,
and was half asleep in the saddle, thinking—
nearly dreaming, perhaps — of the ruined *fazenda* and its past history; vaguely speculating,
too, on the chance of a meeting with coffee

thieves, when the halt of his mule recalled him in a moment to a state of complete wakefulness. Instinctively he grasped his revolver and prepared for action. For some time, as he advanced, he had heard, without listening to them, the various ordinary night-sounds of a swamp — the dabbling and splashing of waterfowl and the endless chorus of frogs.

But now he became conscious that a fresh sound was added to these — a sound he had been hearing every day of his life lately, — the quick, regular beat of a water-wheel and the steady rush of water through the sluices! In a moment it occurred to him that the long-expected thieves had arrived early, intending to make a night of it, and were coolly clearing the *fazenda* coffee with the *fazenda's* own machinery, which, though old and rusty, was still in a condition to do its work in a sort of way. A touch of the spur set the mule going again, and in a few seconds she and her rider were round the bend, and looking at the upper storey of the *Enghenio*, as it towered above the orange-clumps. To Jack's intense surprise, the whole place seemed to be lit up. He guided his mule off the road in order that her hoofs should not be heard, and, revolver in hand, cantered through the orange-grove. His astonishment may be imagined when he got an end view of the *Enghenio*, and could see that some of the windows were open, and that through them broad streams of light flowed across the drying-grounds, which were literally crowded with blacks!

He could distinctly see the dusky forms of the slaves flitting backwards and forwards between the *Enghenio* and the drying-ground, as they carried in large baskets of coffee. Several had torches, and there were a couple of overseers directing the work. The blacks were all working silently and " at the run."

The first thought that occurred to the astounded spectator was, that one of his worthy neighbours, well known to be quite capable of robbery or any other crime, had brought down the whole of the people on his own plantation, intent on making a clean sweep of the *fazenda*. Insensibly Jack slackened speed as he picked his way through the last clump of orange-trees. As he did so, a thicker wreath of mist seemed to seethe up from the marsh; the ruddy glow of light from the windows apparently faded and disappeared; and hurrying slaves, whom but a moment before he had seen so distinctly, melted into darkness and vanished. Another stride carried him clear of the trees, to a point within twenty yards of the *Enghenio.* He pulled up with a quick jerk, utterly bewildered. For there, close before him, was the drying-ground with its regular heaps of coffee, not one displaced — nothing moving, nothing visible — the whole place as silent and solitary as when he had left it the night before!

He sat there for a while, unable even to think, but with a strange feeling of awe creeping over him; for, up to that moment, it had never occurred to him that he could be the victim of an illusion. Even now he could scarcely force himself to believe that what he had positively *seen* was not real, and he waited half expecting again to behold the troops of blacks come hurrying out of the *Enghenio.* But no! not a light or sound was there in the desolate place. Then he remembered the great water-wheel. He had *heard* that going, and could not have been mistaken.

With a feeling not far from dread, he rode past the Enghenio towards the sugar-house, which was the right wing of the building — the machinery being in the centre. As he rode slowly along the front, he saw that the windows, from which shortly before streams of light had issued, were, as usual, tightly closed; the shutters, gray and steaming with damp, shining coldly in the pale moonlight. The centre door, leading into the machine-house, was fast, and the rusty padlock untouched. The sugar-house was open on one side, and into this he rode his mule, dismounted, and explored the building. Nothing seemed changed. There was no trace of any one having visited it. He made his way to the part of the building partitioned off for the water-wheel. He knew *that* must satisfy him. Several of the planks had rotted and fallen back into the watercourse below: they had left a large gap in the partition, through which he looked at the wheel. A cold chill passed through him as he did so, for the broad floats were as dry as tinder, and the wheel itself was held locked by a fallen rafter which had passed through its arms. It had not moved for a year!

Far below was the water, unconfined by sluice or shutter, running silently along the shoot, and not even *touching* the lowest float of the wheel. Two or three bats, disturbed by the lantern he carried, fluttered past him, the only signs of life visible. Then he knew that what he had seen could not be real; but in that case, how account for the noise of the wheel? His head ached as he sat in the sugar-house puzzling over the weird sight till near daylight, when he rode slowly home. He could eat no breakfast, but still he insisted on going out to see some fresh land that was being cleared. However, he soon began to feel very ill, had to be taken home, and by evening was down with swamp fever, and raving.

He had a pretty bad turn, and made a good deal of noise; but the odd thing was, that when he recovered he could remember many of his delusions as if they were facts, while the real facts he had entirely forgotten.

Whether it was the fever that brought him the negro ghosts, or the ghosts that brought the fever, is one of those things which no man can decide. But it does seem possible that in some overstrained, receptive conditions of the mind, strange things may be seen, — things invisible at other times, when the consciousness of the body overpowers that of the soul.[1]

[1] Jebb afterwards wrote the story of "The Haunted *Eng-henio*" for 'Blackwood's Magazine.'

CHAPTER V.

IN THE FAR WEST.

NOW an attack of malaria as severe as that just described fixes on a man with a deadly grip not easy to shake off. So it came about that after he had recovered, and commenced work again, very few weeks of riding about in the mid-day sun and the evening dew induced a relapse, with a fit of shakes which brought Jack to the verge of the grave. To add to his troubles, it had been a bad coffee year, and there was little to show for his labours.

Of course the owner of the plantation was "seeing life" in Paris, from which paradise he had no intention of returning to live in a fever-stricken swamp, so long as one "mad Englishman" was left who would do so for him. Moreover, when of the two parties to a contract one is in the interior of Brazil, and the other in the heart of Europe, it is not easy to enforce the fulfilment of that contract, and Jack began to find that he was going to be "left" in both senses of the word. By this time he was getting so used to the persistent ill-luck of all his ventures, that he was more disappointed than surprised when he had to make up his mind that he might as well leave the *Enghenio* before wasting more time and money upon it. No doubt he was partly helped to this conclusion by the native doctor, who told him that unless he speedily betook himself to a colder climate nothing could ward off another attack of malaria, which, in his weakened condition, would probably be the last. He therefore acquainted the Visconde de B. with his intention in a very plain-spoken letter, installed the only Englishman in the place as manager, and then sailed for New York, having acquired a good deal of insight into the working of a coffee plantation, learned a fair amount of bad Portuguese, and lost yet a little more money.

Fortunately for him, he had some "expectations," one of which opportunely fell in at this period, giving him a little ready money with which to carry on the war.

He had now knocked about the world long enough to have made a good many acquaintances of various social grades and very different characters in most of the places he had visited. Accordingly, he had not been long in New York before he ran up against an old guide, whom he had met in one of his excursions on behalf of the White Star Line, and whose business it was to show the guileless tenderfoot how to hunt buffalo. There were still a few buffaloes left in those days.

The guide, an old frontiersman called Bob Harker, told Jack that he was then about to start for the plains, where he would procure a waggon and team, pick up his companion, a half-breed Government scout and hunter called " Mudeater " — of Cherokee blood — and then spend some months hunting and camping-out. He asked his English acquaintance if he would not like to join the party, and Jack quickly decided that he most emphatically would, especially as the free life and bracing air of the plains would be more likely than anything else to drive the last germs of fever from his blood. His preparations, consisting chiefly as they did of rifles and ammunition, were soon made, and the two men started by rail to a little station on the Kansas Pacific Railway, whence they struck out south. After the first day they "joined parties" with five buffalo-hunters, also bound south. Their new comrades were not exactly agreeable companions, being mostly on, or over, the edge of delirium tremens; but the Rapahoes were reported " out," and only a fortnight before a hunters' camp had been surprised, and five men and a woman killed.

Therefore, as eight straight rifles are better than three, to say nothing of as many revolvers, the two parties joined forces, for the march at all events.

The first day out there were no incidents. The strangers were sleeping off their potations in a comatose condition at the bottom of their waggons, though always keeping one of their number sober enough to drive. Jack got two antelopes out of a band that galloped past, while the driver grabbed his rifle and missed them clean. He rubbed his eyes, swore feebly, and remarked that he had missed them through seeing *two* herds of antelope and shooting at the wrong one!

The party passed a wretched night, camping

at a mud-hole, with burnt prairie all round, and with no food for the stock except their corn. The coyotes howled dismally, like lost souls in purgatory, while the five drunken hunters spent most of the night in furious quarrels. When day broke, it was found that there was only enough water for coffee, and none for washing, as the horses had trampled the only water-hole into a mass of mud.

There was a long day's march to the next water, a creek near which they expected to find buffalo; but the early morning air was keen and bracing, and was made to do for a wash. So after a hasty breakfast on antelope-steak, the team was harnessed up and the travellers started due south. Hour after hour they toiled over the endless prairie, broken only by long, shallow depressions, which during the rainy season might carry water, but now were dry as dust and sun could make them.

The guide, Bob Harker, had been a Confederate during the war. He had also filled the positions of stage-driver, prospector, and preacher. Many and strange had been his adventures, and many a tale could he tell of the war, or of the stirring times " out west " in the sixties. He was a typical pioneer — strong as a bear and quick as a cat — a strange combination of simplicity and shrewdness, a splendid shot, and a noted tracker. He was outwardly pretty much in the rough, but at times would give evidence that if his reading had not been extensive, it had at least been varied. He once took Jack to visit his " home," a snug log-cabin on the head waters of Ute Creek, where he kept a shelf of miscellaneous volumes — " Prescott " flanked by Byron and Scott, while between a treatise on the mining law of California and Ingersoll's lectures was a copy of Paley's ' Evidences.'

" You see, boss," he explained, " when one spends long evenings alone, one wants something solid to read, though one can't always make out what the fellow meant who wrote it. As to them ' Evidences ' — well, it's only the square thing to give both sides a show, but *I* think Bob Ingersoll ' lays all over the other duck.' "

To return to the journey. They toiled along, mile after mile, until, sick of the eternal jolting, Jack descended from the box-seat, and taking his rifle, started off in advance. The half-breed was behind with the second waggon, to which he was attracted by the hope, if not the certainty, of whisky. Jack soon got half a mile ahead, looking carefully into each sweeping valley before showing himself on the sky-line, as he was now nearing the buffalo range, and might at any moment run on to an out-lying old bull.

As he was stepping steadily along, his meditations were suddenly interrupted by the distant report of a rifle, and the whizz of a bullet a few feet over his head. He turned quickly, and not 300 yards off saw the half-breed " Muddy," who stood out clearly on the crest of the next ridge, while the puff of smoke still visible made it clear that the shot came from him. When he found himself observed, he began advancing towards Jack, who, by the irregularity of his progress, could see that he was drunk, and as he came nearer, could distinguish on his features a propitiatory, depreciative grin. Jack sighted for the middle of his chest, and kept him covered as he advanced, but " Muddy" showed not the slightest sign of uneasiness.

" What do you mean by shooting at me ? I've a good mind to do for you ! " pacifically remarked the victim.

" Don't be mad at me boss," pleaded " Muddy." " I'm real sorry; but s'help me, I thought you was a jack rabbit."

Now, to be fired at by a noted shot, in a country where all shoot well, is distinctly annoying. But to be mistaken for a jack rabbit into the bargain is adding insult to injury, and for a few seconds Jack was not quite sure whether or no he would join in " Muddy's " laugh.

At last he said, " Look here, Muddy, when you are sober you can shoot straighter than I can, but when you're drunk I can lick you every time, and when next you fire at me I'm going to shoot back. I promise you I won't miss."

" All right, boss," replied Muddy, " that's a square deal; but you can bet your boots I won't fire again — thar, shake ! "

And facing south once more, they tramped on amicably together, Muddy diving into a long story of a recent *rencontre* with a Sioux chief, whose cartridge belt he was then wearing; from which fact it may be inferred that the meeting was unpleasant in its results for the Sioux. He was in the middle of his tale, and they were crossing a low divide between two long depressions, when he crouched suddenly and threw forward his rifle, whispering, " Down, boss, down ! there's a man hid in the willows, and he may be on the shoot."

" Where is he ?" asked Jack; "I see nothing."

" He's down to the left," was the reply. "But I don't see his horse anywhere; and he can't be a hunter, for we ain't on the range yet. He's a white man, for I see his boots; but he ain't moved an inch since I first saw him. Can he be dead, I wonder?"

The two men began to creep along the shelter of the ridge towards the still figure, but they had not gone ten yards when a solitary buzzard slowly rose and circled high into the air. *That* made things clear to them, and shouldering their rifles, they advanced without further precaution. A moment later they could distinctly see a man lying on his back with his feet towards them. When they got closer they saw that he who lay there with his face upturned to the unresponsive sky was a tall and powerfully built man, while, judging from the clothes he wore, his profession was that of a miner. His attitude was so natural that he might have been sleeping, but that the shrivelled, lead-coloured features told a different tale, while a round black spot in the centre of his forehead explained how he came by his end. Muddy kept silence for a moment, though his eyes were busy searching every tuft of grass around the place where they were standing. Then he delivered himself of the conclusions he had drawn.

" There's been no fight here, or there'd be some empty shells about; likewise there ain't no horse-tracks. Some one has ' laid for ' this poor fellow and got him before he knew it. It wasn't an Indian either, or his hair would have been lifted; nor a ' road agent,' or his pockets would be empty; and see here," taking a handful of dollars from the murdered man's pocket. " No, I guess I know, who done this job. Just you open his shirt and see if there's anything wrong with his chest."

Muddy's manner was so impressive that Jack felt a thrill of horror go through his frame, even before he did as he was told, and gently touching the dead man's shirt, exposed to view a large deep cross-cut on his bared breast.

" I thought so," said Muddy, placidly.

" What did you think? What does it mean? " asked Jack, anxiously.

" The tale's too long to tell now," said Muddy — " the other chaps'll be here directly ; but I'll tell you all about it as we go on. I don't mind letting you know now, that there's buffalo not far off, 'cause this poor chap's been here a week or more, and the coyotes haven't been to look for him yet, as they certainly would if they hadn't a big herd somewhere near to feed upon."

Soon the first waggon appeared on the crest of the divide, and, in obedience to a signal, rolled slowly towards the silent little group, followed shortly by its companion. None of the men knew whose the body was, but they all seemed to be well acquainted with the strange sign it bore.

"I heard that fiend had begun his tricks again," said Bob Harker, "and sure enough it's true!"

"I should like to get within shooting distance of him once — just once!" murmured Muddy softly.

"They say there's a reward out for him," broke out one of the other men.

"No, there ain't," said Bob, "'cause the council's afraid some one would go and shoot a wrong man and bring him in to get the reward!"

Jack listened and wondered, but, as became a "tenderfoot," offered no remarks on a subject of which it was evident he knew only the results and not the cause. He suggested at last, however, that something must be done about giving the corpse a securer resting-place. They had no spades, and the ground was hard as flint, whilst they were still ten miles from the nearest water. So one of the hunters was bribed with a five-dollar bill (on which he saw a reasonable chance of shortly getting drunk again) to take a led horse and ride back to the post to report the matter. Then he was to guide a burying-party to the spot, and rejoin his companions later. The two waggons began to move on meanwhile, Jack and the half-breed walking a little in advance as before, while Bob took charge of their waggon.

Jack, of course, was eager to know who was suspected of being the assassin of the man whose body they had found, and Muddy soon plunged into the following story. Colorado and its neighbourhood was just beginning to settle down into a fairly respectable place, where murders were infrequent, and where such as did occur were usually considered to be richly deserved, — the perpetrators not being interfered with by the remarkably *short* "arm of the law" in those regions.

Such was the state of affairs the previous summer, when the driver of the Colorado spring-stage brought in news of a murder having been committed in Ute Creek. Probably no one would have been greatly disturbed by this announcement, but for several curious features in the case. The murdered man had been shot in his tracks, and then marked with two deep gashes, in the form of a cross, upon his chest. His scalp was still where nature placed it, and he had not been robbed, so that his death was not the work of either " road-agents " or Indians. Therefore it must have been the result of sheer spite or " cussedness." The whole thing seemed queer; but probably, as the murdered man was a stranger, the manner of his death would soon have been forgotten, but that a few days afterwards news was brought of two more murders — one on the road below Georgetown, and the other nearly a hundred miles off. Both were apparently the work of one hand, for neither had been robbed, and both bore the fatal sign of the deeply-cut cross on the chest; while stranger than all, although so far apart, they both appeared to have been killed the same day! Nothing had made such a stir since people first penetrated into those mountain-passes; for it looked as though some one were at work who killed for the mere pleasure of slaying, and no man knew if his turn might not come next. Search-parties were sent out, but with no result, except that they came to the conclusion that a gang was at work, for the road near the murdered man in each instance was covered with horses' tracks, but with so many, and going in such different directions, that it was useless to attempt to follow them. A week later, yet another body was found, about twenty miles south of Denver, evidently recently killed, and in the same manner, and marked with the same sign as the other three!

People now were thoroughly scared, and didn't care about going through the mountains alone, for so far no *parties* had been molested, only solitary men, who were evidently lain in wait for and murdered without the chance of a fight for their lives. The *vigilantes* took the affair up, but with no success whatever; and week after week news would come of other ghastly crossed bodies found perhaps as much as two hundred miles away from the last one; until, by the time the snow began to fly in November, there had been over twenty murders committed by that secret band of assassins. After the first snow they abruptly stopped. Evidently, then, it was old hands who were at work, and who had no idea of leaving tracks in the snow, which any " tenderfoot " would be able to read. All that winter not a man was missing, and not a ray of light was cast on the mystery! But when spring came round again, before the roads had been open a week, the South Park stage driver brought in word that another man had been found shot and crossed, some fifteen miles up in the mountains!

During the next month two more murders were added to the long list — one near Blackhawk, and one near Manitou — and people were beginning to think with a cold horror of these murdering fiends whom it seemed impossible to trace or find. The Eastern papers, too, got hold of the story, and began to have articles on the territory, saying that what between Indians, " 40-rod " whisky, and secret murders, as a law-abiding section it wasn't a success, and ought to be looked after. This made both the city council and the *vigilantes* mad, and they redoubled their efforts to find the authors of the trouble, but never a sign could they discover. The wretches knew their work too well.

" And now," wound up Muddy, after his long story, " *we've* come across the last of these jobs, and perhaps we're being ' stalked ' ourselves at this moment."

CHAPTER VI.

AN ADVENTURE ON THE PLAINS.

ON THE MARCH — PRECAUTIONS AGAINST INDIANS — "SIGN" OF BUFFALO — A BLOODY CONSPIRACY ON FOOT — A SCOUT'S LOYALTY — FURTHER ATROCITIES — BREAK-UP OF THE HUNTING PARTY — JACK JEBB JOINS IN PURSUIT OF THE MAN-SLAYER — THE PROBABLE CRIMINAL AND HIS RENDEZVOUS — TRACKED — A DESCRIPTION OF "LOST PARK" — THE SCOUT'S MODE OF ATTACK — RETRIBUTION AT LAST — A GRUESOME DIARY — THE CAREER OF "BIG FOOT" — THE LONG-CHERISHED VENGEANCE OF A MEMBER OF A SOUTHERN RACE.

AFTER the half-breed's last inspiriting remark, the pair trudged along silently for some moments, when Jack said that he thought on the whole he would rather hunt these murderers than buffalo, in which sentiment Muddy quite agreed with him, — but, as he observed, buffalo left tracks by which they could be found when wanted, while these human brutes had, so far, been careful not to do so. "All the same," he concluded, "they'll be taken some day; and then I don't think their trial will last long!"

Muddy then volunteered to change places with Bob, and got into the waggon, driving the tired team along as though they were the wretches he had been talking of. The travellers were not far from their journey's end by this time, and they reached water about sundown — a half-stagnant creek, which here and there opened into big ponds black with wild fowl. With some trouble the waggons were got over, as on the opposite side was an ideal camping-ground. The creek made a regular horse-shoe bend, surrounding some four acres of land, and leaving only a neck about forty paces broad opening into the prairie, so that both flanks, together with the rear, were well protected, while there was plenty of space for the stock to feed comfortably. The two waggons were drawn across this neck, and the tongues interlaced. Jack pitched his small tent on one flank, and then helped to build a fire of buffalo-chips on the other. The men spread their blankets either below or under the lee of the waggons, while two of them were sent to scout up and down the creek for any sign of neighbours, red or white — particularly *red*, for on his native prairie the noble red man is apt to forget the beautiful ideal set up for him in Fenimore Cooper's immortal works, and to cause

his society to be little cultivated, and less sought
for, by the unromantic hunters who know his
" little ways."

When the scouts returned, reporting that all
looked quiet, the watch was set, and a sumptuous
supper of rashers of bacon and antelope-steak
was cooked over the camp-fire, and washed down
with hot coffee. Then pipes were produced, and
each man made himself comfortable according
to his lights, for after the fatiguing day's march
they were all glad enough of a rest. Some talked
and speculated over the events of the afternoon,
while others discussed the probability of finding
buffalo next day, as during the last few hours
they had come across unmistakable " sign " of
being on the track of a large herd, which, as it
would be certain to work down to the water on
which they were encamped, they might be pretty
sure of overtaking early in the morning.

Neither Jack nor the guide felt much drawn
towards trusting their companions with the post
of sentinel during the night, as, if they didn't
murder or rob the party themselves, they were
sure to be too drunk to interfere with any stray
Rapahoes who might have a similar design ! So
it was arranged for Jack to take the first watch,
and for Bob Harker to relieve him at 1 A.M.;

the reason for this being that, when Indians make a night attack, they usually choose the hour before dawn, and therefore it was best for the old frontiersman, with his trained eye and ear, to be on duty at that time. Jack took up his post on the crest of the bluff, about fifty yards from the camp, where there was clear ground and a sky-line to watch. He had been there about half an hour, and was beginning to enjoy the desolate grandeur that was spread around him, when suddenly, and without the slightest sound, he found Bob Harker standing by his side!

"Don't make a noise, boss," said the guide; "I came over here because I have something to tell you, and if we are overheard, it'll mean an unhealthy time in store for both of us. You know them nice beauties we're camping with? Wal, I kind o' misdoubted 'em from the first, for they're a pretty tough crowd. So, just now, I thought I'd go and take a look at 'em before turning in; and I wormed myself round behind the waggons to where they're lying, with the half-breed along of 'em, and the very first words I heard was them discussing whether they hadn't better wipe you and me out. It seems they're mighty keen set on your shooting-irons, and they've found out that you've got a keg of whisky in the waggon. They allowed that *I* might give some trouble, but they didn't think much o' you, boss! One of them was to pick you off when you was stalking game to-morrow, while the other three settled me!"

"And Muddy," asked Jack, "is he in this precious plot too? I could have sworn he meant honestly by us."

"And you'd be right," was the reply, "for Muddy's on the square this time. When the others had done talking, he sat and thought for a minute, and then he says, 'Look here, boys,' says he, 'there's only four of you, now Charley's gone back to the post for the burying-party, and there's three of us. Now, I can lick any two of you, and Bob wouldn't grumble over the responsibility of the other two, while the boss saw fair-play. So I rather think we've got the draw on you this time, and you may as well chuck up the game.' Of course they growled a bit, and they tried to make him see things different, but the half-breed he stuck to his guns, and so they said they'd give it up; but we'd better keep our eyes peeled, all the same."

"Bravo, Muddy!" said Jack. "Somehow I felt sure he was straight. I'm glad you've told me this, because of course I'll keep a brighter lookout; but if it comes to blows, there's no fear of our not being able to lick those blackguards."

"Oh, we'll soon settle with them if they begin to play tricks," replied Bob; "but I'm going to turn in now, so call me at one o'clock, and — good-night."

The hours passed quickly and with no further incident, rather to Jack's surprise, considering the afternoon's adventure, the character of their companions, and the fact that the Rapahoes were reported "out." He found his vigil, in the silent charm of the prairie at midnight, so little irksome that it was nearer 2 than 1 A.M. before he called Bob Harker, and himself lay down to rest.

When he awoke the sun was up, and the camp busy over preparations for an early start. A plunge in the creek, followed by a hearty breakfast of the inevitable antelope-steak, and the party were ready to begin the day's march, hoping to come up with a herd before long, and to have a good "bag" to show by nightfall. But —

> " The best-laid schemes o' mice and men," &c.,

and they had not gone very far from their camping-place when Jack fancied he could discern a man standing on a low hill about a mile in front of them. The guide's attention being directed to the figure, after a moment's scrutiny he declared that not only was there a man on the hill, but that he was in distress of some sort, for he was standing with his arms outstretched in the attitude of crucifixion, which in the language of the plains meant that he needed help badly. So the two waggons began to make the best time they could to the hills, crossing the trail in front of them. As the party drew nearer, the man came down to meet them, and then they saw that he was not alone. Lying in the road within twenty paces of him were two stiff and rigid figures, which at the first glance could be seen to be beyond the reach of help or sympathy, even if the slightly disarranged shirt of each body had not quickly taken the travellers' thoughts back to their adventure of yesterday.

"Good heavens!" Jack exclaimed involuntarily, "this must be more work of the same hand!"

"Ay, and I'll find out *whose* hand before I'm much older," said the man who had signalled for help. "I don't know who this is," touching one corpse lightly with his foot, " but this one's my brother George! He was coming from Denver, and wrote me he'd be about here by sunrise, so I rode out to meet him, and I found him like this!" Then the poor fellow broke down completely.

"Say, ain't you Pete Taylor?" the guide asked him presently.

"Yes, and you're Bob Harker; but I was so took up with this dreadful business that I didn't recognise you at first. Look here, this whole-sale murdering has got to be stopped! You're a good tracker: won't you help me to find the brutes that's doing it?"

" Of course we'll all help," answered Jack and his guide simultaneously, while Muddy was heard to murmur something about " shooting at sight," which probably had no reference to the present company.

The rest of the men remarked that they guessed they wouldn't be of the search-party, as they could not afford to miss the chance of finding buffalo that day if they stuck to the trail. After what he had heard of their amiable intentions the previous night, Jack was very glad to get rid of them on such easy terms, and the others concurring, they got into their wag-gon and were soon lost to sight, though not at all " to memory dear."

When they were gone, the little group of men around the bodies began to look about them for tracks.

In the first place they noticed a lot of hoof-marks going backwards and forwards in the road, the newest crossing the others from north to south. They were all made by unshod horses, but none went up to the bodies. The next thing was to carefully examine these; and although they knew it would be there, each man felt a chill throughout his frame as he saw on each breast that ghastly cross.

The ground on the hillside was rocky, and hard to carry a trail over, but they soon discovered that one of the men must have seen his murderer advancing upon him and turned to run — quite fruitlessly — for he had been shot in the back and dropped at once. As for George Taylor, he seemed to have fallen in his tracks without a struggle, shot clean through the head. After examining the two corpses, Muddy knelt down and began to scrutinise the gravel, on which could be seen a few marks. He looked at each in turn, lifting a fallen leaf from one or blowing away a little dust from another. Then he moved up-hill, observing every inch of ground, until, seeming to have made up his mind, and beckoning to the others, he led the way to a rock with some dwarf pines above it, just on the shoulder where the hill dipped both ways. From this point it was possible to see for miles while being perfectly concealed from the view of any one passing along the road. Beyond the rock they found the scrub-pine boughs were bent down to make a shade, and the grass was flattened in two places facing the road. There was the ambush, and there the assassins had hidden: for it was becoming evident that there had been two at least. Jack caught sight of something in a tuft of buffalo-grass, and stooping quickly, he picked up an empty metallic cartridge.

"Winchester carbine did this business," he remarked.

"Right you are, boss!" said Bob. "Now we must find out where the horses were hid, and then we'll follow the trail if it takes us over the Rio Grande!"

They soon discovered that the horses had been feeding and resting a little lower down, for there they came upon a piece of ground which was simply a mass of unshod tracks. Muddy stopped to puzzle them out, while Jack consulted with the old guide as to the best thing to be done.

To find the murderers and give them a "long

rope and a short shrift" they were resolved, but
so far it was impossible to say how many there
were in the gang; and after the long chase they
were likely to have, it would be a pity to let any
of these ruffians slip through their fingers for
want of sufficient numbers, as of course, with the
record they had against them, not one of the
hunted men would allow himself to be taken
alive if he could help it.

It was finally decided that, as Pete Taylor
would naturally be anxious to dispose decently
of his brother's remains, he should take the two
bodies in the waggon back to Alma — the place
from which he had that morning started — and
there despatch a posse, with instructions to meet
the search-party at a waggon-pass on the red
hills, whither both Bob and Muddy felt sure the
trail would lead. Should they prove to be mistaken as to this, one of them would ride back
to meet the reinforcement. Pete agreed to the
plan, saying that he should be of the party starting from Alma.

As soon as he had left with his terrible load,
Jack and his companions held a council of war,
chiefly that Bob and Muddy might compare
their discoveries before starting on what they
all felt would be a desperate undertaking. Both

men were sure that there had been nearly a
dozen horses, though it was impossible as yet
to say how many were mounted.   Also, some of
these horses had been scattered just below, but
all had crossed the road in two bands, and head-
ing south, would be bound to go by the waggon-
road gap.   If on reaching this the trail bent
east, then Bob was certain of coming up with
the murderers by the next night; for in that
case they could only be in one place — a spot
known as the " Lost Park."   Bob said he had
always believed he was the only person who
knew the way into it, but he began to think that
it was the hiding-place of the men they were in
search of.   He added that he was pretty sure
now of the identity of one of them.

" Look at this ! " he exclaimed, pointing to a
mark on the ground which Jack could hardly
see, although in course of time he became no
bad tracker himself — " look at that point !   It's
no more a ranchman's boot than it's a mocca-
sin !   It's a sharp-toed, Southern-made boot.
And don't you two see something else peculiar
about it ? "

" It seems to be a good size, doesn't it ? "
ventured Jack.

" Size !   It's just thirteen and a half inches,

and there's only one man *I* ever heard on as carries a hoof like that around with him! But we mustn't waste time talking, so let's be off."

They mounted the led horses and started in a bee-line for a low range of hills, which they could see from where they had been standing, although the hills were at least fifteen miles off. They reached the gap at which they were to meet the others before nightfall, and as they had to wait three hours or more before the party could arrive from Alma, they got a little sleep, after Bob and Muddy had satisfied themselves that the trail did turn off east, as they had expected. Another trail, coming from the south, joined the one they had been following at the gap. By-and-by the "boys," led by Pete Taylor, began to drop in one by one, and dismounting, asked eagerly for news.

"Wal," began Bob, " I guess we're more than enough to handle the cusses, for Muddy and me thinks there's only two of 'em, with five loose horses running free. There may be more where they're camped, but it isn't likely. We'd better start in about two hours, so as to get into cover of the woods by daylight. There is only one pass into the place they're bound for, so we can follow them at our leisure: we've got the brutes caged this time ! And now I'll tell you, chaps, who it is as you're after: it's that big Mexican cuss they had in the Denver legislature — him and a pard ! I've never seen him, but they say he's the strongest man south of the State line; and as to shooting — well, any of you as gets a chance of drawing a bead on him had better *shoot straight,* if ever you did in your lives."

Two hours later the whole party moved on, and before daylight were safely hidden in the timbered slopes of the range. There was no difficulty about tracking now, for apparently the murderers had felt safe here, and had made no attempt to hide the broad fresh trail, leading ever upward and onward. About noon a halt was called, in order that a hurried breakfast might be eaten. Then with increased caution the men resumed their march, until a small glade was reached, where the horses were unsaddled and turned loose. Beyond this glade the cañon narrowed and became steeper. It was cumbered by fallen trees and immense boulders, shadowed by great yellow pines which met overhead, darkening and obscuring the prospect.

At last the top of the pass was reached, and through the tangle of underbrush could be seen, some hundreds of feet below, an exquisite little park, about two miles long and half a mile broad. This glen was completely walled in by precipitous cliffs covered with dense pine-forests. In the centre of the park was one small clump of timber, from which a thin stream of smoke was visible to the watching eyes that looked down eagerly, certain of their prey at last. Cautiously they made their way along the steep trail, till they reached the heavy fringe of timber clothing the foot of the cliffs, which towered above them. Then they paused for a whispered consultation. The difficulty now, having treed their bear, was how to bring him down; for there was a level sweep of grass, with no shelter, between the pursuers and the pursued, and if they attempted to cross this, the enemy could sit in his thicket and pick them off at his leisure. After some discussion, the men decided to stop where they were until about an hour before sunrise, when the two ruffians would most likely be sleeping — that is, if they ever slept at all — and then, working carefully across the open on three sides, before it grew light, be ready to fire the instant a leaf in the thicket stirred.

"But why not rush the camp, as soon as it is dark enough to get there without being seen?" asked Jack.

" Rush the camp! " repeated Bob, with much scorn; "can't you see there's a lot of dead wood on that grass, and the first twig a greenhorn snapped our birds would be off, and ten to one we should miss them. No; we must wait until we can see to shoot; unless they build a big fire, which, not being tenderfoots, they ain't fools enough to do."

Crushed by this scathing reply, Jack decided not to offer any more advice just then. After a slight and silent supper of cold meat and biscuits, they all lay down to get a little sleep, except, of course, the sentry. The night passed quickly. The moon sank behind the mountains, and a denser darkness settled on the valley; but as the sharp chill which precedes the dawn caused the sleepers to turn uneasily in their blankets, the sentry went round, and, without a word being spoken, awoke them all.

In a few minutes the first three men detailed to advance on the pine-clump from the opposite side had started. Ten minutes later the rest, among whom was Jack, moved silently beyond the dense shadow of the wood, and one by one they crouched and crept towards the solitary thicket two hundred yards off in the open. Then a long wait comes, while the stars grow fainter, and the shadows under the great pines of a less opaque blackness — the only sounds breaking the deadly silence being the bellow of a wapiti and the occasional hoot of an owl; until, as the dawn strengthens, even these are still — so still that when a muffled figure in the midst of the pine-clump slowly rises and begins to throw an armful of wood on the dying fire, the slight sound rings like thunder in the ears of the listeners. He stoops, rises again, as a sharp whiplike crack passes through the air, and then falls back, tossing the blanket wildly. Then — for an instant only — another figure is seen leaping a fallen tree, on which two saddles are resting. There are two more hurried shots, and — dead silence!

The party waited a few moments before beginning to advance cautiously through the underwood to a small natural clearing in the centre, from which a steady stream of smoke arose. A fallen tree sheltered one side of it, and behind this, with his glazing eyes staring up to the brightening sky, lay old " Big Foot," the man they had expected to find. A revolver was tightly clutched in one hand, and his grey face was distorted by such a scowl of mingled horror and hatred as haunted those who saw it to their own last day. Near by, fallen right across the camp-fire, lay the body of his nephew and partner in crime. What he might have carried about him was never known, for his clothes were on fire; but in his uncle's breast-pocket they found a mass-book and a diary, and in the diary were twenty-seven dates marked with a black cross, corresponding to the ghastly red signs which he had drawn upon the breasts of his many victims.

Great crimes are not always bred of great injuries, for this was the trivial cause of his fiendish hate and vengeance. It seemed that when Colorado and New Mexico had a joint-legislature, he was one of the Mexican delegates chosen to go to Denver. Of course the two sets of men detested each other, and the Colorado "boys" were for ever playing tricks on the Mexicans, who retaliated when they could. But this particular Mexican took it all in earnest, and when he was finally christened "Big Foot," in delicate allusion to the size of his extremities, he fairly boiled over, and left the court-house, cursing the whole American nation (including the Canadas), and swearing he would be bitterly revenged upon his tormentors. That was the last the joint-legislature of Colorado and New Mexico ever saw of him; but they heard that he had made a bee-line for his own country, swearing like a "singed cat" as he went.   Of course the "boys" were simply charmed when they found they had driven him out, never heeding his threats, nor remembering how a member of a Southern race will keep his hatred warm year in and year out until he sees a safe chance of gratifying it.   And it is doubtful whether even in his last agony old Big Foot ceased to gloat over the achievements of his deadly hate, and the thought that wherever his nickname was heard, there also would be told the story of his revenge.

CHAPTER VII.

SPORT IN COLORADO.

AFTER the bodies had been disposed of, and the
fatigue of the exciting chase and still more exciting " kill " had worn off a little, the party of
trackers began to climb up the steep cliff and
wend their way to the place where they had left
their horses; discussing with much prospective
joy, meanwhile, the rage of the sheriff of the
county when he found that two such criminals
as he was scarcely likely to see again had met
their deserts without his professional assistance !

" He's not a bad sort," said Pete Taylor, " but he's too fond of bringing in the law if he sees a chance, and we don't need no law when we go out to settle up with chaps like them we've been after." In which sentiment the " boys " heartily concurred.

Once started, they met with little or no incident on the homeward way; but it was a long ride, and they were a dusty and weary crowd that rode into Alma a week from the day of their departure, with stiffness in their limbs, but conscious pride writ large upon their faces. Of course, directly their tale was heard, the entire population insisted on "standing drinks." Fortunately it numbered less than a thousand all told; but even a few hundred drinks taken together will prove cloying to the thirstiest soul; and before he got away even Muddy felt that for one short period of Elysium he had absorbed as much whisky as he could hold. As for Jack Jebb! it was considered in the town that any man who could keep his head clear and his legs well in hand after several hours of very mixed refreshments, no longer deserved the opprobrious name of "tenderfoot"; and any Alma boy who heard him so spoken of afterwards, considered it a personal matter calling for the use of shooting-irons. Owing to propitious circumstances, he had seen more of prairie life in a week than the average traveller might in a year, and now he was anxious to pursue the original object of his journey — the shooting of big game. Bob Harker was willing to accompany him; but Muddy decided that he had had enough excitement for one while, and guessed he would return to the quiet pursuits of a Government scout — tracking bands of marauding Indians and warning outlying camps of their coming, always, of course, with the certainty of being scalped if caught. Poor Muddy! It was the general opinion that there was a good deal more whisky than " cussedness " in him as a rule, but it was his fate eventually to be strung up by *vigilantes* for shooting a man — who doubtless would have been beforehand with him had he been as handy with his gun.

Well, Jack and the old guide started afresh with their waggon, and began journeying westward over the wide plains, where the snow-clad Rocky Mountains stretched away in their weird beauty on the horizon, for many and many a desolate league. Frequently for days and weeks the travellers met no living soul, save an occasional band of trappers, or a solitary Indian brave. But the lack of human interest in the scenery was amply compensated for by such sights as great herds of buffalo spreading out as far as the eye could reach, and fading away into a dim brown-blue in the distance; or the graceful antelope feeding down towards water black with wild fowl. Many things they saw which can never again gladden the hunter's heart, for the remorseless tide of civilisation, which, twenty years ago, was chafing and fretting against the long chain of the Rockies, has now burst through their rugged passes. The buffalo is gone. The wapiti is getting scarce. The dirty Indian brave has given place to the not much cleaner cowboy. The trappers' camps and waggons have been superseded by railways and the great American caravanseries called hotels; and one wonders whether the plains have gained in any other way what they have lost in picturesqueness.

Men now hustle and jostle each other, and often fall in the long battle of life, because they have created for themselves so many artificial wants which must be gratified before they can be content; while in the old days, with the keen, fresh air of the prairies about him, the thousand interests of the hunter to occupy him, a man needed little but his bed and his dinner. And surely sleep is never so restful as by a camp-fire, or a meal so refreshing as when one must kill the game, and cook it over the glowing wood, before it can be eaten.

Many a fine old buffalo-bull fell to Jack's gun, in the years he spent wandering about the plains. For the fascination of the free life grew upon him, and this was the beginning of long months of "camping out"— sometimes with the guide, sometimes with a chance companion, and often quite alone. Occasionally when game was scarce he would go to sleep hungry, but generally he shot all he wanted, and did a fair trade in skins besides. Plenty of narrow escapes he had too, from Indians and bears,—the former, eminently serious adventures; the latter, sometimes funny ones. He once "joined camp" for a time with an American colonel, also out after game. Returning to their tent one day, to their delight they came across bear-tracks close to it — the brute being tempted to the camp doubtless by the scent of the fresh meat hanging up. As he made off too quickly for them to get a shot, they set to work to construct a "fall-trap" — a thing rather like a gigantic mouse-trap, built with heavy logs, and usually quite efficacious. The drawback, however, to this apparatus in the mind of the sportsman is, that unless the prey is to be ignominiously murdered by being shot at through chinks in the logs, the door of the trap must be lifted while the hunter takes his chance of a flying shot; with the prospect of an animated five minutes before him should he miss!

Well, after preparing a safe shelter for their expected visitor, the two men retired to rest, and early next morning they went to see if he had arrived. They found him securely fastened down and savagely worrying the logs in his efforts to get out. Of course, his captors were charmed with their success, and at once began to discuss which of them should lift the door, while the other stood at the post of honour and took the shot. They were both good sportsmen, and neither liked to deprive the other of the first chance at the enemy, so they argued the matter for some time; until, by a happy inspiration, the colonel proposed settling it by a game of cards — the winner to shoot, while the loser turned the bear out for him. There happened to be no smooth piece of ground close by, so they adjourned to a flat rock about

fifty yards off, and, with cartridges and buckshot for " chips," settled down to a game of
poker. The game soon began to get exciting
on its own account, as the cards favoured first
one and then the other; and little bright-eyed
chipmunks and busy squirrels ran to and fro
between the players, attracting no notice at all.
They had been playing for two hours, and the
sun had climbed far up towards the meridian,
when with a laugh, the colonel raked in Jack's
last buckshot and won — winning, besides the
stakes, the right to generously present his companion with the first shot. They reloaded their
rifles, and softly approached the trap, Jack getting into a position which would give him an
excellent shot when the bear bolted, while the
colonel quietly stepped on the roof in order to
lift the door. As he did so, he turned his face
slowly towards his friend. A look of misery
and disgust was in his eyes, as, with remarks
that it would take two cowboys and a muleteer
to do justice to, he said, " —— ! —— ! —— !
—— ! if the —— ! —— ! —— ! brute hasn't eaten
his way out, while we've been fooling with those
—— ! —— ! —— ! —— ! cards ! "

This colonel afterwards became quite a noted
bear-hunter in the Rocky Mountains, and strange

to say, he never got " mauled," though on one occasion nothing but straight shooting saved his life. His usual practice was to stalk his game while it was feeding, as, when a bear has got its head well down over its food, and is thoroughly absorbed in the business on hand, the hunter can creep up within easy range and get a capital shot. No old bear-hunter will risk a long shot at a bear in the open, unless there is cover of some sort near, or he is so sure of his shooting that he knows his left-hand barrel can be depended upon if the beast is only slightly wounded and charges him. But on this occasion the colonel, who had been working round the crest of a mountain, suddenly, while crossing a steep gully filled with snow, caught sight of three bears about a hundred and fifty yards below him. He was armed with a double ·500 express, and he felt that the shot was too tempting to be resisted, especially since the snow-slide was so steep that he would have plenty of time for reloading, supposing any of the brutes began scrambling up towards him.

The old she-bear, with her two half-grown cubs, caught sight of him at the same moment that he first saw them, and stood, lumped together, looking up at him as he shot at them with both barrels. One cub rolled over dead, and the mother was evidently hit, for she went spinning round, savagely biting at her shoulder. But there was plenty of fight left in her, for in another instant she and the remaining cub were floundering and scrambling up the steep snow-slide towards their aggressor. He reloaded quickly, and was in the act of crouching down again to get a steady shot, when his foot slipped from under him, throwing him violently on his back, and before he had time even to think, he was sliding rapidly down the slopes of frozen snow towards the two bears, who were climbing up to take their revenge for the death of the cub. Down, down he went, almost falling over the old bear, which made a vicious grab at him with her paw as he passed; but fortunately her wounded shoulder failed her, so she contented herself with turning round, and half sliding, half rolling, she followed him down. The colonel slid gracefully past the dead cub, and so did its mother; but luckily for the hunter, she managed to stop herself an instant to growl over her defunct offspring, which maternal tribute of affection gave the colonel time to get to the bottom of his involuntary

slide. It was probably less than ten seconds
from the start when he found himself standing
on *terra firma* again, badly shaken, and minus
both his cartridge-pouch and an important portion of his attire !

He had kept his head better than he had his
footing, and had never let go his rifle, which,
thanks be given ! was loaded. The bear was
now scrambling down again; and with not a
tree in sight, and his cartridges lying round
loose on the mountain-side, the colonel knew
that a miss, or even a poor shot, would seal his
fate. It was life or death, and he was still shaking so much from his rapid descent through the
air that he could scarcely hold the rifle. He
dared not shoot, and the bear was only thirty
yards off. A quick backward glance showed
him a boulder not far away; he backed towards
it, got behind, and waited. On came the great
brute: she passed the end of the snow-slide,
made a short rush over the rocks, and then
reared up and sprang forward, not five paces
from where the colonel awaited her, his hand
steady enough now. The express rang out,
and she dropped dead, literally at the hunter's
feet. Not fifty yards away the half-grown cub
was making off, pausing a second to look back

for its mother — a fatal pause, for there was still another cartridge left, and an instant later the cub was rolling down the slope.

The colonel's escape was a narrow one; but he always maintained that three bears made a very good " bag " for the small expenditure of four cartridges and a pair of old breeches.

Life in the Rockies was never wanting in incident in those days. There were times when the scattered camps wished that it had been; when, for instance, the Utes were reported restless, and there were rumours of the sun-dance being held, and of the young braves insisting on being paid nothing but ammunition for their furs. Then those white men who were wise fell back quickly on a common centre; but sometimes an outlying camp would be surprised, and then, no matter how desperate the fight, its result was certain, and soon nothing was left of what a few moments before had been a busy active community but a pile of quivering bodies and scalpless heads.

A rumoured Indian rising once gave Jack Jebb an excellent opportunity of getting even with a beef-contractor who had sold him an old work-ox for a steer, by frightening the man nearly out of his wits. Jack had arrived safely at a large camp, and with several others lay sheltering from a cutting wind among some rocks, when he caught sight of the contractor and a couple of men some hundred yards below, also hastening into security from the dreaded Utes. He thought first of putting a bullet into a tree-trunk close to the contractor's ear, but a better plan suggested itself. Half-a-dozen men lay down behind the rocks, pointing their rifles over them, while the contractor and his companions went on climbing placidly, until, when within about thirty yards of the top, they stopped and looked up at the rocks above them. Their looks of consternation and amazement when they saw six rifles deliberately aiming at them *may* be imagined, but cannot be described. They had no cover, not a chance of escape, and not the smallest glimpse of anything to shoot at. Almost automatically their three rifles fell to the ground, and six arms were held high above three horror-stricken heads.

"For God's sake, don't shoot!" they yelled. "We ain't armed."

"Then will you swear never to run in an old work-ox on us for good steer-beef?" they were asked.

"D—d if we'll swear!" was the answer; "we thought you was Indians, sure."

It was about this date that Jack first met General Fremont, the discoverer of California; and, fired by his glowing accounts of the " Golden State," he resolved to inspect it at the first opportunity — partly because he had never been there, which with him was always an excellent reason for starting to the ends of the earth, but chiefly because he wanted to see what the placer-mining was like, in which nearly the whole population of California was then engaged. Moreover, he felt that somehow he must soon begin to make money himself, for the years were slipping imperceptibly past, and he was still in very much the same position as when first he found himself thrown upon his own resources. In those days a buffalo was worth about $1, 50 cents, and a bear not much more; so hunting, though a fascinating, was not a very profitable pursuit. Then, too, all the world was beginning to get infected with the mining craze, whether gold, silver, placer, or otherwise. Nothing was talked or dreamt of but the hidden riches which could be found for the seeking. Denver was at that time a little outpost of about 5000 inhabitants, while Leadville, regarded as a mining centre, did not exist at all. In fact, a far-seeing speculator with a few dollars in his pocket could have bought up the land containing the wealthiest mines of Colorado. Mining was just the sort of risky business, both physically and financially, to suit Jack Jebb to perfection, so none of his friends were surprised when he caught the contagion. Together with another man he already owned a small property in the mountains, which so far they had been unable to develop for want of working capital, although they had each put both money and labour into it. But at this juncture some wealthy friends of Jack's who had seen the little mines and become interested in them came forward with an offer of co-operation; and while his partner returned to England with these people in order to arrange details, Jack paid his first visit to San Francisco.

How lovely it looked with its blue sea and towering mountains, its gorgeous flowers and abundant fruits, and the stately palaces which even in those days were beginning to rise upon its rocky eminences. It is true that the people were less cultivated than their surroundings, and that a six-shooter was as necessary an article of attire as trousers; still the *vigilantes* were hard at work improving all that, and the charm of a new civilisation makes up for many defects.

Jack soon pushed on to Sacramento, then at its very worst and rowdiest; for the gold-fever was at its height, and all the sweepings of Europe and America were gathered there, drinking and gambling, fighting and murdering, with little restraint and less compunction — a " straight shot " the only reputation of any importance. Jack had long ceased to be a " tenderfoot "; nor, with his stalwart frame and strongly-marked bronzed features, did he look like one: so he managed to steer clear of " rows," despite the damaging facts that he neither drank nor played, and had the misfortune to be a " Britisher." For one thing, he did not stop long in any particular mining-camp, but moved on from one to another, trying to get some general idea of the " lay of the land." Crowded as it was with a large and usually unwashed populace, Sacramento could scarcely be described as a health resort at the best of times, but there was one part of the valley deadlier than the rest, where the air that was breathed and the water that was drunk — supposing any one ever did drink water — seemed to be impregnated with the germs of fever.

Of course Jack's usual luck induced him to make a week's stay in this place, and long before the end of the week his old enemy had found him out, and he was down with a bad attack of fever and ague. The local medical talent — an Irish apothecary's apprentice — insisted on his stopping in bed, taking quinine by the pailful, and above all, never indulging in a single drop of water either outwardly or inwardly. Jack bore this treatment for some days, the quinine of course making his head ache furiously, and engendering a wild longing for even one dip into anything cold. Then he revolted, and watching his opportunity, the first time he was left alone, he rolled himself in a blanket, crawled out of the hut down to a creek which ran a few yards below it, there discarded his blanket, and sat down to rest in the creek! The water was only up to his neck, but he could obviate that misfortune by ducking, which pastime he indulged in cheerfully for the next hour. Meanwhile his medical man returned to find the patient missing; and fully believing that, in the united delirium of fever and quinine, the invalid had destroyed himself, he roused the whole camp to search for "remains."

The camp nearly had a fit, between horror and surprise, when it came upon the supposed corpse placidly enjoying life in the creek! He was promptly hauled out, and told that although not dead yet, he might shortly expect his decease after such an escapade. But, strange to say, the fever appeared to have left him; and when the turn of the "shakes" came round they failed to arrive, so that his fatal immersion seemed really to have cured him! — a fact which can only be accounted for by the general contrariness of his affairs. Any one else would have died; he therefore recovered.

Even diphtheria took on a different form for his benefit. Some years later he was living alone in a log-hut, several miles from his nearest neighbour, when he began to feel ill and feverish, and to experience an increasing difficulty in swallowing. This went on for a few days, until matters grew so serious that one morning he found himself unable to rise, while not only was it impossible to swallow anything, but it was rapidly becoming equally impossible to breathe. With a horrible feeling of imminent suffocation, he started up in bed in a last endeavour to shake off the invisible power which seemed to be clutching at his throat, when — possibly induced by the sudden movement — a violent fit of coughing came on, in the midst of which what he afterwards described as a thick white skin, several inches long, tore itself away from his panting throat, and he immediately discovered that his breathing had become perfectly easy and natural again. In fact, so well did he feel that, seeing no particular reason for stopping in bed, he shortly afterwards got up and went about his business; and it was not till later on that it dawned upon him that he had recovered from an attack of diphtheria which ought to have killed him, alone and unaided as he was, and which could only have failed in doing so through sheer " cussedness."

But to return to Sacramento valley. Having now spent as much time there as he cared to, Jack began to retrace his way to Colorado, being accompanied for some distance by a party of miners who, having made their " pile," were hastening to New York as the most promising place in which to get rid of it with the least delay.

CHAPTER VIII.

FURTHER PURSUIT OF GOLD.

WHEN Jack returned to Denver he found his friend awaiting him there, with the financial prelimi-naries of the projected syndicate so satisfactorily arranged that they were not only able to continue working the small mines they already possessed, but were justified in buying some adjoining property which they had long wished to add to their own. The present owner was selling be-cause he preferred a reasonable sum down to large but uncertain dividends in the future — thereby showing himself to be wiser than his generation — and he was very glad to respond to the overtures the partners made to him.

The mines rejoiced in the prophetic name of the " Great Whale," bestowed upon them probably in modest allusion to their supposed superiority to all other mines; and no more suitable title could have been found, though for an entirely different reason, for they were destined to swallow all that was thrust into their capacious maw. Jack's contribution was about £3000, which a year of steady work was to develop into £12,000, besides a large number of shares. The syndicate was an entirely private one, and the arrangement was that Jack, who one way and another had picked up a good deal of mining experience during his years of wandering, should take a large part of the management on himself — thereby both saving expense and obviating much of the reckless waste that often ruins a promising property.

Jack wished for nothing better than the laborious but free and unconventional life of the Rocky Mountains, and he was quite willing to take up his abode there altogether. No one knew better than he the difficulties and dangers to be contended against, especially in winter, when it was almost impossible to get from place to place, through the driving storms, and when frozen extremities were among the pleasantest of the accidents likely to happen to the belated traveller. But in spite of all this, the keen dry air of the Rockies was delicious, and Jack started in high spirits for his headquarters — a log-hut near the principal mine — with many anticipations of the fortune he was to make, and of the steam-yacht in which he would immediately invest it.

To his great satisfaction he found that some old Boston friends were going to spend a few years on a mining property they possessed not many miles from his own location; and as there was already one family within fifteen miles, and his own partner would be backwards and forwards frequently, the neighbourhood was evidently going to be quite populous — for Colorado. The little log-cabins each had a huge stove in the centre of the room; for no ordinary fireplace could keep out the bitter cold when the temperature was below zero, and water froze within a yard of the fire. No one particularly objected to this state of affairs, however, as for one thing it stopped the operations of " road-agents " during the winter, while even the Rapahoes scarcely cared to go out shooting stage-drivers, with every

chance of perishing themselves in the snow.
Still they made occasional sallies, and one afternoon a driver came in with an arrow through his
cheek and a loose tooth in his throat — the part
of the matter which most troubled him being
that, in these circumstances, he was unable to
swear properly!

After getting the machinery up and the mines
at work, the next thing to be thought of was a
stock of provisions for the six months during
which the trails would probably be snowed up.
Game was plentiful, and Jack soon supplied the
larder with sufficient meat, while groceries were
carted from the nearest settlement. Once the
snows began, it was the rarest thing for any one
to leave the mines before spring. Now and then
a man would go for the mails, but probably not
once a-month. Therefore Jack found that he
would have to make the expedition alone when
he wished to visit the various mines in the district, all three of which were chiefly under his
control; so that he was likely to get quite as
much solitary snow-shoeing as he wanted before
the winter was over. He usually travelled at
night, partly to get an extra day at whichever
mine he was bound for, and partly because the
snow is then in better condition, and there are

fewer chances of an avalanche above timber-line. Of course the only way of getting about at all was on snow-shoes, as without them there was nothing to prevent the traveller sinking in up to his neck; and floundering through loose snow is a process that would quickly exhaust the strongest man in the world.

On one memorable occasion, Jack started on a nocturnal journey at 1 A.M., and, blessed with a good moon, he made capital time, reaching the crest of the range by daylight. The snow was in excellent travelling condition, the crust being just soft enough to let the twelve-feet Norwegian shoes he was using bite well. All the lower branches of the pines were covered, and in the gulch below the snow must have been at least twenty feet deep. On the crest it was blowing hard, and the wind having swept the ridges clear, he had to carry his shoes for half a mile or so, to where a long valley through which his road ran headed up to the highest peak — 13,200 feet above sea-level. Of course it was frightfully cold up there, and the wayfarer was well pleased when he caught the first glimpse of the pine-clad valley below, and saw that he was just in the right place for starting the run down-hill — the most enjoyable part of the journey, after the first mile or two, which was rather *too* steep to be pleasant.

One of the advantages of the Norwegian snow-shoe is, that it cuts into hard snow just deep enough to give a grip without sinking so far as to stop the pace, and on a steep down-grade it is possible to go at almost any speed, if the balance-pole be used carefully.

Jack fastened his shoes on again, and started down-hill, going slowly at first, and then faster and faster as the plateau dipped off towards the head of the valley. He had run about half-a-mile, and was travelling almost at top speed, when suddenly he found himself in the air, and got a fall which nearly stunned him. He had struck a sheet of ice, and of course the shoes lost their bite instantly, depositing their startled wearer on the broad of his back without a moment's warning! Naturally, they both came off, and although he clutched at them instinctively, he only succeeded in saving *one* — the other was already beyond reach, sliding rapidly out of sight down the mountain-side. As he watched it disappearing, Jack felt sick for a moment — which may have been the effect of the crack on the head he had received in his fall, or the punch in the ribs from his revolver, but it was probably the knowledge that if that shoe was really gone, he might reckon on his fingers the number of hours he had to live. The snow around him was very deep, and though it was harder some hundred yards above, he did not think he could get there; while even if he succeeded in doing so, there were still four or five miles of snow, from ten to thirty feet thick, between himself and his destination. To get through that was impossible; and even could he flounder as far as timber-line, build a fire, and camp there, it so happened that he was not expected home for four days, and if any one tried to follow him later, his tracks would certainly be snowed up.

Before him were twenty miles of mountain and valley to the nearest camp. And to stay where he was meant being frozen to death in a few hours. There was plenty of choice, but of nothing agreeable. Then he began to think of the possibility of following his shoe, which would of course slide down the steepest grade it could find, and would therefore pass into the lower valley by means of a rocky gorge, which Jack could see from where he stood, and which was a thoroughly break-neck place, with mountains of snow in and around it, whence it would be impossible to climb up again, should the quest

be unsuccessful.   However, *any* chance was
worth trying in such a desperate case, and Jack
thought that as the shoe he had would naturally
follow its mate if placed on the same grade, his
best plan would be to lie down upon it, start
sliding, and trust to its being stopped by whatever had arrested its fellow.

Of course the odds were that the first shoe
had gone over a precipice or splintered on a
point of rock, and that the same fate would over-
take the second, together with its burden; but
if a man *must* die, then a quick death is better
than the slow torture of freezing or starving, and
Jack decided to risk his fate and start in pursuit.
Accordingly, he carefully found the place where
the accident had happened, put the remaining
shoe on the track, and then lay down along it,
rounding his chest as much as possible and
steering with his elbows.   Down they went! —
sometimes sliding along gaily, sometimes ploughing heavily through the soft drift: on and on,
it seemed to the anxious traveller, interminably.
He watched keenly for any trace of the lost
shoe; at the same time keeping a bright lookout for any ghastly header that might be in
front of him.   At last he came to a turn in the
gully, and could scarcely believe in his good

fortune when he caught sight of the lost shoe sticking out of some drift in front! Slowly and anxiously he extricated it, fearing lest the toe might have struck a rock and splintered. But no — it was all right ; and in a moment more he was safe, and sweeping down into timber.

How homelike and friendly the tops of the pines looked too, after the bare bleak slopes above on whose freezing heights he had expected to remain until he also was cold and rigid as they. Although he had now lost a good deal of time, yet when he got to the mouth of the valley he was so wet, cold, and hungry that he decided to stop there for a rest. So he built a good fire and made himself as comfortable as circumstances would admit. It had now begun to storm, the clouds boiling up blacker and blacker every moment, and the snow blowing past like steam. This made snow-shoeing very difficult, as newly fallen snow sticks to the sole and drags terribly. But Jack had already made up his mind that all the delay which had occurred would prevent his reaching his destination that day — the days being very short — while the night was evidently going to be a wild one.

About two miles farther on was the site of an

old-time mining-camp, which had once been a busy place, but was now deserted, and had but a few log-cabins left standing. The stream had shifted its course and swept most of the village away; but one or two huts still stood, filled half-way to the roof with tailings that had silted in through the unchinked logs. In one of these ruins Jack now decided either to spend the night altogether, or to halt until the moon gave light enough to show the way; so he started afresh, toiling on hour after hour, until it was nearly dark when he entered the clearing surrounding "Gold Hollow." Here and there blackened stumps or the gaping rafters of a cabin stuck up through the snow; then came the solitary chimney of an old forge, from behind which Jack remembered getting a good shot at a deer in the previous autumn, and a little farther on were the bare walls of two more huts. He wondered if any human being had visited the place since he was hunting there three months before, and he also wondered whether — outside the North Pole — there was any one else in the world likely to have so solitary and dreary a camp as he was in for that night. It had stopped snowing, but was darker than ever, as, wet and weary, he dragged himself along. There were but a few hundred yards more before he reached the centre of the village, where he remembered seeing two cabins with roofs on, which, if they could not keep out wind and weather, could at least be used for firing. As he walked he noticed that a trail of some kind crossed the smooth belt of snow which defined the main street; but it was too dark to see clearly, and, moreover, he felt too tired to think or care about it. But a few yards farther on it occurred again, and stooping down he tried to look at it, but could make out nothing, so bending lower he carefully *felt* it. There could be no mistake about it then; it was a bear's track, and a big one at that! Jack pushed on faster to the old cabin, now in sight — wondering what had brought the brute out a good month before they are accustomed to be disturbed by the pangs of a six-months' appetite. Once inside the cabin, he thought, with a good fire started and a few logs against the door, he could keep out any fool of a bear who risked catching cold by experimenting with the early-rising movement.

Again and again he saw the tracks dimly as he hurried along, and reaching the hut, threw off his snow-shoes and slid down the steep bank of snow the wind had eddied out, to the door, which still hung on its raw-hide hinges. There he paused, for the ground was simply padded over with tracks, and while in the act of stretching out his hand towards the door, he fancied he heard a slight sound within. Then it flashed through his mind that the mystery of the tracks was solved. The old bear had " holed up " in the cabin. Jack stood perfectly still and listened intently; but the faint rustle he had heard was not repeated. Everything was silent as the grave. Noiselessly he unsheathed his knife, and took the blade between his teeth; noiselessly he freed his revolver and ran his fingers over the points of the bullets. A full minute had passed since he heard the sound from inside, and it had not yet been repeated; so he took out three or four wax matches, and was ready for the worst. He was sure of being in for a desperate fight, in which the chances were that he would go under, but if he tried to retreat, the brute would rush after him; besides, he was cold, tired, and savage, and possessed by a sort of indignation, that with the whole mountain to choose from, the bear should have taken to the particular cabin in which he himself was quite resolved to spend the night.

He was so angry, in fact, that he would almost as soon fight as not, and he decided that the best plan would be to strike a bunch of matches, kick open the door, and shoot while the glint of light was in the bear's eyes, trusting to his knife for the rest. He struck his matches on a piece of rusty iron nailed across the door, kicked it in, and was in the very act of pulling the trigger, when, as the light flamed up, instead of the green sparks of a bear's eyes, he saw the muzzle of a rifle pointing straight at his head! Instinctively he jerked aside, as the wind, whistling round the cabin, blew out the matches, and from the darkness of the hut a scared voice said, "For God's sake, stranger, don't shoot! I thought you was a b'ar!"

"And I thought you were another," replied Jack. "A nice five minutes you've given me! Who are you, anyway? And what are you doing here?"

In another moment, when an armful of dry pine-tassels was blazing up the chimney, Jack discovered his "bear" to be an old prospector whom he had met occasionally during the last two years, and who over a tin pot of hot coffee began to explain his reasons for keeping house in that most unlikely neighbourhood. It seemed that he had struck a lead of free gold up the gulch in the autumn, and fearing lest any of the " boys " should discover and stake it out before he had time to do so himself, he decided on taking up his winter quarters in the ruined hut, in order to get to work the moment the snow would let him. He finished by begging Jack not to tell any one of his location and prospects, as he " despised a crowd."

" All right," said Jack, " if you'll tell me how you came to make ' bear '-tracks, for I'll swear that I wasn't mistaken about seeing those."

" Oh, that's easy done," was the reply. " Ever since I got my feet frozen two years ago, they're mighty liable to freeze again, so I just cut up the gunney sack I toted my traps here in, wound it round my toes, and padded about that way. I daresay it *would* look like b'ar-tracks."

Well, the belated traveller passed a much pleasanter night than he had hoped for at some stages of the day's experiences, and in the morning, the snow having ceased, he started once more on his journey, reaching the mining camp without further adventures. Once there, he was soon telling his misfortunes to a sympathetic crowd of " boys." When he got to the

bear part of the story they laughed, and said
that their camp cook had also suffered a beautiful fright a few months ago. It appeared that
he had come home one night with only one
boot on, his hat gone, and his appearance generally dishevelled. Moreover, he was carrying
the barrel of his rifle in his hand, the butt being
broken off short.

"Why, what's the matter?" he was asked.

"H--ll's the matter," was the amiable reply.
"I've broke my rifle, and had the worst kind of
a time with a b'ar!"

"Did you kill him?"

"Not much. It was like this. I thought
this afternoon that I'd take a bit of a hunt on
my own account; so I wandered about a bit seeing nothing, until I came to those thick patches
of yellow pine down there. I just had time to
notice that a log had been turned, and some
rubbish rummaged about, when, just as I was in
the thickest of the timber, I see a patch of
brown fur with the wind ruffling it, just between
two trees not twenty paces from me. In course
I turned my rifle loose without any proper aim,
and you should have heard the roar! Now,
you know how pesky thick them woods are?
Wal, *I* thought they were too, up to the moment

that b'ar roared, and then I'm blamed if there
seemed a tree to the acre that was fit to climb.
So I ran, and I guess I made good time, but the
darned b'ar he ran too, and I reckon he covered
the ground quickest! At last, when he was
nearly on me, I got a chance at a good-sized
pine. I dropped my gun and up I went, but
the b'ar clawed at me with his paw and just
caught the heel of my boot and ripped the sole
off! *That* made me go faster than ever, and
I clumb so fast without thinking, that I clumb
right out of the top of the tree!"

CHAPTER IX.

THE ROCKY MOUNTAINS DURING WINTER.

A MOUNTAIN STORM — A SECOND NIGHT'S CAMPING OUT — HAS A MISHAP IN COOKING WITH A POWDER LABELLED "BORWICK'S" — A TOILSOME JOURNEY — THE VERY LOW TEMPERATURE OF THE SEASON — DISCOVERS THAT HE HAD TAKEN STRYCHNINE — FALL IN DESCENDING A MINING-SHAFT — ANOTHER "NEAR THING" — AN EXCEPTIONAL WINTER — PLAN OF DOMESTIC MANAGEMENT ADOPTED BY JACK JEBB AND A COMPANION — ON SHORT RATIONS — REDUCED TO THE LAST EXTREMITY — AN EXCEPTION TO A WHOLE LIFE'S BAD LUCK — A SUPPER OFF ELK — THE SNOW LIFTS — HIS REFLECTIONS ON THE EVENTS OF THE PAST MONTHS.

OF course, although generally pretty rough Jack's winter journeys between the mines were not always so eventful as the one just described ; but, oddly enough, his return on this occasion was destined to be rather worse than his outward trip.

To begin with, he made a bad start; being detained at the mines until late in the morning, when, in order to reach the crest of the range before night, he should have been on his way by daylight. Then there had been a partial thaw in places which made the snow sticky and difficult to travel over, so that by afternoon he had to make up his mind to "camp" again for the night. Unfortunately he was not going straight home, or he might have taken refuge with his friend the prospecting "bear." But he was now bound for a mine 12,800 feet up the range, and quite out of the track of the ruined village. However, at the edge of the wood, which extended as far as the beginning of the precipitous climb up the mountain, Jack knew of a log-cabin with two walls left standing, which was used in summer as a half-way house to the mines. To this he determined to make his way, especially as it was now beginning to storm so violently that in passing through a belt of dead wood with patches of trees still unfallen, he could hear their withered branches crashing down on all sides. When he reached the cabin his first act was to begin to clear out the snow with the help of an old shovel he found in a corner. Behind the shovel he had noticed a flour-sack, and on examination it proved to be half full of damp flour — a mouldy blessing which was received by the traveller with much thankfulness, for he had only one sandwich left in his pocket, and had been reflecting for some

time on the extreme probability of his having
to make it serve for both supper and breakfast.

When he had scraped all the snow from one
side of the log-wall, he cleared a space for a fire
a little in front of it, so that by sitting between
the two he would get shelter on the one side
and warmth on the other. As, with no roof and
only two walls to his bedroom, he was sure of
all the fresh air that even a sanitary inspector
could desire, he thought he might as well ward
off unnecessary draughts, and was proceeding to
fill up the chinks in the logs at his back with
pine-boughs, when, half hidden by a broken
rafter, he caught sight of — a tin of Borwick's
baking-powder! He began to think of his nur-
sery days, and the extraordinary luck of "The
Swiss Family Robinson," who, when wrecked
on a desert island, always found everything they
happened to want ready to hand. Jack reflected
that after all there must be something in that
wonderful book, for a similar fate was befalling
him. He had found a house (ruined), a shovel
(worn out), a sack of flour (damaged), and now
a tin of baking-powder with which to make the
flour rise. He had the cup of his flask, in which
at a pinch water could be heated; and carefully
treasured in an inside pocket was a small screw

of tea. He felt that he could ask no more of fate, except perhaps a blanket; but however luxuriously you propose to live, you must draw a line somewhere, and Jack drew it — involuntarily — at the blanket.

Directly there was a good fire going he began to cook his supper: first course, a flap-jack baked on the shovel; second course, half a sandwich, with tepid tea — tepid, because the metal cup grew so hot over the fire that it was impossible to drink its contents warm. He made the flap-jack by first mixing snow with the flour, and then giving it a plentiful shake of " Borwick's " to make it rise. But it steadfastly declined to rise at all. It burnt into a brown sodden mass, and its flavour was so bitter and disagreeable that after one mouthful only, the disappointed cook put it aside, to be eaten next day if he were on the verge of starvation, but otherwise carefully avoided. So he ate the whole of his sandwich, drank his tea, and then lit his pipe, determined to be as comfortable as circumstances would allow. But — there seemed to be something very wrong. Within an hour he was suffering intense pain; then he became violently ill, and throughout that long dreary night he experienced all the joys of a Cook's excursionist crossing the Channel for the first time.

When morning came he was feeling thoroughly weak and ill. He had nothing to eat, and couldn't have managed it if he had; while there were four hours of hard climbing to be got through before he could possibly reach the mine. To add to his other troubles, the storm was still raging furiously, and he felt very doubtful as to whether his little remaining strength would hold out until he got to the top of the range. His only chance, however, was to try; so he began to plod along, stopping to rest every few minutes, and each time pushing on again for a shorter stage. As he won his way upwards, leaving the shelter of the valley behind, it became colder and colder; and when after hours of toil he reached timber-line, the wild icy gusts, laden with impalpable dust-snow, which came roaring down the steep gullies, seemed almost to cut him, passing through his clothes like a million needles. At timber-line he left his snow-shoes; for above him was a climb over bare rock and ice, where they would be worse than useless. He finished the last teaspoonful of rum-and-ginger that his flask contained, and then started out into the bleak hurricane. It was only when clear of the trees that its force could be realised; for the farther the traveller climbed upwards into the heart of the black driving clouds, the colder it grew. Often he had to crouch down and wait until some fierce blast passed by him.

When about half-way up, he began literally to freeze. There was a sudden queer sensation in his mouth, and putting up his hand to his cheek he found that it was frost-bitten. He stopped and rubbed it right again with snow, but a moment later the eye on the windward side was fast. Then came the feeling of intense drowsiness, the *longing* to sleep, which, once given way to, means never more awaking. Jack had courage and energy enough left to rouse himself and keep up his circulation at all costs; so again and again he gave himself heavy blows in the face — one upper cut under the chin proving very effective. The hardest time of all was when he got near the top of the range, and was crossing a sheet of ice filling a steep gully — probably five feet wide. He was carving his way, step by step, with a little axe he always carried in his belt on these journeys, when down swept a gust which seemed as though it *must* tear him from his foothold and dash him to the bottom of the precipice! He drove the axe-head deep into the ice, and held on like grim death, while the wind pinned him down. He began to count, and got as far as 150, thinking meanwhile that unless the blast decreased in strength he would be gone before he got to 200! But it did pass, and he struggled on. He was quite dazed by this time; his wet clothes were frozen as hard as boards; his hair was a mass of ice, and in spite of all he could do he was frost-bitten both in hands and face. At last, looming up through the drifting snow, the end gable of the mine-house came into view. It was not more than twenty yards distant, but it seemed a mile to the exhausted man, who crawled along until he pitched heavily into the porch. Then he tried to shout, but his voice was gone, so he stumbled through the woodhouse, past the open mouth of the shaft, and into the inner room, where he flung himself down on one of the bunks which lined its sides. Most of the men were down the mine, but one was leaning over the stove, preparing dinner. He stood and stared for a moment at the forlornlooking apparition on the bed, and then began to warm some coffee, remarking meanwhile that he should not have thought any human being would have chosen this sort of weather for a stroll! Though close to the stove, he was buttoned up to the chin in a pilot coat, and from the low roof of the hut hung icicles a foot deep. Just *how* delicious the first cup of steaming coffee tasted, Jack could scarcely have told, and within an hour he was thawed out, could take some food, and began to feel himself again. He was curious to know if the weather had been as bad as this for many days on the top of the range, and asked what the thermometer stood at.

"She don't stand, she just sits," was the reply; " and it's my belief she'd have knocked the bottom out of the bulb to get lower, if she could. The mercury's just froze solid! It's the third time she's been took that way this winter, and where *mercury* freezes, a *man* hasn't a square deal."

The men soon began to come up to dinner from the mine below, and were sufficiently astonished to find the " boss " there.

" Where did you spend the night, sir ? " the foreman asked ; and Jack began to describe his sufferings, and to ask if any one knew who had last camped in the ruined hut, and left spoilt flour behind him.

" Oh," said one of the men, " there were two chaps from Denver there in the fall. They called themselves taxidermists, but *I* took 'em for tenderfoots."

" Yes," chimed in another, " they were pre-serving skins and suchlike up to the first snows, and said they should be back in the spring for more; and I believe they did say something about a tin of strychnine for poisoning wolves that they'd mislaid. I guess that's what you thought was baking-powder, sir."

Of course that was the explanation of the flap-jack that wouldn't rise. Jack reflected soberly that it was very lucky for him it didn't, because as one mouthful had half killed him, the entire baking would certainly have done so quite.

When dinner was over he felt so " fit " that he thought he would go and have a look at the mine, as he was specially anxious to see if any ice had formed below a shaft which was not then being used, but would have to be in order before spring. He found that there were no lad-ders to this particular shaft, so he elected to be lowered by the windlass. There was no cage, and it was necessary to hold on tightly to the rope, keeping one foot in a loop at the end of it. He settled himself firmly and swung off, the rope in his right hand, and a candle in his left, which served to show the copper-stained walls of the shaft as he slowly descended. This shaft was about three hundred feet deep, and he was half-way down when he leant forward to examine a stain of decomposed copper, and, as he did so, in an instant his foot shot out from the noose. It was coated with ice, and he had forgotten that a solid crust had formed under his boot. His candle was jerked out of his left hand, while his right hand slipped down the icy rope like lightning and closed on it with a death-grip! It all seemed to pass in the fraction of a second, until he felt himself swinging by one hand to the end of the rope and instinctively reaching up to the loop with the other, only to find it a smooth coat of ice which gave scarcely any hold at all. He knew that he could never hold on long enough to be hauled back to the mouth of the shaft, even if he succeeded in making the men hear him. The shaft was pitch-dark, and it was therefore impossible to judge if he were being lowered slowly or fast as he hung — literally between life and death — with every faculty strained to the one act of clinging to that rope! His hands were rapidly becoming numbed with cold, and little by little he felt them slipping, — another moment, and down he went!

But not far; for when he let go, he was not three feet from the bottom of the shaft. All the same he felt decidedly shaky, as he groped about for his lost candle. It had been a very " near thing," and he had been through too many close shaves lately for his nerves to be strong enough to enable him to think without a shudder of his sensations when first he felt himself falling. It was entirely characteristic, however, that after finding his candle he went about the business he had in hand before signalling to be drawn up again.

Altogether, he had passed a rather lively week; and when, after a few days spent at this mine, he arrived at his headquarters without further adventure, he felt a chastened joy in the reflection that by the time he had to make the journey again, there would probably be a change for the better in the weather. But it was an exceptionally severe winter, and for some weeks even the mines were snowed up; so the men went off to the nearest settlement to wait, leaving Jack with an English mining superintendent whom he had lately engaged to keep house alone.

Domestic management does not seem to have been a strong point with either of them, although they succeeded in simplifying it greatly. Neither objected to doing the cooking, but what really did

appal them was the washing-up afterwards. The
dishes *would* slip out of their hands, giving rise
to forcible and pointed remarks; then the greasy
water was unpleasant; so that altogether they
looked forward to meal-times with dread, until
they hit upon the happy expedient of using first
the right and then the wrong side of each plate,
afterwards piling them in a corner till every
scrap of crockery in the house was dirty, when
they would have a field-day, and wash the lot.
Then the process would begin again! Their
house-cleaning was performed on much the same
principles. In a bedroom at the back of the
house stood a large deal table. It seemed a
pity not to make use of it, so they began by
covering it with their boots, clothes, portmanteaux, &c., and they found it such a convenient
receptacle for anything they wished to get rid
of that they gradually added ties, hats, papers,
pistols, brushes, and in fact all their worldly
goods, until the pile reached such a height that
it was necessary to fetch a chair when anything
was required from the top layer. This would
be endured for a week or two, and then voted
a bore, when they would tidy up by the simple
and obvious method of upsetting table and
contents on to the floor and sorting out their

respective possessions, which they carefully kept apart for a few days. Then, as a rule, the sight of the empty table proved too great a temptation to be resisted, and another monument of order — or disorder — began to arise.

A little later on, owing to the great length and severity of this particular winter, the two men found that they were very likely to run short of provisions; and as snow was heaped up twenty feet deep all round them, and still fell heavily, there was no hope of getting a fresh supply. They allowanced themselves carefully, taking first two and then only one meal a-day; but with all their pains they saw their stock of food gradually getting lower and lower day by day, while the storm outside raged unceasingly. Finally there was nothing left but a box of sardines and two biscuits. They divided these equally and made them serve for a meal — so frugal a meal that they were glad to go to bed early in order to forget in sleep the pangs of hunger, which were already beginning to make themselves felt. The next morning they scraped out the crumbs from the biscuit-tins and fried them in what remained of the sardine oil, so as to make them go a little further; but at best there were only a few mouthfuls, and Jack and his companion tightened their belts with a feeling that it was all over with them. With the nearest camp fifteen miles away, over snow-covered mountains, on which no trace of a trail could possibly be found, the chances of rescue seemed very slight. That day they spoke little. At times they felt faint and sick, otherwise not much the worse for their fast; but next morning they awoke racked by violent pains and a ravening hunger. They searched the house despairingly for any small fragments of food which they might have overlooked. Not a vestige of anything eatable was to be found. Then they went to the door of the hut and looked out. The wind was still blowing a hurricane, but the snow seemed to be lessening in thickness, and Jack resolved that if it stopped that day he would take his rifle and try to get something to eat before he became too weak to do so, even if the storm abated. Better to be lost in a snowstorm and freeze to death, he thought, while trying to save yourself and friend, than to sit supinely at home waiting for a horrible fate. So they both set to work with spades to clear an exit from the house, growing exhausted and stopping to rest every few minutes, — still, making way slowly.

By the afternoon there was a decided lull in the storm, the wind had dropped a good deal, and the snow ceased entirely; so Jack fortified himself with a hot glass of spirits and stepped out into the white desert, realising fully that should it begin to snow again before he could return, his tracks would be covered up, and he might wander round and round the house until he dropped, without ever seeing one sign by which to find his way.

However, there must be exceptions to every rule, and for once the bad luck which pursued him all his life gave way to a better fortune; for the snow held up, and he had not wandered more than a mile from home when he sighted a fine elk, and brought it down with the first barrel. It fell in an inaccessible place, and he had to go back for his companion; but between them they soon extricated their prize and dragged it home in triumph. How good their supper was! and how their spirits rose when freed from the awful dread of the last few days.

The storm came on worse than ever that night, but next day abated again, and then gradually died away, not to return that winter; so that, before the last bones of the elk were picked clean, there was once more a trail between the camps, and the worst was over. Jack was not given to shirking danger; but all the same, when spring arrived and the snow began to melt, he felt that, all things considered, he had had more narrow escapes in the last few months than he should care to crowd again into a single winter.

CHAPTER X.

AFFAIRS AT DENVER.

WITH the advent of milder weather the trails became passable once more, the men returned to work, and the dreary inactivity of the past few weeks gave place to all the bustle of a busy mining-camp. Also, of course, Jack's tour of inspection became infinitely easier — but! There seemed destined to be more "buts" in his career than in those of most people, although there are very few unacquainted with the ca- pacity for disagreeableness possessed by that useful word. The trouble now was with the "Great Whale" mines; for with an appetite entirely unappeased by the large amount of money and labour they had already absorbed, they were eagerly clamouring for more.

The fact was, that though an excellent group of mines in themselves, they required more development than the purchasers had expected, before beginning to pay the large dividends, which seemed as far off as ever. There was no doubt about the whole thing being a sound going concern, but it is the experience of all who have had to do with silver-mines that before getting any money out, a vast amount has to be put in. Altogether, a consultation with the other members of the little syndicate appeared to be necessary, and Jack thought it best to see them before affairs got worse. So after making arrangements for a couple of months' absence, he started for New York, *en route* for London. A few days after reaching the former place his business took him on to Boston. He had been there before, but never after so long an interval of "roughing it," and at first he found its luxurious clubs and its hospitable people a little alarming. For some days he lived in a chronic state of terror lest he should dip his knife into the salt-cellar at a dinner-party, or commit some other solecism which would shake the cultured city to its foundations. Mercifully, however, he was preserved from dragging the "Wild West" into the domesticated East, and as he already had some friends in Boston and quickly made more, he thoroughly enjoyed his taste of civilisation.

As compared with Americans, notably New Yorkers or Bostonians, hospitality in England is little understood. There, you may arrive unexpectedly in the middle of the night, and instead of remarking, as an English hostess certainly would, that there *are* more convenient trains, your Americans will say, and think, how truly sweet of you to give them such a delightful surprise! Or you may write to tell your friends that you are going to pay them a visit, accompanied by your wife and mother-in-law, with their pet dog and favourite monkey, and you will be met and welcomed just as heartily as if you were an eligible bachelor fulfilling a long-promised engagement. It adds a great charm to a return from many wanderings to know that not only will everybody be overjoyed to see you, but that they will have no hesitation in saying so.

Another thing which greatly endears Boston to the stranger within its gates is the number and variety of its religions. You may be a follower of Tom Paine, or a High Church curate; you may believe that only a Plymouth Brother has any real chance of salvation, or that all but the votaries of the Roman Church are doomed to destruction. You may practise any or all of these creeds, and you will be sure to find others who think with you, while those who don't will be convinced that there is a good deal to be said for your side of the question, and will regard you with a large tolerance, considering your soul as much your own private property as your bank-book. There may be Boston missionaries — probably there are — but if so, they confine their propaganda to the heathen, who *may* like their ministrations, and in any case have to put up with them, on the principle of "No work, no pudding"; but they allow their cultivated fellow-citizens to indulge peaceably the faith that is in them.

Among the various schools of thought in the "London of America" there is a large spiritualistic element; and into this circle, both by circumstances and bent of mind, Jack was drawn. Whatever is newest in the world of spiritualism takes its rise there, so that whenever our traveller found himself in Boston he always went to one or two lectures or *séances.* Of course some of the latter were very palpable humbug, while sometimes, when they took place in private houses and with non-professional mediums quite above suspicion, it was difficult to account naturally for the things which occurred.

For instance, he once took what purported to be a spirit hand in his, and closing his fingers tightly over it, determined to see what would happen if he refused to release it. That was soon seen, for the hand gave a slight flutter and was gone, without his having in the least relaxed his grasp! Incidents of this sort might be multiplied indefinitely; but while few people nowadays doubt that there is "something" in spiritualism, probably the majority would agree with Jack Jebb that it is scarcely worth while to spend much of the short life accorded to us in penetrating into those supernatural mists which must one day be made clear to all. He was sufficiently interested, nevertheless, to join the Psychical Research Society, later on, in London, while it was under the presidency of Madame Blavatsky. After some years, during which he was too seldom in England to see very much of its proceedings, he took his name off its register for the entirely characteristic reason that a man whom he *knew* to be a fool had joined!

But to return to our story. Between business and pleasure two or three weeks slipped rapidly by, and Jack was soon on board an Atlantic liner once more. When he reached London, he found that it would take longer than he had expected to conclude his financial arrangements; so while they were pending he had an opportunity, which had not occurred for years, to see something of his family. The aunt in Yorkshire (Mrs Miles), with whom he had always been a great favourite, was delighted to hear of his return, and insisted on his paying her a visit at once. She was a strong-minded, autocratic old lady, with a *penchant* for arranging the affairs of the entire family, most of whom stood rather in awe of her. Now Jack was a man of equally decided character, who preferred making his own plans, and was not at all disposed to have them overruled even by an elderly aunt with a large fortune. Therefore, though really very fond of each other, they usually quarrelled whenever they met, and the amount of money for which Jack was down in Mrs Miles' will fluctuated accordingly.

On this occasion it was the family tree which brought them to grief. Mrs Miles had been regaling her nephew upon it for an entire afternoon, until at last his patience gave out, and in a tone of bland inquiry he asked, "Do you *really* believe all that?" She never quite forgave him for this remark, although at her death some years later she left him a few thousands, which were all the more acceptable for being scarcely expected.

Meanwhile Jack soon had to hurry back to town in order to finish the business about the mines. While there he spent a good deal of time with his other aunt, his mother's sister, also a strong-minded wealthy old lady from whom he had expectations. At her house he met a young Canadian lady, whom he fell in love with and eventually married. She was then about to return to Canada; and when he had concluded his financial arrangements he followed her there, and her parents raising no objection, they were married at once, starting for the mining camp in the Rocky Mountains shortly after. It was not a happy marriage; but as Mrs Jebb only survived it a few years, it is not necessary to go into details. She left one child.

When the newly-married pair got as far as Denver, on their way to the mines, they succeeded in finding an Irish domestic, who for a large consideration consented to accompany them, and once there, devoted the whole of her time to making herself, not useful, but ornamental, for the behoof of the miners. There were now three or four families settled within a radius of about fifteen miles, and in the summer they managed to meet frequently; but of course the winters were as usual cold, stormy, and lonely. If November were sufficiently open for a large enough supply of elk and deer meat, willow-grouse, sage-hen, and blue hares to be obtained occasionally, with perhaps an odd bear, it was pretty certain that no one but Jack would enter or leave the camp for the next six months. The other supplies were procured from the nearest settlement, but once in a way itinerant vendors would make a tour of the various camps, which were only too glad to get their provisions brought to them instead of their having to waste a week in taking a waggon to fetch the necessary stores.

Jack bought a load of potatoes one summer from a ragged and dirty-looking creature whose face could not be distinctly seen, as what remained of his hat was pulled down over his eyes, and he wore a muffler which hid the lower part of his face. But something in his voice struck Jack, who tried in vain to enter into conversation. The man, however, seemed surly, and would not respond. So Jack concluded the bargain and went back into the house, thinking to himself, " I'll swear that's an Englishman down on his luck!" Indeed he was so haunted by the thought that he went out again to make another effort to overcome the man's reserve. However, the potato-vendor had quickly disappeared, so the matter remained unsettled. Years afterwards, when the mysterious pedlar had come into the title to which he was then only heir-presumptive, he was constrained to confess that he had once gained a precarious livelihood by hawking potatoes when more than usually hard up. He explained that his objection to being recognised was not on account of his occupation, but because of the dirt inseparable from it. Therefore, when Jebb went a second time to look for him, he hid behind the waggon, and eventually got away without being found out.

That year, when the last of the steers for the winter supply had been driven in and butchered, Jack noticed bear-tracks every morning in the vicinity of the slaughter-house. He tried sitting up for several nights, but never got a chance of a shot, so he decided that " trapping " was the best plan ; and accordingly a trap was set just where the fence of the stock-corral came down to a little creek, overgrown with willows. The trap was carefully powdered with snow, and from a tree above it were hung some tempting scraps of offal, within easy reach of an enterprising bear. The next morning Jack, with one of the men, started to investigate a little before daylight, and as the trap was close to the slaughter-house — not half-a-mile from the camp — they promised to send for the others to see the fun should the brute be caught. When the two reached the place, they found the ground covered with tracks; but not only was the bear invisible, the trap also had disappeared. They peered silently in every direction, carefully scrutinising each rock sticking up through the snow, and closely examining the back of the slaughter-house, without finding a sign of their prey, when, just as they were beginning to think that the wily animal had outwitted them, they caught sight of a patch of black-and-silver fur hidden in a thick clump of willows covered with snow. They could not make out his head for some time, but at last got a glimpse of it, sunk on his fore-paws and half-buried in snow. He was kept prisoner by the chain and toggle on his leg having caught round a willow-root.

When they had discovered this fact, Jack and his companion softly retraced their steps a few yards, quickly deciding that the latter should go to fetch the other " boys," leaving his rifle with the " boss," who, armed with this and his own revolver, could easily "'tend bear" until the arrival of the camp to see the sport. It was a bitterly cold morning, freezing hard, and Jack found that he had a very chilly bit of sentry-go before him. The rifle felt cold enough to burn his hand, so he cleared a stump from snow and laid it across, taking care to point it towards the willows. It seemed like an hour before the sun rose, and even then it gave no heat; so that the solitary watcher was glad enough when first a few, and then more figures, came in sight, until there were about twenty lookers-on. They all took a glance at the prostrate bear, which had not moved an inch all this time, afterwards bestowing themselves in various coigns of vantage — the fence round the slaughter-yard for preference.

Now, the man who had gone to fetch the

others was to have for reward the first shot; but as Jack did not want to see the poor beast baited, he determined to give it a *coup-de-grâce* with his revolver — a navy-pattern Colt — as soon as it was wounded by the rifle. Therefore, as the man moved cautiously towards the willows, Jack followed closely. The former stepped to the edge of the creek, a few paces to the right, to get a clearer shot; but as he raised his rifle the crust of snow on which he stood gave way, and down he went into the dry bed of the creek! There was a roar of laughter from the spectators, echoed instantly by another and a different roar, as with one wild pull at his chain the bear charged straight at Jack! Most of the men were armed, but as he was between them and the furious animal, they could not fire, while the only member of the party near enough to be of any use was swearing volubly, on the broad of his back, in the creek. For an instant the great brute's charge was checked as the chain tightened up to the toggle, but his impetus was too heavy to be long withstood. Something gave way, and in a second more he was rearing up, and almost on his victim. Then Jack fired, taking him in the centre of the chest, a little low; and with a sort of sigh the bear sank down, all but touching his adversary's feet!

The whole affair was over in five seconds, but considering the amount of lead a bear will sometimes carry away, it was a strange fluke killing one with a single pistol-shot; and Jack always maintained that if he had not been so taken by surprise, he should have bolted too. For the charge was so sudden that the "dress-circle" perched on the high fence had one and all started backwards, thereby causing the top rail to give way, so that they all took a header into the snow behind them, from which now protruded a large variety of wildly gesticulating legs! A little to one side, three men were frantically trying to swarm up a small pine-tree, not big enough for one; while from the blind ditch into which the foremost sportsman had fallen still issued sulphureous sounds. They picked themselves up by degrees, and went slowly homeward, wiser and sadder men. It was not considered polite to allude to that bear-hunt for a long time; and when other camps got hold of the story and began to "chaff" the men, they were at once gently but firmly silenced by the simultaneous production of every shooting-iron in camp.

There were occasional incidents of this kind to vary the monotony of life in the heart of the cold and silent mountains, but nothing occurred worth recording until the year of the great eclipse of the sun — 1875 — which Jack saw under conditions such as were probably vouchsafed to few human beings. He climbed to the topmost crag of one of the highest peaks of the Rocky Mountains in order to enjoy the magnificent sight to the full, and he was not disappointed.

To the east the great table-land of the plains stretched out below him like a vast greenish-brown ocean, far as the eye could reach. To the south Pike's Peak towered up in solitary grandeur; while to the north and west arose a tumultuous sea of snowy peaks, piled range behind range. At first there was not a fleck of cloud in sight; then far away the distant western horizon was seen to darken; the white ridges changed into violet, then to blue, and soon faded away, leaving only a faint ghostly outline. The valley grew darker, and even as the solitary spectator gazed, seemed to form long tongues of grey-blue shadow, leaping towards him from its depths. The clear air became dusky, and glancing upward, he could see the sun already partly obscured. Then a great dim shadow swept up with a hideous velocity from the west, as if a crape curtain, becoming thicker and thicker each instant, were being thrown over the vast background of mountains and precipices.

A complete silence settled on the earth, the air grew colder and colder each moment, and an indescribable sense of desolation and death pervaded the atmosphere. The stars sprang out in all their still beauty, and as the icy blast swirled along the crags, of a sudden it was night. The scene on the mountain-top, in the moments of totality, was terribly grand, for a dark veil of night brooded over the world for sixty miles around. Beyond this belt of gloom, in the north and south, was a clear yellow band ; the faint blue range, distinctly visible, as it dipped down to the far-off plains, fading away by exquisite gradations of colour into the hazy north. Above, in the dark sky, a black ball was hanging, surrounded by a faint pale disc, streaming out and vanishing into space : then a speck of intense golden light. Larger and larger it grows; farther and farther does the black shadow draw off from the glorious sun, until the last vestige of the stupendous phenomenon has passed, and the beholder stands shading his eyes from the glare, while a frightened band of antelope a mile off, which had been rushing about wildly, sobered down again now that the unknown terror had swept away.

It was a sight worth living long to see, and, strange to say, it proved of some practical utility, for the marvel so utterly demoralised a party of Utes meditating a raid on the mining camps, that they gave up the idea and went off stealing Rapahoe ponies instead.

It has been mentioned elsewhere that some old and valued friends of Jack Jebb's were living at their own mine a few miles from his head-quarters. They were a charming couple — an American lady and gentleman, in the true sense of the words: clever, cultivated, witty, — perfect types of the best that wonderful nation *can* produce, and occasionally *docs*.

If the friends had been attached before, it may easily be imagined that years of hardship endured in common, and an almost entire dependence on each other for society, had made the bond between the two families stronger than ever. Therefore when, during this winter, on returning from one of his periodical journeys, Jack found a message awaiting him from the other camp, saying that Mr A. was taken seriously ill, he promptly put on his snow-shoes again and started for his friend's house.

When he arrived he found the state of affairs even worse than he had expected, as Mr A. was in a very bad way indeed. The nature of the complaint is immaterial, but it was something which required immediate medical attention, and there was no doctor nearer than the settlement at the foot of the range. It was something, too, which grew worse with every hour that the patient spent in that freezing air; and there were no means of getting him lower, unless he could go on snow-shoes — a manifest impossibility. Mrs A. was outwardly calm, but it was easy to see that her anxiety was terrible in face of her helplessness to do anything to save her husband, who seemed to be fast slipping out of existence simply for want of aid. Jack at first despaired of being able to help, but at last he thought of a plan which, though it might cost both his own and Mr A.'s life, might on the other hand save the latter, if successful, and was therefore worth trying, as he would most certainly die if nothing were done. Mrs A. caught at the idea when it was suggested to her; but she utterly refused to let Jack take any risk for her husband which was not shared by herself, and after some argument she was allowed to have her own way.

The plan was for the invalid to be enveloped in furs and carried to the edge of the ridge, which hung over the next plateau, only to be reached by a circuitous trail. Then a stout rope was to be secured round him, and afterwards passed under Jack's arms, leaving them as free as possible, in order that he might use one for steadying Mr A. and the other for the terrible descent down the rocky mountain-side which he contemplated. His idea was to climb from plateau to plateau of the mountain, finding a foothold in the projecting rocks, and thereby performing the journey more quickly, if more hazardously, than by the circuitous trail. The rope was to be held above by the miners — not a man of whom would have grudged his life if spent in Mrs A.'s service; and if the two friends reached the bottom of the range in safety, she was to be fetched by Jack, if he were not too exhausted, and taken by one of the men if he were. Of course, if his strength failed him on the first journey, nothing could prevent both his charge and himself being dashed against the rocks by the jerking of the rope, when a hideous death awaited them. But it was the only chance.

It is difficult to imagine which suffered the most when that perilous journey had commenced

— she who waited above in sickening suspense and fear, or he whose arm grew numb with the heavy inanimate weight he partly carried, and whose hand was torn by the jagged rocks as he held on for his life, and step by step fought his way on narrow footholds from ledge to ledge, pausing for a moment on each, until at last he stood with his charge in the valley below — triumphant, but spent.

Once at the bottom, the rest was easy, and help was quickly obtained from the village close by; Jack allowing himself a brief breathing-space, while Mr A. was put into a litter and carried to the inevitable hotel which every American collection of a dozen houses can boast. Fortunately this particular settlement rejoiced in the rarer possession of a capital doctor, and between his services and the mild air of the sheltered valley the invalid quickly recovered, with, if anything, an exaggerated idea of what he owed to Jack. Strangely enough, fast friends all their lives, "in their deaths they were not divided," for, years afterwards, the two men, living on different sides of the world, went down into the Valley of the Shadow they had faced together, almost at the same time.

But to return. Directly Jack had seen the

husband safely housed, he went back for the
wife, knowing well what she must be enduring,
ignorant as she was of their fate. She might, it
is true, have joined her husband by snow-shoeing over the path which wound from the top to
the bottom of the mountain; but this, besides
being a terrible journey, would have taken the
whole night, thus leaving Mr A. alone with
strangers at a time when he most needed the
care of his wife. Unweighted by any burden,
in the ascent Jack could allow himself to be
simply drawn up as he signalled, without much
effort on his own part; therefore when he reached
the top he felt perfectly able to take Mrs A.
down in safety, as of course she would require
less help than the invalid had wanted. So he
insisted on accompanying her, and once in the
valley for the second time, he stopped there long
enough to see his friend well on his way back to
health and strength, before returning to the camp
by the longer but pleasanter road of the ordinary
trail.

CHAPTER XI.

LAST EFFORTS AS A PIONEER.

THERE is yet one more " pioneering " incident
to be told, and with that the tale of Jack Jebb's
experiences in the Rockies may be concluded;
for though he remained there until about 1881,
the years passed evenly, and without more adventure than might occur to the casual traveller
in any " new " country.

It was in the winter of 1878, one of the sever-
est which ever passed over Colorado. Rumours
were current of trains being snowed up for days
at a time out on the plains, and of buffalo-hunters and even Indians being frozen to death,

while cattle perished by thousands. But high up in the mountains, though the weather had been wild, and the cold, doubtless, far more intense, people suffered but little; for in those deep pine-clad gorges there was always shelter.

At one of the mines in which Jack and his partners were interested, and which was situated far above timber-line, the works had been frozen since November, and the camp practically deserted by all but an old man, three women, and the lad who drove the teams in summer and experimented in cooking during the winter. But as this was the nearest point and lay on the best trail to the other camps which Jack must visit periodically during the snows, he resolved to take up his winter quarters here. December set in badly: storm followed storm, piling up the snow a good six feet around the house, while at the head of the gulch it was twice as deep. But the great fall commenced on December 18, and from that date until January 6 there was not an hour's cessation. The snow came down ominously day by day, and what the intensest cold was, no one ever knew, for again and again the mercury was found frozen in the bulb, although the thermometer was sheltered in an outhouse! The meat was literally as hard as boards, and venison-steak had to be cut with a saw, being afterwards hammered into *splinters !*

It was practically impossible to go out of doors, so for three weeks the distant camps remained uninspected. At length, one Saturday, there were some signs of a break in the weather; and as they had been striking rich ore in one of the mines when the storm began, Jack decided that he would at least make an effort to get to it. Accordingly he set off, although the wind was still blowing with almost hurricane force down the valley, and it took him four hours to reach timber-line — a distance of only three miles. Beyond that there was of course no shelter, and the blast roared over the bleak slopes. Now and then he caught a glimpse of the high ridge of snow-covered precipices forming the backbone of the range, but more often he could see nothing but whirling clouds of drift-snow flying past, while the air seemed filled with a wild, weird music — the sharp hissing of the gusts sweeping over the frozen fields in front, and the roar of the wind through the pine-trees behind.

Once for a moment he thought he saw the " Bear " mine barracks, to which he was bound,

and which were now only a mile farther on;
and he began to have visions of the hot bowl of
coffee and the warm welcome that awaited him
from the old Cornish foreman, who, with his
wife and child and four miners, constituted the
winter garrison of the mine. But they were
destined to remain nothing more than visions,
for as he left the shelter of the pine forest and
struck out into the open, a cross eddy of wind
threw him violently down. He rose and tried
again, but found it impossible to force the
long Norwegian snow-shoes up-grade against
the blast — it was like trying to pole a canoe
against the rapids above Niagara; and he was
always blown back. He then took a short rest,
and discarding the snow-shoes, tried to reach
the mine on foot, trusting to the frozen snow-
banks bearing his weight between the occasional
caps of rock which showed here and there.
Quite in vain — for within five minutes one ear
became frozen, and after another halt to repair
damages, one hand was in like case; besides
which, the snow did *not* bear, and falling and
wallowing through the drifts was very exhausting
work: so, beaten by weather for the first time
in his life, Jack reluctantly gave up the expedition, and with the wind at his back scudded

down-hill to the camp in half an hour. The next day the snow was worse than ever; but as it now came down in flakes instead of drifting, the impatient peripatetic miner made up his mind that the storm was breaking at last, and that he would not be kept prisoner much longer.

Sure enough, the next morning, Monday, it had almost ceased, and he was peering out to see if there was any use in venturing again, when he caught sight of a man on snow-shoes coming from the direction of the other camp. From the instant Jack first saw him approaching he felt a strange presentiment that the man was the bearer of evil tidings, and when he drew near enough for his face to be seen, it was plain from its expression that some worse calamity than usual had befallen the exposed mines above. But no one was prepared for the full horror of his first words, " The ' Bear ' camp is *gone*, and every soul in it lost ! "

The messenger was one of a party working the second mine, about half a mile from the " Bear," and this was what he had to tell. On the previous night, a man minus coat, hat, and boots, dazed with cold and fear, and at first unable to speak, had crept into their cabin. After being revived

with scalding coffee and generally cared for, they
found that he was one of the miners from the
"Bear" camp — what had been the "Bear"
camp, at least — for he managed to let them
know that of all the household alive and busy in
the morning, he was the sole survivor that night.
He said that, having finished his breakfast that
day before the others, he got up from the table,
leaving the rest still seated there, and went out
to the powder-house to fetch a roll of fuse. While
inside he heard a great roar, and felt the room
lifting with him. He remembered little more,
except that twice after a violent shaking he found
himself on the surface of the snow; the second
time stationary, with his head and shoulders free.
Somehow he dug himself out, leaving portions
of his clothing behind. He was terribly scared,
of course, and began to make his way up-hill to
tell his brother and sister-in-law — the foreman
and his wife — of the narrow escape he had
experienced.

He found that he had been carried down about
two hundred yards, but it never occurred to him
that he had been struck by only the outer edge
of an avalanche, which had expended its full
strength on the cabin above, and that even at
that moment his relations and companions were

lying dead twenty feet below. As he climbed, he suddenly stumbled over a fresh, broken board, and a few shingles came hurtling past like leaves. That told him all. He had no recollection of how long he wandered about searching for some trace of those he had left alive and well a few moments before, but at last he started for the valley below to ask for help.

How it happened that, half-dressed as he was, he did not freeze to death, no one could tell, unless the intense excitement from which he was suffering kept him warm. At last he reached an old sawmill, and resolved to camp there; but he had only just lit a fire, when another avalanche crashed and roared down the steep mountain-side, cutting a broad swathe through the forest, and sweeping away the end of the mill as if it had been made of paper. This must have completely shattered the little nerve the man had left, for instead of going on down the valley to a camp, he turned back up the range, and only by the merest chance, or God's mercy, reached the cabin where the other miners were wintering — the only living men on that mountain.

Now, in Colorado there used to be an eleventh commandment which was generally better observed than the orthodox ten, and it was to the effect that if a man dropped in his tracks, or chanced to be swept down by a snow-slide, all that his comrades *could* do to find the body and give it decent burial must be done. No one liked the idea that it might fall to his own lot to be dug up by foxes or stray bears; and when men carried their lives in their hands as often as not, it was a sort of satisfaction to feel that a search-party would be out as soon as any one was missed.

Therefore Jack's course was clear. The man who had brought the news was too exhausted to be of any further use; but Tom, the old man in camp, was a seasoned vessel, as was Jack himself in those days. The cook-boy wanted to join in the search; but he was only just recovering from rheumatic fever, and his joints were still too swelled and tender to admit of his doing such wild work. He insisted, however, on carrying the news to the lower valley, with a view to sending on all the volunteers he could gather; and half crippled though he was, he made splendid time on his snow-shoes.

So Jack and the old man started, carrying with them a blanket each, some frozen meat, biscuits, tea, and a couple of bottles of brandy, which, with long-handled shovels, that also served as balance-poles, was about as much as they could manage. They reached timber-line easily enough, and were fully expecting to arrive at the mine before night-fall, when by some mischance Jack's snow-shoe broke, and he found himself up to the neck in fine drift-snow. It took him nearly two hours to cover the next hundred yards, but probably the exertion was all that saved him from freezing. His companion, meanwhile, had gone on to the other mine for a spare shoe; but as it was nearly dark by the time he returned, they decided that they must spend the night at this camp, instead of trying to get to their destination. They found the poor fellow who had escaped, lying there in a bunk, snow-blind, and so stiff from the bruising and wrenching he had been subjected to that he could scarcely move.

That was a terrible night, and no one slept, for though the snow was deep above the log-hut, and its inmates were comparatively safe, it was not reassuring to hear two more avalanches roaring down the mountain no great distance away. About midnight Jack thought he heard a faint shout. It seemed impossible that any one should be there; still he went out, climbed the high snow-drift round the door, and showed a light, firing a shot at the same time; when, sure enough, another faint cry came down the wind. A few minutes later a man hove in sight, in whom Jack recognised an old soldier, who, after bearing his part in the war, had gone out West, and was now one of the best known trappers in the State. Powerful as he was, he was almost exhausted by the fifteen miles he had just travelled in the dark and against the storm. After getting him into a bunk and doctoring him with a hot drink, Jack naturally asked why none of his companions had accompanied him.

"Wal, boss," was the reply, "there ain't none of the mining hands in the valley just now, and I guess them ranchers ain't much count, for they allowed there warn't no show for getting the bodies out before spring, and it was giving live men for dead 'uns to try. So of course I came on alone, though there ain't one chance in ten thousand of our finding any of 'em alive now. Still we've got to do our best."

Between 4 and 5 A.M. there was a slight lull, while here and there a star could be seen; so the party started on their melancholy errand, and in little more than an hour they reached the plateau, just under the precipices of the horse-shoe bend, where the lost cabin had stood.

And now came the question, Where to dig? for not one familiar landmark remained. So tremendous had been the avalanche which had descended on the place, that at least fifteen acres of ground were covered, ten to twenty feet deep, with hard-packed snow. Of the buildings there was no trace to be seen, except a few fragments of wreckage scattered for five hundred yards over the mountain-side. However, after sinking a number of trial pits, they became pretty certain of the spot, and began to drive an incline intended to reach to a little below where the house had stood, shouldered against a great rock too deeply imbedded to be shaken, even by an avalanche.

As the sun rose, they caught occasional glimpses through the driving snow of the great horse-shoe above them, and the line of crags beyond that, which appeared to be bearing up thousands of tons of fresh snow on the place from which the fatal mass had fallen. The newly formed pile of white flakes seemed ready to give way at any moment, and added an un-looked-for risk to those which the searchers were already incurring. Fortunately the wind

was now blowing direct into the horse-shoe and
helping to hold the snow back.

Very soon a more immediate trouble overtook
them.   Old Tom ceased work, utterly worn out.
Then the old soldier began to bleed from the
lungs, where a Confederate bayonet had nearly
found his life, at the battle of the Wilderness,
years ago.   At a little distance was a single out-
building which had escaped the general destruction, and here Jack built a fire, setting the
two exhausted men to warm by it alternately —
the one on duty to stand at the door and watch
the great drift overhead, so that at the first
symptom of a slide, the men digging below
might be warned, and have some slight chance
for their lives.   They were of course sheltered,
and their work kept them warm; but the sick
men had a hard time of it, for in that icy hurricane it was impossible to mount guard for more
than ten minutes at a time without beginning to
freeze.   Deeper and deeper dug the forlorn-hope,
meanwhile, and soon fragments of the wreck
became frequent — pieces of broken crockery,
billets of firewood, the door of a stove, and once
a large piece of uncooked beef, which at first
they took for *something else.*

Hour after hour they worked, and had sunk

an incline thirty feet deep, when about two o'clock Jack found a pipe-stem sticking up. He gently removed the caked snow about it, until he saw the whitish-grey fingers of the dead man to whom it belonged closely clutching the bowl of the pipe. The tobacco was just scorched, no more: he had been lighting it when death overtook him. Lying partly across this body was that of another man who had been taken in the act of pulling on his great miner's boots. The face of each was covered by an ice-mask, which when broken showed the features beneath it undisturbed, untroubled by pain. Death had come quickly, and they slept.

Soon there was a change in the hard-packed snow, which the diggers found thawed away from the kettle and the overturned stove. Thrown across the latter was the body of the dead foreman's little child: it was frightfully mangled and burnt, but they thanked God she could not have suffered, for a breaking beam had crushed her head. They had now reached the ground, and were working up-hill. They came next to part of one end of the house, where the boards had formed a sort of floor; and never to his last day could Jack forget the ghastly horror of the face he found there, with frozen glassy eyes looking into his! It was the foreman's wife, who had been hurled backwards. An overturned table and some planks had by chance fallen over her, resting at the same time against part of the stone foundations, and entirely protecting her body from the crushing weight of snow above. Her arms were pinned down, and there was a splinter through her cheek; otherwise she was uninjured, and the awful horror of her terrible fate was stamped in full consciousness upon her features.

One by one the awed and silent searchers bore their sad burdens to the old storehouse. The last to be taken was the foreman, a huge and burly Cornishman, who, though far heavier than Jack, seemed to the latter to weigh nothing, as in the intense strain of nervous excitement he carried the body up the incline. Even when all was done, he did not at the time feel tired, nor did he notice that his gloves were cut to ribbons, and his hands a mass of blisters. But two hours later, when they had nearly reached the camp, he began to feel strangely done up. He had occasion to make some remark, and found that he had entirely lost his voice. The last two hundred yards he could scarcely keep his feet, and once indoors — he sat down and cried like a child! Sheer bodily and mental exhaustion, of course. He had been digging desperately since daylight, and altogether had passed through the hardest day he ever spent in his life.

The rest of the winter sped quickly and un-eventfully, except for the vagaries of the mines, which seemed to be almost human in their contrariness and misfortunes. Directly a rich streak of ore was struck, they would take the opportunity to get snowed up, or the machinery would break down ; and if these resources failed, the find would turn out to be only a " pocket," and consequently not of much value.

Surely there is no other Will-o'-the-wisp so fascinating to its possessor as a mine. There it is before you, clad in its robes of gold or silver, luring you on with hopes of the brilliant future it promises, and when it has absorbed all that you have to give, the glittering vision fades from sight, leaving you probably too infatuated with its elusive charms to wholly believe how shadowy they are. What happened in the present case was, that much of the ore did not pay for working, and the capital of the little company gave out before they got to the rich veins which they knew to be there. They naturally clung

to their property as long as there was a ghost of
a chance of doing anything with it; but at last,
about 1881, they were obliged to shut down the
works and retire, utterly beaten and heart-sick
by the long years of hopes and fears, hardships
and dangers, which had led to such meagre
results. The usual irony of fate was fully exemplified by the fact that the mines were pur-
chased by a company which, beginning with
fresh capital just where the others had left off,
of course reaped the benefit of their labour, and
quickly made the business into a flourishing
concern.

With the work of years wasted, and his capital
vanished, Jack found himself back in New York
again at rather a loose end. But surely no one
can be seriously unhappy for long in a city
where the sun shines most of the year, and
oysters are only 7d. a dozen! where you can
dine at Dorlon's too, not Delmonico's, and for
a reasonable sum can have (usually waking)
dreams all night of Boston stew, soft-shell crab,
and roasted lobster, followed by a Welsh rare-
bit such as can be found in no other place.

Jack knew a good many financial people by
this time — though that fact is not put forward
as an unmixed joy — and his services were very

soon invoked for the formation of what his friends at home always insisted on calling the Omelette Company. It was really a small company started for the introduction of a new invention which was intended to take the place of eggs in domestic cookery, and which was cheap and not outrageously nasty. The company (consisting of the original promoters only) is still dragging out a precarious and unappreciated existence somewhere in the States; but, of course, Jack Jebb never made anything out of it, nor probably was it ever intended that he should. His own ready belief and honesty of purpose always made him an easy prey for any sharp man of business who knew how to utilise his capacity for hard work without letting him discover that some of the work might be a little soiled. When he did find out anything of the sort, like most trustful people, he never forgave the person who had deceived him.

The Omelette affair kept him travelling between London and New York for some little time, and the commissions with which he used to be charged by English friends for relations on the "other side" were truly remarkable. He took a lady in to dinner once who asked him if, while he was in New York, he would try to see a little

of her nephew in Arkansas; and another sent a
parcel to meet him at Liverpool, which she said
she should be greatly obliged if he would personally deliver in Washington. If the average
Britisher is rather vague about American geog-
raphy, however, the Americans do not treat us
with much more respect; for in Texas there
used to be a school manual which, after dismiss-
ing England and Scotland in about six lines,
remarked briefly, " Ireland, a small island mis-
governed by the English." To see the terror of
many Administrations thus summarily disposed
of, was a sight to fill the down-trodden Britisher
with awe and admiration.

During the years he had spent "out West,"
Jack, of course, had often been to Texas on one
pretext or another; but as nothing worse happened to him there than once having to spend
a Fourth of July in a rowdy little town where
the day was celebrated by pistol-shots in the
intervals of orthodox fireworks, it has been unnecessary to chronicle his journeyings in detail.

When the egg business was organised, it
seemed — for a time — in a fair way to do well;
and as there was little that he could do towards
its general management, Jack turned his attention to other business while awaiting further

developments. Therefore, when some overtures were made to him in London with a view to his going out to Mexico, he was delighted at the prospect; especially as the object of his journey was to inspect and report upon the capacities of a group of mines — work which he both liked and understood. The mines were situated in a remote part of the country, and reaching them would necessitate some rough travelling — also, in his eyes, a distinct gain.

He was now, with the exception of his child, once more alone in the world, and his remaining aunt having taken charge of the little girl, Jack felt free to resume — if, indeed, he had ever left off — his wandering life.

CHAPTER XII.

THE LAND OF MONTEZUMA.

THERE are several ways of getting to Mexico. You may go direct from Southampton to Vera Cruz, touching at many of the West Indian islands *en route*, and sailing smoothly over summer seas, until you begin to feel like a lotos-eater, ever "falling asleep in a half dream." When the dream and the voyage are alike over, and you have to awake to everyday life again, it is some time before you can take up your burden exactly where you laid it down. Or if you want to call at New York on your way, and yet perform the journey by sea, you can get a ship from there taking you past Hatteras — where you will probably meet with "weather" — along the coast of Florida, and so into the calm blue Gulf of Mexico. These ships all touch at Havana; and supposing there is not *too* much "Yellow Jack" about, you may land to take a look at the pale Cuban beauties, who, in their cool white gowns, seem to be ever sitting at their barred windows, gazing down on the turmoil of a life in which they bear so small a part. With their black eyes and hair, their beautiful teeth and delicate olive complexions, many of them would be lovely could they only be content with their natural charms. But alas! they are one and all covered with a thick white powder, which makes their faces into ghastly expressionless masks, only the brilliant eyes and gleaming teeth showing through to tell of the passionate nature beneath.

Leaving Havana, the ship calls at various half-Indian villages scattered along the coast of Mexico, and while she is unloading her cargo the *élite* of the town crowd on board — usually clad in last year's Paris fashions except as to their hats, and where those come from no human being has yet discovered. Huge erections, covered with lace, ribbon, feathers, and flowers, apparently taken up in a bunch and thrown on haphazard, they are a sight to make the simple European gasp for breath! He usually does gasp — with relief — when the ship is on her way again and the visitors all gone; for they each have a theory that they know how to play the piano, and all the time the vessel is in port they make " Napoleon cross the Alps " and " The Maiden pray " unceasingly. Their *répertoire* is not extensive, and those two horrors of one's school-days usually comprise it. Altogether, in taking this route, the unsophisticated traveller is not sorry when the white walls of Vera Cruz are in sight, and he can land at about the hottest, the dirtiest, and the most forsaken-looking city in the world. After a night spent on a bed composed of a piece of sacking stretched across a bedstead, and in company with a class of mosquitoes whose desire for human society no curtains can thwart, he is only too glad to arise at 5 A.M. to catch the daily train, which, after a day spent in climbing through stupendously magnificent scenery, lands him, 8000 feet above sea-level, in the city of Mexico by evening.

But if time is an object, it is best to go on from New York by rail instead of taking either

of the pleasanter but much slower routes. There
are comfortable Pullman cars, on which for the
first three days you can get your food. After
that the train stops at miserable little stations at
odd hours for the refreshment of the passengers,
and you may have to eat your breakfast at 5
A.M., with the option of going without and not
getting another meal until the train stops again
perhaps at 5 P.M.! The road runs for the most
part through a perfect Sahara of dust and dreari-
ness; but as the entire journey only takes six
days, it is possible to live through it, though you
emerge at the other end feeling a shaken, dirty,
and aged wreck.

This is the route that Jack Jebb took on his
first visit to Mexico in search of that El Dorado
which had eluded him so long. If omens go for
anything, he was not likely to find it even now,
for the journey was most inauspicious. He had
not gone far when he discovered that somehow
he had miscalculated his expenses; and not quite
midway between New York and Mexico he found
himself with only half-a-dozen dollars left, and a
draft which was useless anywhere except at his
destination. On an American railroad you pay
for your ticket before you start, but your bed
has to be paid for nightly at $1 a night, and your

meals at the same price, as you take them. Therefore, Jack was confronted by the stern necessity of going either sleepless or hungry for four days. All things considered, he chose the latter, because after paying for his berth he would still have $2 left, which even at a Western station would buy bread enough to keep him from starvation for four days, while he decidedly quailed from the prospect of sitting bolt-upright for four nights on the chairs which a thoughtful railway directorate provides for day use only. He soon found to his dismay that his choice entailed remaining thirsty also, for the water on the cars was warm and dirty — a sort of concentrated essence of microbes. His means, of course, would not allow of " drinks "; and though not usually deficient in moral courage, he felt incapable of asking for water at an American refreshment counter! — especially as the last two days he had to be very careful in his purchase of bread, for even that commodity is dear at a wayside station.

It was the middle of summer, and the sun beating down on the cars all day made them intolerably hot; while the dust outside was so thick that not only was it impossible to open a window, but even with every aperture hermetically closed, the fine choking sand seemed to blow into the train in clouds. The thirst was worse than the hunger to endure, and how slowly the hours went by on the last day no one who has not suffered in a similar fashion could imagine. At last Mexico was reached! Jack called a cab, drove straight to the bank, got his draft cashed, and with much speed betook himself to a restaurant, a solid meal, and a long, long drink of "Bass's Bitter."

He wanted to be at the mines as quickly as possible, and therefore did not then linger long in the big, dirty, old, old city, which seems always to be haunted by memories of those brave and silent Aztec warriors, who looked on with rigid expressionless faces while the conquering Spaniards tore down their impenetrable stone idols, setting up the Inquisition in their place.

The way to the mines was easy enough at first — a day's rail, and then a night spent in a clean little hotel in a clean little town, where every second building is a church, and where the inhabitants are so truly devout that they occasionally arise and (literally) stone Protestants to this day! After this came two days on muleback; and although a mule *may* be possessed of excellent qualities, he does not often allow himself to reveal them to his rider! Still, the scenery was lovely enough to compensate for a good deal of discomfort in the survey. The road wound through deep cañons and rocky gorges — where the sound of a voice reverberated like thunder — until it came out at the foot of the mountains leading to the Indian village for which Jack was bound. The last thirty miles, though it took seven hours to ride, was well worth the trouble; for the narrow mountain-track, going ever higher and higher, led through picturesque ravines lined with varying ferns, and around precipices where, by the least false step, a man might fall, to remain for eternity a shapeless heap at the bottom. Not a crevice of the mountains but had its history of the brave handful of faithful people who held their own in the rocky fastnesses against four times their number of rebels, in the struggle which sent Maximilian to his unmerited death.

The Cacique who ruled, and virtually owned, these sierras where the little mining-town slumbered peacefully, had been working the mines in a primitive way all his life, but had at last awoke to the superiority of nineteenth-century methods, as against those employed at about the time of the Otomies. Hence Mr Jebb's mission. It turned out that he was the first

European who had ever penetrated into this mountain abode of unmixed Indians, and the old Cacique was a little doubtful of his reception by the villagers. He therefore had an escort awaiting him on his arrival, consisting of a captain and six soldiers, and Jack afterwards learnt that they had orders to shoot at sight the first person who cast an unfriendly eye on *El Inglese*. They did their duty nobly, never leaving his side for an instant. He used to fall over them sleeping outside his door in the mornings, and run against them down mines, up mountains, and in every sort of unlikely place.

He was once exploring a peculiarly dangerous and ruined old "fox-earth," politely called a mine, and had got about three hundred feet down a monkey-pole,[1] when, looking round, he found that he was being closely followed by a couple of cavalrymen in full regimentals! Their carbines were slung across their shoulders, their swords dangling between their legs; and their faces of ghastly horror, as they crept down those poles, were worth seeing. They had both been under fire, but had never been under-

[1] A monkey-pole, it may not be generally known, is a long pole in which at regular intervals are cut notches for the feet to be placed in when descending a mine that possesses no cage, and considerable nerve is required for its use.

ground before, and they said that as a matter of personal safety they preferred battles. Later on, when the works were in full swing, and several Englishmen employed there, a company of infantry was quartered in the town to take care of them. But the natives had taken kindly to Jack from the first, and did not seem inclined to interfere with the others. So the lieutenant in charge — an amiable *caballero*, with a cultivated taste for Scotch whisky — grew tired of a post which was such a sinecure. His desire for employment grew upon him, until one day he said to Jack, " Are you *sure*, señor, that no one has threatened you since you have been here? "

" Not in the slightest degree," he was told.

" Well, then, has any one been at all uncivil to you? " was the next question.

" On the contrary, they have all been kind and helpful," was the reply.

" Then, señor," asked the lieutenant, " *is there any one you don't like?* Because," and he tapped his revolver significantly, " my men have nothing to do, and idleness is bad for them ! "

Fortunately for the unoffending natives, Jack loved them all — or said so — and the officer withdrew in a highly dissatisfied mood. He had taken possession of a primary school (lately

started by the Federal Government) for a barrack, giving the children six months' holidays —
which goes to show the freedom, the liberty, and
absence of tyrannous practices in a republic.

As the natives of the sierra soon began to recognise the advantages of regular work and regular pay with the English company — a state of
things to which they were totally unaccustomed
— their attitude became so friendly that the
guard was withdrawn to the headquarters of the
regiment, and the strangers were left to their
own devices.

The mines being entirely satisfactory, and the
company likely to take root, one of the first con-
siderations was to build some sort of accommo-
dation for the staff. Accordingly a number of
peons were set to work to erect a small wooden
house for the superintendent, and a continuous
line of rooms a little farther off, which, from the
blank bareness of their appearance, were immediately christened " Poverty Row." One of these
was turned into an office, Jack appropriated a
couple, and the rest were used for the reception
of the clerks, &c., and for the storing of dynamite. Everybody settled down steadily to work,
and the superintendent sent for his wife and
family — the latter a large and turbulent quantity

— who arrived much dilapidated by the long journey. The children were made free of the place, with the needful exception of the dynamite stores, which were strictly forbidden to them. Probably for that reason this was the only part of the entire village for which they seemed to have any real affection; and they were constantly caught hanging round the rooms, to be dismissed promptly with a caution.

They had not been seen about there for some time, and it was thought that they had forgotten the subject, when, going home to bed early one morning, after sitting up all night with a re-fractory furnace, Jack happened to notice that the outer door of a room containing giant pow-der was ajar. Thinking of the gross careless-ness some one had shown, he went to shut it up, when, glancing inside to assure himself that all was safe, to his speechless horror he saw the whole half-dozen children sitting on the various cases trying to see which could make a match burn longest. There was enough explosive substance in that room to have blown up the entire town, and it seemed extremely likely that was just what was going to happen; for it passed through Jack's mind in a flash that if he startled the children at all, they would probably drop their matches anywhere and run, when the result was pretty certain. They were too busy to have caught sight of him, so he moved gently a little way from the door, and then called to them softly. Probably his voice was a little shaken by what the novelists call "conflicting emotions"; for at first the children did not recognise it, but at the second or third call they came gingerly out of the room, fearful lest retribution for their disobedience might be about to befall them. Directly the last child — carrying a still burning match — crossed the threshold, Jack rushed in to the store-room just in time to extinguish a smouldering match-head on the floor, and after a searching look around to see that all was safe, he went out again and locked the door with a gasp of relief. Then he marched those children off to their father, with whom, judging from the sounds, they spent an exciting half-hour. Anyhow they concluded that, regarded as an amusement, an explosive substance was a failure, and they were never seen near that part of the building again.

Of course not one of the natives had the slightest idea of the working of an English household ; and the superintendent's wife, with whom all the Englishmen boarded, found at first that she could get no domestics at all, and when she finally succeeded in catching and taming a few young Indians, it was exceedingly difficult to make them understand that they were occasionally expected to do a little work. The ordinary Mexican servant is often good-tempered and faithful to a degree, but loafing is his profession, and he does not see why he should forsake it because a *gringo* is grasping enough to want some return for the wages he pays. Then, too, it is difficult to say very harsh things to a person with eyes like those of a sorrowful Madonna, and whose name may be Dolores Velasquez!

Altogether, the domestic establishment of the *Ingleses* was run on peculiar lines. For one thing, the cook could never be brought to distinguish between salad and lamp oil; which idiosyncrasy frequently imparted a good deal of flavour to the dishes, — when there were any dishes, for sometimes in a fit of generosity she would give away a whole day's commissariat to her relations overnight. Then the housemaid was a source of much tribulation to her mistress. She was a bloated capitalist, who, on the strength of having saved $20, was known as the

"Heiress of the Sierras," and was much sought after by fortune-hunters. She was rather like a Burmese idol in the face, and resembled a Thames waterman in the figure, so her wealth *must* have been the attraction. Anyhow, it was discovered that, like the cats, she used to hold *levées* on the roof, after every one else had retired; and as she could not be brought to see any impropriety in the proceeding, her further services had to be gently but firmly declined.

The superintendent's wife soon started a garden, which entailed the employment of a gardener, who also looked after the pigs, and acted as maid-of-all-work to the bachelor establishment in Poverty Row. As the lady did all the gardening herself, and the pigs wandered about the town at their own sweet will, while none of the rooms in Poverty Row contained more than a camp bedstead, a table, and a chair, the gardener might have struggled through his duties without seriously endangering his health, had it not been for the quantity of water which the "señores" insisted on his providing them with each morning. He considered that washing in it was a wicked waste of clean fluid, besides entailing labour — a thing to be carefully avoided. He himself retired to a secluded part of the garden once a-month in company with a damp lettuce-leaf, with which he sponged himself all over. He was regarded, therefore, with much awe by the rest of the villagers, who considered that he had reached the highest European standard of cleanliness.

After a time the mistress of the establishment took to fattening her own chickens and turkeys, and when she had got one of the latter up to the requisite degree of plumpness, she ordered him to be killed for the next day's dinner. But when his presence was required in order that his neck might be wrung, he was discovered to be missing! He could not have gone away by himself, so therefore he must have been stolen, and the services of the one policeman were called in. He had no doubt of being able to find the missing bird, and started at once on his search, which he conducted on the simple principle of walking into every hut in the town until he came to one where a turkey was hanging half roasted over the fire. The ingenious officer seized it, and marching off to his employer, asked if she recognised her fowl? She explained that she found a difficulty in doing so, as the last time she had met him he was arrayed in all the glory of feathers, and looked rather differ-

ent from the denuded, half-cooked object before
her. "Never mind," said the intelligent native;
"nobody in the village would dream of killing a
turkey of his own on anything but a very supe-
rior saint's day;" so leaving the defunct bird
with the cook, he returned to the culprit, whom
he marched off to the judge. A little later,
while sitting at dinner, the entire tableful were
convulsed with laughter by a message arriving
from the judge to ask what the señora would
like him to do to the thief? If she had replied
"Shoot her!" there is no reason to suppose that
the sentence would not have been carried out!

It will be gathered from these instances that
life was conducted on primitive lines in the
Mexican sierras; but in the eyes of the new
settlers, that rather added to than detracted
from its charm. In any case, the climate went
a long way towards making up for other defi-
ciencies. Always cool enough up in the mountains for a fire of pine-boughs to be very welcome
in the evening, winter was yet unknown, and
day followed day of unclouded skies and brilliant
sunshine; while the purple shadows on the distant heights looked so like the bloom of heather,
that little imagination was needed to fancy one's
self living on a Scotch moor in a perpetual June.

Then, too, it was pleasant to feel on good terms with the whole community, as, with one exception, the Englishmen were. Even the old Padre had come round by now, although at first he preached long sermons on the desirability of turning the *hereticos* out of the place. But he was a person of much perspicacity, and when he found that regular pay meant more fees for himself, he gave the entire village leave to work on all but the very highest saints' days. Indeed he impressed upon them from the pulpit that there were many *ordinary* saints in whose honour it was not at all necessary that they should take a day's holiday, as they had been in the habit of doing; on the contrary, it was much better for them to keep on working for *him* and for their families — that was the relative order in which he put it. With all the odd *reals* and *pesetas* that he could squeeze out of his parishioners, his reverence was by no means wealthy, and as marriage fees were higher than any others, and formed his principal source of revenue, he promoted holy matrimony as if it had been a limited liability company. Left to themselves, the Indians would have dispensed with it as a superfluous and expensive commodity; but their priest kept a very wide open eye upon them, and at the first symptom of love-making, took them off and married them at once.

A little later on, this padre grew tired of his mountain cure, and resolved on going to the city of Mexico. But he reflected that it would be a pity to leave any more money than he need, to be gathered in by his successor. So he made it widely known that before going he would marry any one who wished him to do so for the low sum of $10. He gathered in a few devoted couples at that price; but as soon as no more were forthcoming he dropped his fee to $5, with a pathetic reminder that he would soon be far from them, and unable to bind them together any longer. This brought in several more lovers hovering on the verge of matrimony, who thought the offer too cheap to be resisted. As soon as the holy man was sure that there was not another $5 in the entire bachelor community, he said that he would perform the ceremony for a sheep, then for a pig, and so on, down to a fowl, until the whole country-side was married, and he departed with a rich harvest, leaving his successor to groan over the prospect of no fees coming in until some of the children grew up!

Of course all Mexicans, Indians included, are

devout sons of the Church — and yet ——!
There are out-of-the-way corners of the sierras
where sometimes stray fragments of strange,
wild stories can be heard about temples
yet devoted to Aztec gods, which are hidden
away in mountain fastnesses, and whose whereabouts are known only to the few tribes who,
through all persecution and change, have
kept the faith of their fathers. Outwardly devoted to the religion of the Spaniards, in secret
they do homage and sacrifice to the old, old
gods, whose day is over and whose power gone.
There may be a little truth in these tales. No
man knows how much. Indian races can keep
their secrets well, and Mexico is a country where
all things are possible, and most things come to
pass.

CHAPTER XIII.

A BRUSH WITH BANDITTI.

TREACHERY IN CAMP — THE EX-MANAGER, DON EDUARDO, AND HIS SCHEME OF REVENGE — THE GATHERING OF THE ENEMY — A DISCONTENTED *PEON* — SEBASTIANO DRUNK AND SEBASTIANO SOBER — THE PLOT LEAKS OUT — PECULIAR ARRANGEMENTS FOR DEFENCE — A SMART CAPTURE —AN INSTANCE OF SUMMARY JUSTICE — POWER OF THE DISTRICT CACIQUE — A SUPPORTER OF THE EMPEROR MAXIMILIAN — AN OLD BATTLE-GROUND — THE CACIQUE'S DESCRIPTION OF THE FIGHT — DEVOTION OF THE TRIBESMEN TO THEIR CHIEF — THE CLANNISH FEELING STILL EXISTENT IN MEXICO.

ALL things considered, for a mining camp the picturesque little Indian town was pleasant enough, and the Englishmen thought themselves in a perfect Garden of Eden, compared with other places they had known. But, like the original garden, this one too had its little snake. In the present case the serpent took the shape of a former Mexican manager of the mines, who, before the advent of the English company, had been a person of much importance, able to cheat and bully the peons to his heart's content, with

little fear of being called to account. He had
tried to continue this process under the new
rule, and had been dismissed in consequence.
Therefore he thirsted for the blood of every
foreigner in the country, but especially for that
of the superintendent who filled his post. He
had contrived to annoy the entire staff in various
little ways ever since his dismissal, but he did
nothing overt until about a year from the time
that they first arrived in the town. At this
period some alterations seemed to be necessary
in the original form of the company, and Jack
had to journey to England in order to arrange
the matter satisfactorily; leaving the English
superintendent, together with the cashier and
assayer, in charge, during his absence.

The ex-manager, Don Eduardo, thought that
with only three of the hated *gringoes* on the
spot, the time had arrived for him to carry out
a little scheme of revenge which had been in his
mind for a long while. During his management
he had been accustomed to pay the *peons* 60 per
cent of their wages in spoilt beans and maize,
and only 40 per cent in cash. Therefore when
the new company paid them entirely in coin, the
natives thought at first that it would not last,
but finding that the pay-rolls continued to be

met every week, they came to the conclusion —
helped thereto by Don Eduardo — that the foreigners must be enormously wealthy, and that
the office was crammed with silver dollars. A
little judicious talking quickly spread this rumour
through the sierras, whence it soon percolated
down into the plains, where — as any hillman
will tell you — the people are all *ladrones*, or, to
speak plainly, thieves. So it came to pass before long that a good many shady characters
found their way up into the mountains, in the
hope of being able to appropriate to themselves
some of the riches which were now wickedly
wasted on *hereticos*. Don Eduardo knew a bandit or two himself, and was careful to drop them
a hint that there might be plunder shortly;
whereupon several of his friends decided that
change of air would be beneficial to them, and
made their way to the sierra accordingly. They
dropped in to the mining camp casually, one at
a time, in order not to create suspicion, explain-
ing to all whom it might concern that they were
in search of employment. So they were!

Now, working in the mines was a *peon* named
Sebastiano, who, having been set to do something he did not like, struck work after the most
approved European fashion. In order to con-

tinue the resemblance between an angry Aztec
and a discontented docker, he also got drunk,
and went about abusing his employers roundly.
One of the loafers in the town overhearing his
tirades, took him aside, saying that, as he evidently hated the foreigners, he had better go to
the house of Don Eduardo, where he would find
others of the same way of thinking. Sebastiano
was charmed at the prospect of sympathy with
his wrongs, and immediately repaired to the
house, where he met a miscellaneous assemblage
of men, only two of whom, however, were fellow-
townsmen. After his tale of woe had been listened to, he was sworn to secrecy, and then told
that it only required a little courage on the part
of a few brave men like himself to secure two
things to be devoutly wished for, — first the loot-
ing of the office, and then the annihilation of the
hereticos, who ought not to be allowed to live,
anyhow. It further transpired that as the towns-
people were weak enough to tolerate and even to
like the strangers, about forty outsiders were to
be engaged in this excellent work. Of course
the Englishmen, and perhaps their servants,
would fight; but with so many men all armed
with knives and revolvers, there was no doubt
whatever as to the issue of the affair. Now that

one of their enemies had started for the doubtless pestilent country to which he belonged, the sooner the blow was struck the better, and they need only wait for the arrival of a few of their comrades, who had not yet put in an appearance, but would be on the spot within a fortnight.

Now, like a certain Philip, Sebastiano drunk and Sebastiano sober were two perfectly different *peons*. So when he awoke in the morning, having slept off the fumes of the *mescal* imbibed overnight, Sebastiano was a very frightened Aztec indeed. He didn't half like the conspiracy into which he had been drawn, especially as he remembered that his uncle, who was captain of the mine, lived near the English quarters, and would most assuredly be in the fray. Probably he would be killed; but if he lived to inquire into the matter, then would Sebastiano certainly soon cease to ornament the earth. This reflection decided any wavering he might have experienced, and he forthwith told his uncle all that he had heard. The uncle, Don Carlos, took counsel with the head men of the town, and partly from the joy of possessing a secret, and the still greater joy (to a Mexican) of postponing the telling of it, and also for reasons which will appear, they all agreed to

keep the Englishmen in complete ignorance of
what was taking place. Meanwhile, Sebastiano
was to go on conspiring and — reporting.

When, in a few days, he was able to tell them
that the last bandit had arrived, and that the
attack was fixed for an hour before daybreak
the next night, the party decided that it could
scarcely be called premature if they acquainted
their employers with the peril in which they
stood. So a little after dark, three head men
dropped casually into the superintendent's office,
and mentioned that it would be attacked about 2
A.M. Also that there had been a lot of strangers in the town for the last three weeks who had
arranged for the Englishmen's murder to take
place at the same hour! Surprise naturally
kept their astounded listeners silent for a moment, and an awful moment it must have been
for the man whose wife and children would have
to share whatever danger menaced him. During the pause Don Carlos proceeded to explain
that all the reliable men had been armed with
machetes, and would rush to the defence of the
office at the sound of the first shot, as, if they
attempted to sleep there, it would be found out
that an alarm had been given, and the attack
would be put off. Don Eduardo was of course

the moving spirit, and Don Carlos added that if it would not inconvenience the Señores, he should like to have the shooting of the ex-manager himself!

"Oh! by all means," replied the superintendent; "but if you have known of this precious plot for the last month, why the devil didn't you warn us sooner?"

"Señor," said Don Carlos, "we thought that as you were always so busy it might annoy you, and besides, would be sure to frighten the Señora. You see, we knew all the *ladrones'* plans, and in order to be *quite* safe, we have had armed men sleeping in your garden every night."

"I'll send a runner to the Cacique to ask for troops," exclaimed the superintendent. "Thanks to your delay in telling me this, they'll probably arrive in time to bury our remains. Still, it is our only chance."

"Señor," was the reply, "the troops are by now on the road. The fastest runner in the sierra started at noon. He will have reached the general an hour ago, and the soldiers will certainly be here in time."

"Well, you have shown *some* common-sense at last," said the superintendent; "but, for the life of me, I cannot understand why you have run it so fearfully close."

"Don't you see," he was told, "that at head-quarters, down in the hot country, Don Eduardo has many friends; and if we had sent for the troops sooner, rumours would certainly have reached him in time to cause him to change his plans, or even to get away altogether — and so!"

Light began to dawn upon the startled Englishmen. They had been used as a bait to catch Don Eduardo in his own trap, which, though an excellent plan, regarded as a piece of strategy, might prove to be unpleasant for the bait. It was evident that the Mexicans saw their way to paying off plenty of old scores during the night, and were simply "spoiling for a fight"; while, should they get the worst of it, there would be the troops to fall back upon. Of course the opposition were better armed than they; but then they could raise double the number of men for a scrimmage if need be, and besides, in the dark a *machete* is a rather more dangerous weapon than a revolver.

As these reflections occurred to the three recipients of the news, they began to feel a little easier than when it was first sprung upon them, and they said good-night to their visitors with some hope that, when they met again in the small hours, it might still be with whole skins.

After some discussion among themselves, they decided to take books, papers, and what little cash really existed, over from the office to the house, where they would all sit up and await events. This was accordingly done; but while the superintendent's wife was still about, not a word of the threatened danger was said. Directly, however, she had retired, windows and shutters were carefully examined, and the lower part of the house was put into as good a state of defence as might be. Hour after hour passed slowly by, the silence broken only by the crowing of the innumerable cocks, or the barking of the multitudinous curs which infest every Mexican village. Twelve o'clock tolled from the distant belfry, then one — the watchers growing ever more watchful. The moon was sinking low, but they could see clearly down the village, where all was quiet as death. Then two o'clock boomed out, and the excitement grew intense, for the attack was fixed for half-past, and surely the troops must be near by now!

Presently, as the three men gazed, they thought that they could distinguish three or four points of light on the road, where it dipped into the valley. In a moment more a dozen appeared. It was the welcome sight of bayonets and rifle-barrels glistening in the moonlight. The soldiers were in time. A few seconds, and they could be seen filling the *arroya* below Don Eduardo's house; then came a shower of heavy blows, and a crash, as one by one doors were forced in, and the waiting ruffians behind them dragged out to take a different part in the surprise from that which they had planned. Not a shot was fired, and very soon all was quiet again; but in the grey dawn an indistinct crowd of men might be seen a mile away on the road to the plains, surrounded on all sides by the glittering bayonets of the Federal troops! Except for the few *peons* who, rising from among the cabbages and rose-bushes in the garden, yawned wearily, and pulling their red blankets closely round them, slipped off to their huts, with a "*buenos dias*" to the three Englishmen, it seemed to the latter as if the whole thing must have been a dream, so quickly was it all over, and the village settled down to its slumbers again! Of course they heartily congratulated themselves on the capture of their enemies and the prompt

settlement of the whole affair. But Don Carlos
took a different view of the matter, as he explained when he called at the office later in the
day. In the first place, Don Eduardo had seen
the soldiers coming in time to get into bed and
pretend to be asleep, whereby he would probably be able to prove an *alibi ;* then those who
were captured had been taken to the plains,
where they would secure lawyers who might
get them off. Lawyers had been known to do
equally outrageous things, and Don Carlos
crossed himself as he spoke of them. But he
brightened up when he mentioned that some
of the bandits had escaped, and would make
for a certain point in the sierras where, thanks
to the Virgin, there were no lawyers, and he
had already sent a runner to arrange for their
reception — and despatch — at the hands of
the chief of the district!

Three months later, on Jack's return, he was
riding across a *mescal*-covered plain, accompanied by an escort of troopers, when he
noticed a fresh little hillock, and asked the
man nearest to him what it was. Nothing of
consequence, he was told; it only contained a
few of the men who had escaped the soldiers
on the night of the expected attack on the

foreigners! Two had been got near a *pueblita* close by, and three more down an *arroya* at a little distance.

On reaching the camp Jack heard that most of the others had been sent to Yucatan, but that the head and front of the whole plot, Don Eduardo, had been acquitted in consequence of his father being a *compadre* of the colonel of the regiment. But the Cacique had told him that if he gave any further trouble he would be shot at once; and as there was not a man in the country but knew that the "Tiger of the sierras" kept his word in such little details, the English community felt quite safe from further molestation.

This Cacique, who was also General of the army and Governor of the State, and in all three capacities exercised rather more power than the Czar, shared Don Carlos' dislike to lawyers, none of whom would he allow within his jurisdiction. A little prior to this date, three men had done something — I forget what, but something sufficiently bad to induce the General to send a party of troops in pursuit, who, after a very long and hot chase, came up with them eventually, down on the plains. The three malefactors proved to be well-connected men, who managed to communicate with their friends. These procured an order delivering them over to the civil powers, and to their extreme disgust the troopers had to give up their hardly-earned prey. Their indignation was great, but it was nothing to the rage of the General when he afterwards heard that the criminals had employed a clever lawyer who had got them off.

"Got them off!" he exclaimed, purple with wrath; "and my men spent a hard week tracking them down. All wasted work! But it shall not happen twice! No lawyers shall talk, talk me out of my prisoners again! The men shall have instructions always to shoot at sight!"

And they had!

Both for business and for pleasure, Jack often took the thirty-mile ride down into the hot country, where the cast-iron old chieftain lived on his hacienda in the midst of his vassals, dispensing open-handed hospitality and rough justice to all the countryside, like a feudal lord in the middle ages. Long and interesting were the conversations that took place round his eccentric board, where the soup was frequently served in delicate Sèvres *teacups*, and the kid, roasted whole in honour of the visitor, was eaten with black-handled Birmingham knives, but with forks hammered out of blocks of solid silver! The General had been a strong Imperialist in Maximilian's time, and had done his best to save the gentle, kindly, deceived, and betrayed Emperor from his fate. He was preparing for a feint on Querétaro, when the Republicans got wind of his intentions and sent 5000 regular troops against the General and his handful of clansmen, who, after five days' and nights' incessant fighting high up on the pine-crowned precipices of the sierra, were too utterly exhausted and reduced in number to commence a campaign. But they were victorious over regulars who numbered ten to one against them; besides, they so harried the retreat of their assailants that only 2000 ever reached the plains again, out of the 5000 who a month before had started confidently for the sierra.

Jack rode one night with the Cacique over the battle-ground of twenty years before, where the latter had fought and struggled over those narrow ridges, with friends and clansmen falling fast around him. But the enemy fell still faster below, as they crawled and scrambled up the inaccessible gullies, striving to win the ridge, only to find that when won, there was a still higher and steeper crest beyond, also lined with glittering arms, as tireless and deadly beneath the cold bright moon as through the long hot day. The General began to tell his eager listener the story of that desperate fight, and it is best repeated in his own words.

" This is the place," he said. " We lined this ridge nearly all the second day, and I had my men strung out for half-a-mile, although there were less than 600 of us! But we were all well armed, and knew how to shoot straight; besides, we had fair cover, while our enemies had next to none. Still they were brave men, and came up time after time, though we shot them down in crowds. They made their best charge up that *arroya* you see to the right. They massed 1000 men there, and I saw it was impossible for us to hold the ridge longer, especially as they were flanking us besides; so I let them come to within fifty yards. All were ' men of the plains,' and it took them a long time to climb our sierras; so at fifty yards I gave them another volley, and then every man of us rushed down the other side of the hill and scaled the ridge behind, so that when they reached our former position, we were all safe at the top of the next hill, and our enemies had another stiff climb before them! I left a third of my men there to hold the ground and to skirmish, while with the rest I marched nearly all night. Before morning we got round behind the troops, to the crest of the hill they had driven us in from the preceding day, so that they had to face about and do their work all over again. We also captured some baggage and ammunition. It was pretty hard work, though, for we never got any sleep, and no food either, except a few tortillas the women managed to bring us from time to time. Well, it's long over now; and down there in the glade they say that more than 400 of them are lying! But, *quien sabe*, there was no time to bury the dead in those days!"

How devoted his tribesmen were to him, probably the General himself scarcely realised. A few days after listening to the foregoing story, Jack, who was very much interested in the whole history of the revolution, was talking to one of the peons, and asking if he too had been in the war. The man replied in the affirmative, and Jack then inquired if he had served with Maximilian or with the Liberals.

"Maximilian!" said the man; "I seem to remember the name, and I think he was on the same side that I was, but *I* was fighting for General —— ! "

He had never troubled even to ask what the war was about! His Cacique told him to fight, and he had done his best unquestioningly. It seemed like a dream to Jack to find still existing in the heart of Mexico the old clannish feeling which in long-past generations enabled the squire of every English village to march to battle followed by the men who had grown up beside him, and were willing to die for and with their master and friend.

CHAPTER XIV.

MEXICAN HISTORY AND LEGEND.

THE subject of Maximilian's martyrdom is full of pathetic interest, and it seems impossible to leave it without a few words about the lonely figure on the Cerro Del Campana, which for a short space held the world breathless with pity and suspense. Even his bitterest foes allowed that the Emperor was an honest man, and one who strove anxiously for what he believed to be the good of his adopted country, — a man whose brain was filled with schemes for the improvement and development of Mexico, but whose hands were not strong enough for the work. His cause became hopeless from the moment that Napoleon III. accepted the ultimatum of the United States and withdrew the French army of occupation. Had Maximilian been wise, he would then and there have given up the useless contest; but he was surrounded by men whose interest it was to keep him in a fool's paradise. He was made to believe that the bulk of the country was with him, and he was told that the patriot bands who, under Juarez, Diaz, and others, had never ceased to resent the French occupation of their capital, were no better than herds of marauders, as much the enemies of Mexico as the bandits who had long been its curse. Later, when the stern logic of war had proved the vanity of his hopes, and he had suffered the pang of seeing many of his traitorous advisers desert to the enemy, he was too proud and chivalrous to fly. Again and again, under all temptation, he refused to abandon the few who still stood by him, and whose danger increased as his star waned.

It is now well known that he might have escaped at almost any period of the three months during which he was beleaguered in Querétaro. All preparations were made, and the step was urged upon him by his closest friends; but, like the true gentleman he was, he chose to stay with the little army that still fought for him, though he knew by then what his choice implied. Although both besiegers and besieged fought magnificently at Querétaro, it is more than doubtful if the former would not have shared the joy of the latter had the Emperor escaped. The President and his Cabinet had no desire to cover themselves with the odium that the execution of Maximilian would undoubtedly cast upon them; while at the same time it was felt that should he be captured, an example must be made which should for ever deter any other prince from attempting to play the *rôle* of Emperor of Mexico. It is equally certain, though less well known, that in the Presidential army there were many who, although they fought well, were still anxious *not* to take Querétaro. Of the 35,000 men who besieged the city, a large proportion were very irregular troops indeed.

Bands of guerillas, enlisted bandits, the scourings of many a jail, were to be found in the ranks; and to these men the fall of Querétaro meant the end of the war, and the loss of free rations, together with all chance of legitimate and illegitimate loot. Altogether, there were plenty of people, from those highest in authority to the lowest privates in the army, who would have been delighted had Maximilian broken through Escobedo's lines and reached the coast in safety, as he might easily have done. Twelve hours' ride would have placed him beyond pursuit among the clansmen of his devoted follower, General Mejia, where he might have held out for an indefinite length of time, or have proceeded at his leisure to the coast.

But it was not to be. The empire was quenched in blood, and the subtle, iron-willed Juarez firmly seated in the Presidential chair. Few men who knew him would have cared to match themselves against the President in wit or *finesse*, for with all the wiliness, and perhaps cruelty, of the old Aztec stock, he combined immense ability and resource; while from the days when, as a ragged boy in the streets of Puebla, he gained a precarious living by peddling oranges, until he had attained the summit of his ambition as ruler of the country, he was never known to trust any man, or to take counsel with any but himself.

The present President — then merely General Diaz — is probably the only man alive who can

boast of having beaten Juarez with his own
weapons; and the story is worth telling, as illus-
trating Mexican methods of those days, although,
of course, it is a digression from the subject of
these sketches.   Still, it shall be given as it was
told to Jack Jebb.

Among the prisoners, after the fall of Querétaro, were two young *hacienderos* of good family,
who had taken an active part in the defence.
As they were both wealthy, and of great local
importance, Juarez thought they would be just
the right men to make an example of; so they
were tried by court-martial, and condemned to
be shot.

The most urgent appeals were made to the
Dictator on their behalf; bribery of high officials
was tried in vain; every influence that could be
secured was brought to bear, without the slightest effect. Juarez was inflexible. As a forlorn-
hope the family appealed to General Diaz,
begging him to ask the President to give him
the lives of the two prisoners, in consideration
of his own great services — for he was then fresh
from the storming of Puebla, and the most popular man in the country. He was also the head
of a strong party, and in every way a power to
be reckoned with. So, when he consented to do

his best, and called upon Juarez, with a ready-made-out pardon in his pocket, the latter after much hesitation, consented to sign it. But — the instant Diaz left the palace Juarez sent off a courier, with orders to General Escobedo to hasten the execution, and have the prisoners safely shot before the pardon could arrive; thereby, as he thought, securing his revenge, and at the same time obliging his ally! His anger and surprise may therefore be imagined when, four days later, General Diaz presented himself at the palace accompanied by two travel-stained young men, who had ridden day and night to thank him for the lives he had saved, and to make their acknowledgments to the Presi-dent. In his astonishment, Juarez blurted out the fact that he had expected the execution to be over before the arrival of the pardon.

"Ah, your Excellency," said Diaz, " I believe *your* messenger did not start until 2 P.M., while *I* had a mounted orderly waiting in the courtyard until you had signed the pardon. He was on his way to Querétaro with it five minutes after-wards, and as he had relays of horses posted along the entire route, I think that will account for the little mistake! I really ought to apologise to your Excellency for being in such a hurry! " he wound up, with a smile.

The President looked him straight in the eyes with the genial expression of a dog whose bone has just been snatched from him, as he said, " Yes, you have been too quick for me this time, but I should advise those friends of yours to go straight home, and to leave politics alone in future."

To those who have lived in the land of Montezuma, the strange mixture of absolute freedom and military despotism which still forms her government, and the even more singular mingling of cunning and simplicity in her people, are subjects of which it is difficult to tire; but I will have mercy, and will return forthwith to the tale of Mr Jebb's adventures.

As a matter of fact, they were not numerous at this period of his career. There was little to break the monotony of life in the mountains — to the joy of the dwellers therein, for such events as did occur were usually of an unpleasant nature: accidents in the mines, for instance, or a break-down of the machinery. The latter once collapsed so effectually, that a fresh smelting apparatus had to be procured from the United States. The order was sent accompanied by a stipulation that the separate pieces must be small enough to admit of their being dragged

up a precipitous ascent by mules. When Jack
received notice of the arrival of the machinery
at the foot of the sierra, thirty miles from the
mines, he rode down to look at it, and to arrange for its removal. To his consternation he
found that his instructions had been disregarded,
and that each piece weighed a ton or more. As
there was only space for two mules abreast on
the narrow trail up the mountains, and as har-
nessing them tandem would probably result in
the amiable animals kicking each other over the
precipices, the situation was decidedly embar-
rassing. The latter course had to be tried,
however, and the result was half a mile's progress in twelve hours! The mules, with the
"infinite variety" which distinguishes their
character, had turned sulky instead of restive;
and even that half mile was won only by a constant attention to business on the part of the
drivers.

Jack felt a little discouraged, but hoped for
better things next day. Quite in vain, as events
proved, for every mule in the countryside seemed
to have struck work, and it took just one month
to get that machinery a distance of thirty miles!
The entire staff kept riding backwards and forwards to look on and to help, and although they

admitted that their feelings were difficult to express, they afterwards confessed that they thought their language had done justice to the situation. When the cumbrous pieces of iron at last reached the topmost ridge, and were promptly put together and set to work, the company hoped for some months of uninterrupted progress, with large dividends looming in the distance. They *did* loom, constantly, but somehow, they never seemed to get any nearer. In the first place, the furnace, when up, refused to work for a long time, although Jack and the superintendent hovered over it all day, and sat up with it all night, like affectionate parents with a sick child.

When that difficulty was overcome, fresh ones arose. For instance, a portion of one of the mines fell in, undoing the work of weeks, and almost costing the lives of the men who were labouring below. They were only saved by the heroism of a little Indian lad of twelve. He was employed near the entrance to the mine, and while busy there one day, he noticed something wrong with the shaft. Looking closer, he saw that it was giving way, and would fall within a few minutes. Being near the mouth, he could easily have escaped before the crash came;

but that did not seem to have occurred to him, and he rushed back into the depths of the mine, shouting to the miners to run for their lives. They threw down their tools and fled, while the boy went farther in, to make sure that all had heard his warning; then he, too, began to think of saving himself. He turned, and ran after the others, most of whom had got out safely, but as the last batch were leaving the mouth of the shaft, the trembling mass fell. Some were killed outright, and some maimed for life; and among the last was the brave little lad, who had courted his fate in giving his companions a chance. It is almost needless to say that everything science could do for him was tried, but at the best he could never hope to work again.

While the task of clearing away the *débris* and preparing to sink a new shaft in the damaged mine was proceeding, amid much grumbling from the disheartened staff, one of the miners tried to console them by saying that they would get on better now, as it was well known that a mine was always lucky in which a man had been killed! They found that the entire village firmly believed in this sanguinary superstition, and were willing to tell some very "queer stories" in proof of it. One of these was so dramatic in itself, that Jack took notes of the tale as it was repeated to him by an Indian, in whose family it had its origin, and by whom it had been handed down from generation to generation. As all Indian traditions are very carefully preserved, it may be taken for granted that the history is a true one, and is therefore perhaps worth reproducing.

"Don Isidoro de la Vega was a Mexican — that is, although his grandfather had been a Spanish *émigré*, his father had been born in Mexico, and had there married an Indian woman, who traced her lineage back to one of the oldest families of the valley of Anahuac. Her son inherited from her the intense Indian hatred of the conquerors of their country, and doubtless Don Isidoro's sentiments found their way to the ears of the Viceroy, for at an early age he became aware that he was a marked man. No preferment was ever offered to him, and if he had occasion to appeal to the courts for justice, their decision was always against him. In spite of this he, with his mother and his pretty sister Conchita, led a peaceful, happy life in a little rose-covered house on the long causeway connecting the city of Mexico with Pachuca.

"Pachuca was then the most important mining settlement from which the Viceroy could enrich himself while still sending the expected 20 per cent royalty over to Spain. Living on the direct route to the mines, Don Isidoro often saw groups of miserable *peons* and wretched prisoners from the gaols driven along the causeway to a slavery worse than that of Russian serfs in the wastes of Siberia; and he also made the acquaintance of their taskmaster, Don Miguel Gomez, who was the right hand of the Viceroy in squeezing work — ay, and life — out of the unfortunates who fell into his hands. It was necessary to treat this man with respect, as a high official; but he was so notorious a scoundrel that Don Isidoro made a point of sending his sister out of the room whenever Don Miguel stopped at the house on his way to and from the mines, as he soon formed a habit of doing. At first he asked if he might not see the Señorita Conchita, but finding his request politely parried, he ceased to prefer it, and Don Isidoro thought the subject had passed from his mind, until one evening, going home later than usual, he saw a group of Don Miguel's cut-throat followers by the roadside, and heard a wailing cry issuing from the house!

" In an instant he had dismounted and thrown

open the door! There, in the corner of the living-room stood his mother, with Conchita cowering behind her, whilst storming, and threatening, and vainly trying to drive the mother from her post, was Don Miguel Gomez! Isidoro was unarmed, but he had the ruffian by the throat in a moment, and seizing a bridle that chanced to be near, he administered such a thrashing as few *caballeros* of Castile have ever received! Don Miguel yelled for help in a paroxysm of fear and fury; but as his men came running to the rescue, Don Isidoro, with a parting kick, sprang into his own room and seized his sword. At the same moment the Indian mother slipped a knife into his left hand, so that before his assailants could gain the front room, he was waiting for them in the doorway. They did not care to face him, however, when they saw the spectacle he had so speedily made of their chief, for Don Miguel could scarcely stand, and the blood was dripping into his beard from a cut on the forehead, where the hard edge of the bridle had bitten deep. So the party turned away with many oaths, and helping their master into his saddle, they slowly mounted and rode back to the city.

"That night, as the rising moon gleamed

coldly on the snowy steeps of Ixtaccihuatl, and was reflected on the placid bosom of Lake Tezcoco, the little house on the causeway was surrounded by armed men in the uniform of the Viceroy's guards. After a desperate but futile struggle, Don Isidoro was dragged on to the main road, where more soldiers were guarding a group of ragged criminals, — the scourings of the prisons of Mexico, now condemned to a far drearier fate in the mines of Pachuca. Almost naked, half stunned, and bleeding from a dozen wounds, Don Isidoro was forced into the ranks, and securely chained to a ferocious-looking bandit, whose head had been nearly beaten into a jelly while he was resisting capture a fortnight before. As his hurts had never been dressed, even by the faint moonlight he presented a spectacle of blood and filth calculated to send a shudder through his involuntary companion. After a march of about a mile, the village gaol was reached, and into a small dungeon, scarcely large enough for one man, the whole gang of eighteen prisoners were driven for the night. The dirt and misery were more than even the hardened malefactors could bear calmly, but for Don Isidoro it must have been a hell indeed! Before daylight each man received his day's rations — just enough to keep life in their tortured bodies, and no more — and then they were again started on their march. To Don Isidoro, who was an extremely powerful man, the forced marches were a trifle, but some of his weaker companions fell and died on the road. It was the thought of his sister's fate, and of the untold miseries which awaited him, that weighed him down more than the chains about his body. At mid-day the prisoners were halted at a well and allowed to drink their fill, while the infantry guard which had escorted them from Mexico was changed for a detachment of cavalry intended to take charge of them to Pachuca.

" Don Isidoro recognised the officer commanding, and ventured to address him. The latter was horrified at the plight of a man he had long known and respected, but he did not dare to do more than exchange a few words with him. However, in the course of these Don Isidoro learnt with certainty what he had naturally suspected, that Don Miguel Gomez was responsible for the position in which he was placed. The officer had heard at the Palace the preceding night that Don Miguel, covered with dust and wounds, had made a formal report to the Viceroy of some one who had spoken ill of the King

of Spain and had nearly murdered his officer!
Then Don Isidoro knew his fate.

" A week's march brought the convicts to
Pachuca, where they were handed over to the
captain of the most important mine in the district. The column was marched through a
strongly fortified gate into a high-walled enclosure surrounded by sentries, and in which were
sheds where the slaves slept on the bare ground.
In the centre of this enclosure was the mouth of
the mine — 20 feet in diameter, and 600 feet
deep. Down one side of the deep shaft was a
line of poles, notched on the outer surface, and
shouldered against the projecting rocks. Covered with mud and slime, wet, greasy, and frequently rotten as they were, the prisoners had
to pass up and down these poles day and night,
carrying up loads of ore weighing from 150 to
250 lb. each. Don Isidoro de la Vega knew
nothing of mining, and therefore was not engaged in breaking ore, but he was placed in a
gang employed in the deepest workings, to carry
the ore from the place where it was mined to
the bottom of the shaft, where peons long accustomed to the dangerous work on the poles bore
it safely to the surface. The level where Don
Isidoro worked was a ghastly place. The rock

was sharp and irregular above and below, striking the head if the slaves tried to walk upright, and cutting deeply into their unprotected feet in the treacherous mud-holes. The bottom of the level was undrained, and often the wretched men were knee-deep in slush and filth, while the air was so bad that lights would not burn, so they usually had to stagger along in darkness. But there was no halting, no rest; for the overseer's whip was rarely idle, and the fetid air constantly resounded with the noise of blows and curses. There was no hope of pardon for any there. They were too useful to be spared, and death came only to the weak.

" Don Isidoro was a strong man, but a month of this torture made a wreck of him. Each day he was more and more tempted to throw himself from the poles and make an end of it; but he was borne up, not so much by the futile hope of escape, as by the inward conviction that some day he would hear tidings of the fate of his mother and sister. But no news came; and in time his hope died as his body was dying, until he had scarcely strength left to climb the poles. At last one evening, as, racked with fever, with bleeding hands and feet, and tortured by innumerable wounds, he dragged himself up the last ladder, to stagger to the shed where he slept, he heard his number called. The speaker was the master of his gang — a ruffian whose devilish love of cruelty well fitted him for the post. Half-blinded by the setting sun, and stumbling every other step, Don Isidoro went round the great shaft to where the master was standing with Don Miguel Gomez by his side.

"'So, Don Isidoro de la Vega, you are here,' said the latter, with an exultant laugh. 'I hope you appreciate your quarters?'

"'Oh, Don Miguel!' cried Isidoro, 'for the love of the Blessed Virgin, pardon the blows I struck,' and release me! It is a hell underground there!'

"'The half-breed dog seems discontented,' said Don Miguel to his companion. 'One would suppose from his remark that you do not treat your prisoner well, Señor Capitan?'

"'I do my best,' replied the ruffian. 'Only turn him round, and you will see evidences of my care upon his back!'

"'This man is a devil!' broke in Isidoro. 'He has murdered many. For God's sake, have pity on us!'

"'Ah!' remarked Don Miguel. 'You see how he insults you, Señor Capitan; you must

16

have dealt with him too leniently. Give him harder work to do. And now, Don Isidoro, I return to Mexico to-morrow, where I shall see the charming Conchita. I will tell her how you are enjoying yourself, and as you say it is hell below there — go back, you hound !'

" ' I will, and you with me !' shouted Isidoro, as, with one bound, he passed an arm round each of his tormentors, and with an effort of superhuman strength sprang over the edge of the great shaft ! There was one wild shriek of horror and anguish as the three men plunged down 600 feet into the dark depth of the mine — and then silence !"

" Yes, señor," said the Indian, when he had finished the story, " it *was* horrible, but that mine is the richest in Mexico to this day !"

CHAPTER XV.

THE CITY OF MEXICO.

IN due course the damaged mine in the Sierras was opened up again, although the fact of its having claimed its tribute of lives failed to make any difference, for it continued to give trouble of one sort or another to the end. But every one did his best, including the *peons*, who could *not* get used to the idea that if they laboured all the week they would certainly be paid on Saturday, and who stuck to work partly out of sheer curiosity to see how long this state of things was going to last. The one fact of which, from their past experiences, they felt absolutely sure, was that in order to make the mines pay there must be cheating somewhere. Therefore, if the pay-rolls continued to be met every week, what was more likely than that bad money should be foisted upon them? The result of this deduction in the native mind was that, on receiving his wages, each *peon* retired in turn to the door-step of the office, where he carefully rang every coin, down to the last *centavo*. Even then he was not entirely convinced, but proceeded to bite each piece of money before tying it all up in a handkerchief and making way for the next comer, to go through the same performance.

Under these circumstances it always took an entire day to pay the men off, and by evening it was unsafe to go near the long-suffering cashier! As for the *peons*, once satisfied of the soundness of the money, they went and got drunk upon it at once, in order to waste as little time as possible between Saturday and Monday. *Pulque* — the national drink — is cheap, and for the expenditure of about a halfpenny it is possible to get helplessly drunk, but it takes time to do so; while *aquadiente*, though more expensive, does its work quicker. Therefore the latter was the more popular of the two, though its strong resemblance to methylated spirits might have made some fastidious people hesitate before drinking it.

While referring to the national beverages, it would be a pity to omit the story of a Mexican cook (about the only one in the country at the time) who, among innumerable virtues, had the one vice of having a twenty-four hours' "bust" regularly once a-month. Her mistress, anxious to meet her views, offered to give her a day off whenever she felt an attack coming on, if she would only stick to work meanwhile. But the cook said that she could not be bound by rules in such a matter; and she usually chose the evening of a dinner-party for being discovered fast asleep, with her head in the soup-tureen. Then the mistress, driven to desperation by the dread of having to part with her treasure, offered not only a day's leave, but also to provide the liquor herself! This was too good to be resisted, and the thirsty one accepted the terms; while the excellent woman who arranged them continued to enjoy her dinners with an easy mind.

The little English community up in the mountains worked very hard for a couple of years after the mines were first taken over; their only relaxation being a ride, about sunset, round the narrow trails overhung with maidenhair, and looking down upon deep gorges covered with tropical raiment of palms and ferns. Or if, after a particularly busy day, every one felt too tired to stir, they sat round the ever welcome fire of sweet-scented pitch-pine, whose fantastic shadows on the white-washed walls seemed to help in the building of many castles, then — and always — in the air.

When the preliminary difficulties had at last been overcome, and a regular routine established, it became unnecessary for Jack Jebb to spend all his time at the mines, and indeed he was more useful to the company — of which he was afterwards made managing director — in superintending its financial and general management. This entailed frequent visits to the city of Mexico, and occasional trips to England. The former is a place that grows upon its visitors, as Jack soon found, and he had not been living there long, before he knew and loved every ruined stone that had helped to pile a monastery, or in long past days had looked down on human passion and pain from the walls of an Aztec temple. He never tired of the narrow streets with their grey old houses, which, but for the sunshine and the flowers that ever surround them, would oppress the beholder with a vague sense of wrong and suffering silently endured behind their barred windows. And yet — in spite of its age and the sadness of its history — there is much in Mexican life and manners that irresistibly suggests *opéra bouffe !*

For instance, returning late one night to his hotel, Jack saw a carriage driving furiously down the principal street, with its occupant scattering seditious pamphlets from right to left of the windows as he passed; while galloping after him in hot haste were two of the national guards — the police taking ineffectual pot-shots at the vehicle as it flew along! It turned out afterwards that the man who ran this gauntlet was an emissary of one of the former presidents, who chose this singular method of spreading his propaganda. He did not, however, get into office, which perhaps was just as well, for it was said that when he previously quitted the presidential dignity there were exactly twenty-five cents left in the treasury — they were supposed to have been overlooked!

Another night was the anniversary of the taking of the Bastille, an event which the large French colony in Mexico always celebrates with much enthusiasm; and probably on account of its being an excuse for a holiday, the Mexican *peons* join in the rejoicings with fervour — and drinks.   Perhaps on this occasion they had imbibed and rejoiced more than usual; anyhow, the speeches in the *plaza* at night on the glorious exploits of bygone French patriots excited them to such a point that they began to think, Why should they not hand down *their* names to an admiring posterity, by taking the Mexican prison and releasing all the prisoners at once?

Jack, having listened to a few such speeches, saw there was going to be fun, and placed himself in a position to get a good view. He had not long to wait, for after a little more rousing rhetoric, the mob of about two hundred *peons* began to march on the gaol, not very far from where they stood. When, shouting and yelling, they approached the gates, expecting a desperate fight with the guards before getting them down, to their surprise they found the massive portals left invitingly open! Of course they concluded there was to be no resistance, and marched into the courtyard triumphantly, singing a Mexican Marseillaise. No sooner was the last man safely inside than the heavy gates were clanged together by previously invisible guards, who seemed to start up in hundreds out of the very earth, and the unlucky patriots found themselves thoroughly trapped! They were promptly bestowed in separate cells, and after a night's reflection therein, they were released next morning with a firm resolution in the breast of each man to let the prisoners alone in future. As to Jack, after seeing the *dénoûment* of the attack, he went home shaking with laughter, but with a conviction that the management of a mob is one of the things "they do better abroad."

Just at this time the political atmosphere was decidedly " electrical," and there had been several small conflicts between the people and the police. Simultaneously with the then President's retirement, an unpopular measure was being forced through Congress, and the students were being egged on by the clericals to make a demonstration; so that a row might occur any day, and Jack made a point of being constantly about, in order not to miss it when it came.

One evening as he was going with a friend to dine at a *café*, they saw a mob march down a side street in a dense column, from the midst of which puffed little jets of smoke as the crowd " demonstrated " by firing revolvers in the air! No harm was meant or done then, but the two Englishmen congratulated themselves that the plot was ripening, and that by the time they had finished their meal there might be something worth seeing. On reaching their destination they seated themselves at a table close to a window which looked on the street; but the crowd had gone in another direction, and as it was the midst of the rainy season, with the streets consequently like stagnant rivers, there were few passers-by. The coffee and cigarette stage had been reached, when Jack, happening to look up, saw a child's face pressed against the window-pane. Her eyes were wandering towards the remains of food still on the table, and it did not need the thin little face, with dark rings beneath the shy grey eyes, to tell a story of hunger and privation. She seemed inclined to run away when she first saw herself observed, but in an instant mustered up enough courage to hold a box of matches against the window. Jack motioned to her to come in, which with some hesitation she did; then he gave her a roll to eat, while he asked how she came to be out selling matches on such a wild night.

The child, who was about eight years old, and who had fair hair and an English-looking face, told him between mouthfuls that her father and mother were dead, and she lived with an elder sister, who could not earn enough for both, and just now was out of work altogether. Her grandfather had been an American who was killed in the storming of Chapultepec, which of course accounted for her un-Mexican appearance. Jack was touched by the poor little thing's sad face and evident destitution, so he asked for her name and address, with a vague idea that he might be able to do something for her. Then he bought up her stock of matches at a premium, and bade her " good night," telling her to go straight home, as the streets were likely to become dangerous later on. With many " *milliones de gracias, señor*," the child departed, and the two men, after paying their bill, began to wend their way to the Zocalo — a large and lovely garden surrounding the cathedral, where the city disports itself in the evening, and where what correspond to " mass meetings " in Mexico are usually held. In a kiosk situated in the centre of a splendid circle of trees, a military band was playing selections from " Faust," while people sauntered slowly past listening to the music, or talking softly together. It was a perfect night, now the rain had ceased and the clear full moon brought into strong

relief the great white towers of the cathedral, and the long palm-bordered terrace which runs about its base. As Jack and his companion began to walk up and down here, they were accosted by an officer who was evidently on guard. He said he could tell the señores were foreigners, and he therefore advised them to go straight home, as trouble was expected that night, and once firing commenced no one's life would be safe in the streets. The two men thanked the courteous officer for his advice; but almost before they had finished doing so, a succession of shots were heard close by, followed instantly by a large crowd which surged round one side of the cathedral, while from the other side a troop of infantry charged with pointed bayonets! In these circumstances discretion was certainly the better part of valour for people caught between the two opposing forces, and our friends fled down the steps for their lives, just in time to escape being trampled under foot by the excited mob, or spitted on the bayonets of the soldiers! As the fight seemed inclined to confine itself to the terrace on which it began, the pair went over to the band-stand, about a hundred yards off, to watch the pro-gress of events. It was evidently a desperate struggle, and the firing grew continuous, as the combatants fought to the air of the " Soldiers' Chorus," for the band never left off playing. Anything more like a scene from " La Grande Duchesse " cannot well be imagined than the furious battle on the cathedral steps, while the stolid musicians attended strictly to business! At last it became evident that the troops were getting the mastery, as the mob began gradually to fall back, firing at random as it went. Within a quarter of an hour of its commencement the whole thing was finished, and the only sign of anything unusual having taken place was the sight of the soldiers marching off squads of prisoners. The rest of the crowd had melted away as suddenly as it had made the attack.

As Jack and his friend started homewards, having thoroughly enjoyed the show, they found that it was not so entirely over as they thought; for a band of the dispersed mob had chosen the street they were bound for in which to make a final demonstration — *i. e.*, a little wild shooting. Neither man was armed, nor would it have been of much use if they had been, so they kept in the shadow of a doorway until the crowd had passed. To Jack's surprise he found, crouching in terror on the step, the little match-girl he had helped earlier in the evening. She had heard the firing before getting far from the *café*, and being too frightened to proceed, she had lain hidden ever since beside the door where she was discovered. Jack immediately thought that, with the streets in such a dangerous state, it was impossible now for the child to go through them alone; so as soon as the one in which they stood was empty, he told her to show him where she lived, his friend volunteering to accompany them. It was a low part of the city that she led them through, but fortunately most of its population was occupied elsewhere that night, so they reached the miserable hut which she called home without molestation. Her sister met the party at the door, and was evidently glad to see the little one safely back. But of course she ought never to have sent her out alone on such a night; and Jack's companion, who was a fluent Spanish scholar, could not resist the temptation to give the elder girl a little salutary advice. Unfortunately for its effect, he was just in the midst of a beautifully rounded period, when, stepping carelessly backward, he went up to his knees in a pool of green and slimy mud, left in the unpaved roadway by the recent rains. He did not pause an instant in the delivery of his speech; only, instead of moral sentiment, there issued from his lips such a stream of heartfelt objurgations that his listeners became perfectly helpless with laughter at the sudden change in his views.

After this anti-climax to the evening's adventures, the two men betook themselves to their hotel without further delay. Jack, however, did not lose sight of the little match-girl, but finding that her great desire was to be educated, in order that she might some day gain her living by teaching, he began to make her a weekly allowance, which he continued for nearly ten years. From time to time she and her sister came to see him, and as they were both very grateful, and the child always neatly dressed, he took it for granted that everything was all right, and did not trouble himself to inquire how and where his *protégée* was being taught. But at last, when she was (for a Mexican) grown up, it did occur to him that if she were ever going to support herself, it was about time she began to do so. So, with a good deal of difficulty, he found out from her the name of the school she was at, and sent to the mistress of it to inquire if Carmen Lopez were not now sufficiently advanced to take a situation as a teacher.

To Jack's utter bewilderment the answer came back that Carmen Lopez had ceased to attend the school years before, and since then had been living at home in idleness with her sister on some private means they were supposed to have! To confirm the truth of the story, the girl never turned up again for her weekly dole, and on inquiry, was found to have removed from her former address. Of course she and her sister had thoroughly taken in the unsuspicious *Inglese*, and had led a very pleasant life at his expense. It is unnecessary to remark that this was Jack's first and last attempt at philanthropy where the female Mexican was concerned.

The fight at the cathedral was the last disturbance of the sort for a long while. Shortly afterwards President Diaz came into the power which he has now held firmly during three terms of office, and will probably continue to hold for the rest of his life. Mexicans are quite keen enough to see the advantages to trade of internal peace, and to appreciate the clear head and strong arm of probably the only man in the country able to secure it to them. The President is as good a shot as he is a statesman, and he was the principal guest at many a shooting-party at which Jack was also present. Away from the cares of office, in the comparative freedom of a bachelor gathering, the chief magistrate of Mexico was seen at his best, and it was easy to understand the force of character which had helped the soldier of fortune to climb the ladder of life, until he reached his present station. When in Mexico his hours of labour are from six in the morning until eight at night, and probably no man in the country works so hard as he; yet somehow he finds time to acquire an enormous mass of extraneous information. The thing that surprised Jack most about him was his absolute familiarity with any subject under discussion, from the spots on the sun to the qualities of iron pyrites, or from the history of Newton to the latest electrical discovery. He is a man of over sixty, who looks no more than forty, and whose idea of relaxation is a twelve hours' tramp through reeds and marshes in search of sport. Thanks to his uncompromising measures, it is possible at the present time to travel all over the country with little fear of molestation, for he has succeeded in entirely destroying the robber bands which used to scour the roads. As a matter of fact, they now form a considerable part of the army, for at an early stage of his presidency

Diaz gave them the chance of enlisting or of being shot down mercilessly by his troopers. Needless to say, most of them chose to join the army, and capital soldiers they make; while those who held out for the privilege of earning their living in their own way were hunted into their secret strongholds by the regular troops. and almost invariably shot *while trying to escape.* It is said that one bandit begged his captor to tie him on his horse, as then no one could say he had made any attempt at flight.

CHAPTER XVI.

THE "KNIGHTS OF THE ROAD."

ON his shooting expeditions to some of the great fortified haciendas, Jack was by way of hearing a good many tales of the doings of " the knights of the road" in the days when railways were not, and when nothing short of a troop of cavalry could protect the hapless traveller from robbery on most of the highways of Mexico. At one large shooting party the host was the only civilian and Jack the only foreigner present, as they sat through the interminable Mexican dinner discussing the day's sport. They all felt thoroughly soothed and satisfied with the "bag" they had brought in — over a hundred brace of yellow-legged plover, ten couple of duck, and a good number of bittern; so that by the time they reached the stage of such coffee as can only be procured in Mexico, the diners had all melted into a " reminiscent " mood.   Through the windows of the huge dining-room, which had once served as a refectory when the place was a monastery, the last gleams of sunlight were kissing the cold snows of the great volcano that towered above the hacienda.   Some one remarked that even now it might be possible for a gang of the bandits who formerly infested the mountain to attack the place in force and get away with a large amount of plunder before being caught.

" No," said one of the guests, " they dare not risk it now; but twenty years ago I've no doubt our host had some lively encounters with them. Why, the last time I went to Spain, somewhere in the sixties, I was robbed four times in one day ! "

Of course this statement was received with a shout of incredulous laughter, and cries of " Tell us the story, General ! "

" You don't deserve it, but I will," replied the General.   " Well, as I said, I was going to Spain, and fortunately for me I sent various sums to Vera Cruz and to Spain in advance, by means of bills of exchange; so that when I took my seat in the coach at Puebla on the way to Vera Cruz, I had little of value about me except a half-a-dozen *onzas* and an English hunter-watch. It was about 3 A.M. when we started, and in the two hours before the commencement of daylight we should get so short a distance from the city that we thought ourselves secure from molestation. There were four inside passengers beside myself, all too sleepy to talk; so we alternately dozed and smoked cigarettes for about an hour, when all at once we heard a trampling of horses on both sides of the coach, and to our horror we were halted! I was trying to put my head out of the window to see what was the matter, when I was prevented from doing so by the effectual method of having the muzzle of a pistol thrust into my mouth! Then we were all ordered out; though I found time first to slip my watch into my boot. Day was just dawning, and we could distinguish the figures of about twenty men grouped round the coach. They were all on horseback, except those who had dismounted in order to turn out the baggage or to guard us. Our pockets were promptly searched, and their contents vanished as if by magic, while our portmanteaux were being torn open and hastily rummaged. Of course whatever arms we had upon us were appropriated at once; but the search was not so complete as it might have been had our early callers not seemed pressed for time.

"As it was, within ten minutes, and with scarcely a sentence spoken on either side, the bandits were all in the saddle again and riding off at a gallop towards the wooded base of Malinché, leaving us with our rifled belongings strewn about the dusty road, as we stood helplessly gazing at each other. The whole thing was so quickly over that it seemed like a dream. The driver alone was as composed as ever, and removed his cigar from his lips to remark that they must be good people, because they had not harmed the coach by so much as a bullet-hole; though, he added, they might have been afraid of the patrol hearing shots. Well, we repacked our clothing and continued our journey, cursing both the bandits and the Government that permitted them.

" The next few hours passed peacefully, until at about eleven o'clock we were just beginning the rapid descent into the valley of Orizaba, when for the second time we were halted; moreover, it was not by mounted men in a hurry now, but was very deliberately done. At a sharp turn we found a felled tree lying across the road, and looking round, we saw that we were in a trap! Fifteen or twenty men were lounging towards us from the cover of some rocks fifty yards behind, while half-a-dozen more, who seemed to have arisen from the earth, were advancing with rifles at the ' ready '! Alongside the coach, sitting on a rock smoking a cigarette, was a most gentlemanly-looking man, evidently the captain of the band, and some distance up the mountain-side were more men, with quite a troop of horses and mules.

" ' Good morning, señores,' said the captain politely. ' I am sorry to be obliged to go through some formalities with you; but it is the fortune of war, and my men are greatly in need of a few necessaries, as their pay is in arrears. So I must trouble you to alight.'

" I ventured to remark that the regret was mutual, as a requisition had already been made upon us shortly after leaving Puebla.

" ' Still,' persisted the captain, ' I should like to show you some of the beauties of this part of the country,' and he led us off to a clump of pines beautifully situated on the edge of a cliff overlooking the valley three thousand feet below. ' A lovely view!' said our captor, softly, ' and splendid trees. Well, señores, we will now have no more fooling. Doubtless when you were attacked this morning you had time to secrete several trifles that we may find useful. Kindly hand them over at once; and if, when you are afterwards searched, my men find that you have concealed anything, *those trees shall bear fruit*, for you will all be hanged upon them within ten minutes!'

"We could see that the scoundrel was in dead earnest, and I confess that I fished my watch out of my boot at once, at the same time handing over a couple of *onzas* I had slipped into the lining of my hat. One of my fellow-passengers began to clutch despairingly at his throat, and I thought at first that he was going to have a fit. But he was only taking out of his neckcloth bank bills for $2500. Another passenger ruefully explained that under the cushion of his seat in the coach would be found a bag containing twenty *onzas*. The captain took over our effects, thanking us politely; but the outside passengers, who only contributed a few odd dollars, received no thanks at all. In the meanwhile our baggage was being searched, and everything of value annexed. Finally, the *shirts* worn by myself and another passenger were borrowed by the lieutenant and sergeant, who remarked that they were going to a *funcion* that night, and should require clean linen, the latter part of which statement was palpably true.

"'But, señor capitan,' I mustered up courage to say, 'we have had nothing to eat all day, and now when we reach Aguas Frias, where we intended to breakfast, we shall not have a cent among us to pay for a meal.'

"'True,' said the ruffian. 'I shall be delighted to relieve your necessities. You, I think, presented me with a gold watch and two *onzas*. Allow me the pleasure!' and he gave me a dollar, with a bow that would have graced a *caballero* of old Castile.

"'You,' he resumed to another passenger, 'made me a loan of \$2500; pray accept this trifle,' handing out another dollar.

"'You, señor, told us where to find the little bag of onzas,' and with a fascinating smile another dollar changed owners; 'but as for you *ladrones*,' went on the captain, with a complete change of manner to the outside passengers, 'you scarcely contributed anything; so as I can't afford to keep you in idleness, you must beg your breakfast from these noble *caballeros*.

And now, we must really be going, so I will say adieu; but before leaving, I want you all to seat yourselves in a line on this fallen tree, and look up at those rocks about sixty paces from you. Do you see them? Well, I have posted four men behind them, all picked shots, with orders to shoot the first of you that moves within the next two hours.'

" I suggested that if he would return to me the watch which an hour ago was mine, we should be more likely to know when the time was up. He looked affectionately at my gold hunter as he replied, ' I regret that I cannot oblige you to that extent, señor. You will have to guess the time; but I advise you not to be *too soon*, because the consequences would be serious. *Good* morning!' and with a parting bow and smile, our gentlemanly bandit went off in the direction of the horses, followed by his men, and the whole party was soon out of sight.

" It was blowing a norther that day, and an icy wind was driving over the snows of the great volcano above us. We felt half frozen; yet there we had to sit, in a shirtless condition, for what seemed more like four hours than two, and I don't think I have ever quite recovered from that chill. Of course no one liked to move first, for fear of drawing the fire of our unseen guards behind the rocks; but at last we ventured to return to the coach, and when we got to Aguas Frias, the breakfast we ate, at about supper-time, was really surprising. Before starting again we managed to borrow some clothes and blankets, for even down in the valley the night was chilly. Fortified with these and inspirited by our meal, we drove off, hoping to be at last allowed to reach Vera Cruz in peace. Our hopes soon proved to be ill-founded, for about 2 A.M. we were halted by a shot being fired at the coachman, which narrowly missed his nose. These new bandits had an amateurish cut, and were very different from our high-toned visitors of the morning. They were ragged and dirty, and they treated us with no courtesy at all. When leaving Aguas Frias, I and my shirtless companion had placed ourselves next to the windows, thinking that our appearance might prevent our being stopped again, by bearing witness to our poverty. But it was in vain that we now threw back our blankets and showed our unshrouded forms; we were ruthlessly bundled out and stripped of blankets, boots, and indeed almost everything we had left.

" Again we pushed on, in shivering despair. It was a bright night, so we made good time, and had travelled safely into the flat country beyond the mountains, when — it is almost incredible, but — we were stopped for the fourth time. We were passing through endless miles of *chaparral* which might have concealed an army for aught we knew, and to our horror we saw another band of armed men gliding out of the bushes upon us. Once more we were searched, and threatened with instant death unless we handed over our valuables. We looked like a party of damaged Venuses by now, and our condition spoke for itself, but I explained to the principal ruffian of the gang that we had already been stopped three times that day, and, naturally, had nothing of value left.

" ' Holy Virgin ! ' he exclaimed, ' you have been attacked three times ! And pray, why did you not defend yourselves, oh men without shame ? '

" Now, it was really too much for a *ladrone* engaged in robbing us himself to begin calling us names because we had not defended our property, in order that he might take it. I felt that the limit of endurance had been reached, and I am afraid that my reply was couched in very strong language indeed. However, I suppose the gang thought that nothing could be gained by murdering us, so after a fruitless search, in the hope that something might have been overlooked, they went off, swearing discontentedly; and naked, cold, and miserable, we at last reached Vera Cruz, after the most unpleasant journey I have ever taken."

When the General finished his story, a man sitting opposite to Jack said, " I know that tale of woe is quite true, because I was in garrison at Puebla at the time, and we laughed ourselves hoarse over the General's adventures when we heard of them from the stage-driver. But I remember even a worse case than his. The travellers had been treated in pretty much the same way as he, but the coach arrived in the city of Mexico in broad daylight, having amongst its passengers one young lady simply and lightly clad in a newspaper. What's more, it was not so much the costume that she objected to, as the fact that the newspaper had a hole in it, and the sun had ruined her skin ! "

" While we are on the subject of ' road agency,' " said another guest, " perhaps Mr Jebb, as a stranger to the ways of the wily bandit, might like to hear a rather funny experience I had

once in the 'good 'old days.' I was going a
journey by coach, and while on the road we
heard that there had just been a *pronunciamento*
at the town we were bound for, and that a regular
fight was in progress, as, of course, the Government troops were trying to drive the insurgents
out of the place. The report turned out to be
quite true, for we soon heard the booming of
artillery. We were, however, obliged to push on
in spite of the disagreeables which seemed to be
awaiting us at our destination. But when we
were within three miles of the scene of operations, with the town and the smoke from its
guns in full view, we were halted by an advanced
picket of troops. The sergeant in charge was
very polite, but he said that his orders were
imperative to allow no one to pass on the road
without first being examined by the colonel. He
told us that we should find that officer in camp
about half a mile up the cross-road where we
had been stopped. Of course we had no alter-
native but to do as we were bidden; so quitting
the coach, away we trudged, and a very hot walk
we had. We could see no trace of a camp when
we came to the end of our stipulated half-mile;
so we walked on, looking everywhere for the
invisible colonel, until, after half a mile more,

we realised that we had been sold. Hot, dusty, and very ill-tempered, we began our tramp back to the coach, to find, when we reached it, the sergeant's squad coolly plundering our baggage. Two of them covered us with their rifles while the rest possessed themselves of such of our belongings as were light and portable. Then they rode off; but before leaving they carefully cut our harness, so that it was a good hour before we could repair damages and proceed on our way. On reaching the town we went straight to the general commanding the Government forces, to complain that we had been robbed by a picket of his soldiers less than three miles from the town. I shall never forget his indignation.

"'*My* troops *rob* you!' he exclaimed angrily. 'You are either making a mistake through sheer ignorance, or you are trying to insult the Government in my person.'

"With some difficulty we induced him to listen to our explanation, that the robbers had *said* they belonged to his regiment; and, moreover, the uniforms they wore were assuredly the same as those we now saw about us. At this juncture, I regret to say, the general swore.

"'I see it all now,' he said; 'you have been molested by those *ladrones* who are trying to hold our own city against us. Their uniforms *arc* the same — in fact, two of the rebel regiments were in my command until last week. But I'll soon settle this matter!'

" He showed a white flag, and sounded a parley. Within a few minutes an officer came out from the rebel ranks to confer with the irate general, who told him our story with many expletives, expatiating fully on the disgrace to the country of peaceable travellers being robbed by troops who, since they were certainly not his, *must* belong to the insurgent force! The rebel officer was furious, and accused the Government forces of doing habitually what the high-souled patriots he had the honour to command would not dream of when drunk! Of course the general retaliated with personalities about the insurgents and all their ancestors, and the discussion waxed hot; but at last some one had the presence of mind to suggest that while time was being wasted here, the thieves were getting comfortably away. This brought the angry warriors to terms, and they decided upon declaring a short truce. As the besiegers had but little cavalry, the besieged kindly lent a troop, and we soon had the pleasure of seeing a party composed of men who had been gaily potting at each other

an hour before, starting off together quite amicably to scour the adjacent country for bandits.

" The chase was a hot one while it lasted, but
in a very short time the soldiers returned triumphantly with their late comrades in tow. Within
half an hour the *ladrones* had been tried by
court-martial and hanged ! They should have
been shot, only neither of the belligerent officers
wished to waste ammunition upon them. As soon
as this little piece of business was despatched,
the truce was declared over, and in a very few
moments the rattle of musketry could be heard
as the rival armies recommenced hostilities. As
our belongings were all restored to us, I think
both myself and my fellow-passengers rather enjoyed this little comic opera interlude to a serious
battle. I am glad to say that our friend the general conquered, and I am still more thankful to
be able to make my journeys by rail nowadays."

Needless to say that every one at table agreed
in the last sentiment, and they rose with a laugh
and an expression of curiosity as to what had
become of the old professional bandit — such of
him as was not pressed into the army. Jack was
rather inclined to think that he might be employed chiefly in selling mines to the unwary
British investor, or, better still, acting as confi-

dential cashier in the office of the said Britisher
— at least those were the only capacities in which
he had encountered bandits himself during his
stay in the country! A short time after the visit
during which he heard (and made notes of)
the foregoing stories, he happened to be passing
through a little village, where, to about a dozen
huts, he counted no fewer than fourteen churches!
On inquiry he found that the latter had all been
built by repentant robber chiefs who had retired
from business with large fortunes, and who,
having got all they could out of this world,
thought it was time to begin to treat for a good
place in the next!

It has been mentioned that during the first
five years he spent in Mexico Mr Jebb frequently went backwards and forwards between
Vera Cruz and England, but it has not been
recorded that while on one of his short visits
to London he was present at the deathbed of
his only remaining aunt. In many ways she
had acted the part of a mother to him, and he
regarded her house as home — the only one
he possessed; so that he felt her loss severely,
and was only comforted by the thought that at
least he had been with her at the last, instead
of being thousands of miles away, as in his

roving life might easily have happened. She left him a few thousand pounds, but nothing approaching the fortune he had been led to expect. The reason was not far to seek. In common with many wealthy elderly ladies, she was very amenable to flattery, and of course was always able to command as much as she was prepared to swallow; while no hope of future riches could have induced Jack to bestow upon her the smallest quantity of that pabulum, without which even her, doubtless sincere, affection for him languished.

Strange to say, it was again at her house that he met the lady who was to be his second wife. They were mutually attracted at their first meeting; but for various reasons, chiefly financial, the marriage did not take place till nearly five years afterwards. When it did, it was a sufficiently happy one to compensate for the business troubles which, not many years later, began to gather thick and fast. But even that leveller of persons, matrimony, could not succeed in turning Jack Jebb into a respectable stay-at-home Benedict, journeying only between his club and the domestic hearth. On the contrary, after probably the briefest and most original honeymoon on record — it was spent chiefly in cabs — he had to rush suddenly back to Mexico, leaving his wife to follow as soon as she could gather together her possessions. When at last she rejoined him there, they remained in Mexico for several years, save for occasional trips to Cuba or New York.

CHAPTER XVII.

SEARCH FOR TREASURE.

DURING this stay in England, Jack had of course devoted most of his time to the company he represented, and which he had been chiefly instrumental in founding. So far, it was not a success. The mines required far more development than had been anticipated, and even when ore began to be taken out, it was of too low a grade to pay, unless it could be mined on a much larger scale than the resources of the company would admit. This being the case, that unfailing panacea for moribund concerns — reconstruction — was applied, and when Mr Jebb returned to Mexico it was with an enlarged scope of operations, and with instructions to treat for other business. By this time he had a large and particularly mixed circle of acquaintance in the land of Montezuma, consisting of Government officials, great *haciendados*, business men, adventurers, Indian tribes, and Cuban refugees. He probably also knew, and had been taken in by, every curiosity-dealer in the country. Therefore, when he made it known that he was open to receive offers of business, to be carried through by his company in London, practicable and impracticable schemes poured in upon him.

Among the former was the loan for the great drainage-works begun by Montezuma, continued at intervals by the Spanish Viceroys, and destined to be completed by President Diaz. As for the impossible plans, their name was legion; and they ranged from a request to buy up a volcano in order to dig for sulphur inside it, to an invitation to join in a search for the hidden treasure of Guatamoc! There was, perhaps, some temptation to take up the latter enterprise, for while it is a well-known fact that both of the last Aztec Emperors of Mexico had enormous stores of gold and gems, it is equally certain that but a comparatively small portion ever fell into the hands of the Spaniards, in spite of the nameless tortures they inflicted on all who might be supposed to know the secrets of the murdered princes. No one who is in the least acquainted with Indian nature can doubt for a moment that whatever traditions of this sort existed in the time of Cortez, will have been carefully handed down to the present day, in the tribes whose forefathers suffered death rather than reveal aught to their taskmasters.

Through some small service which he once rendered to an old Indian, Jack came very near to finding out one of these secrets. The man was as ragged and dirty as the rest of the *peons* who swarm in the streets of Mexico; but in spite of this, in the little hamlet, a few leagues off, where he lived, there were days of the year on which he received regal homage from his tribe. No Spaniard or Mexican would ever have been permitted to discover as much; but Jack, as an Englishman known by the natives to be in sympathy with them, from time to time was told strange things. The particular Indian in question was the last descendant of the petty king or *cacique* who had reigned in his district for untold generations before the coming of Cortez, and for some reason which for a long

while the man refused to state, he was anxious
to raise a large sum of money, to be returned to
the lender at the end of one month. With
much difficulty Jack at last found out that the
money, if forthcoming, was to be used for the
purchase of a block of land in the suburbs,
about to be sold for building purposes. What
was to be done with the ground when it was
acquired he could not guess, and all his re-
presentations of the impossibility of raising funds
without fuller information were useless for more
than a year after the first application had been
made to him. Then, looking very worn and ill,
the old chief paid him a visit. He began by one
more attempt to get the loan, on his own terms.
Finding that hopeless, he proposed that Jack
should buy one building lot, to be pointed out
by him, on the land in question, and he promised
that within a month he would pay $100,000 for
it. By that time Jack was really interested in
the old man's persistence, and if he had possessed the required sum he would probably have
bought the ground in order to see what happened. But as he could not spare the money
from his own resources, and as even the long-
suffering British shareholder would kick at an
investment which depended solely for success on

the word of an unwashed Aztec, he was obliged to send his visitor away terribly disappointed.

For a long time no more was seen of him; then a message came that he was dying, and had expressed a wish to bid farewell to *el Inglese.* Jack, of course, obeyed the summons at once, to find that it had not come a moment too soon, for the old chief's last fight was almost over! His eyes were glassy, and his voice but a broken whisper, which could scarcely be heard through the sound of the night wind eddying round the hut; but he found strength to motion away a group of women who stood around him, and then telling Jack to stand nearer the bed, he at last confessed his reason for so urgently desiring that piece of ground. He said that beneath it was buried a rich treasure, and that he alone — the last descendant of a line of kings — knew the exact spot. The land had never before been for sale, nor would he have disclosed its secret if it had; but the Englishman had been kind to him, and he wanted him to know that there had been good cause for his apparently insane request. Jack urged the dying man to describe the hiding-place even now, promising to do his best, should any treasure be found, to get it disposed of as the *cacique* might direct. The latter seemed to meditate for a few moments, then he said, " I think you are an honest man, señor; but you have none of our blood in your veins, and if I told you, it might be that the Government — or the Spaniards ——! No; I am the last of my race, and I too shall soon be with my fathers. Who knows that they will not ask the king's treasure at my hands? It shall rest for ever where it is!" And the grim old heathen died, and carried his secret with him to the grave. The suburb was soon built over, none guessing that somewhere in those fifty acres half a million lay hid.

There is yet another story of buried millions in which Jack's participation was desired to the extent of gaining permission from the owner of the property to dig on his land, ostensibly for curiosities said to be hidden there. The suggestion was made in perfect good faith by a Cuban, called Don Anselmo, who himself came across the secret in a rather odd manner. He was much given to dabbling in chemistry, and happening one day to require for some experiments a certain vegetable acid very difficult to procure, he went out on a hill, where he thought it might be possible to find a certain plant which would answer his purpose. While engaged in

the search he became interested in the geology
of the hill, and went contentedly tapping and
prowling about for several hours. At last he
observed that wherever he moved he was followed by some man who, while keeping carefully in concealment himself, was noting every
action of the amateur geologist. The latter endured this unaccountable espionage for some
time, but finding that it seemed likely to continue, he got rather irritated, and shouted to the
spy that it would be well for him either to go
away or to show himself!

This had the desired effect, for some one
crawled out of a *tuna*-bush, who, to the intense
amazement of our friend the Cuban, proved to
be no other than the village *padre*, who was an
old acquaintance. The *padre's* face was full of
rage and suspicion as he asked roughly what
was the object of all this digging and tapping
about a hill which was well known to be private
property? The answer that nothing more serious than a search for rare herbs was in progress,
seemed to infuriate the amiable old gentleman
still more. "It's no use trying to deceive me,"
he said, roughly. "The saints alone know how
you have got hold of a secret which I thought
was known to none but myself; but it is quite

evident that you do know it, although you are not quite certain of the locality."

It was in vain that the other protested his entire ignorance of what could be meant; the priest only became more incredulous. " I was watching you for an hour before you saw me," he said. "and you never went a yard from the spot. You even tapped about the two trees which were planted to mark it. Herbs indeed! " Seeing the uselessness of further argument with the obstinate *padre*, his puzzled listener let-him talk on, and he proceeded to give himself gracefully away! It appeared that the secret which he was so positive had been surprised, referred to a portion of the hidden treasure of Montezuma — that which had been cast away in despair by the flying Spaniards during the massacre of the *noche triste*, to be carefully gathered together again by the devoted Aztecs, and buried securely where there was little chance of its ever being discovered by their enemies. The secret had been kept for over three hundred and sixty years; for, with the undying hatred of the race for their conquerors, no Indian would reveal it in the hope of gain to himself, lest by misadventure any portion of the hidden riches should fall into Spanish hands.

At last a dying *cacique*, before receiving absolution from the priest, said that he must confess something which had long weighed upon his mind. He was the last of his race, and had no kith or kin in whom to confide, or it is doubtful whether even at the supreme moment he would have admitted the *padre* to his confidence. In hushed tones he confessed that he knew the exact hiding-place of Montezuma's treasure, and that he, the last descendant of the royal line, was the only living soul who held the secret. On condition that it should never be given up to the Government, or to any member of the nation he abhorred, he told the priest where he would find plans of the burying-place, and an inventory of the wealth stored therein. So much of the old man's statement proved to be true, that after his death, carefully concealed in his hut, were found measurements impossible to mistake, while the inventory, if a genuine one, promised a treasure well worth winning. It mentioned eighteen large jars of gold, some filled with golden ornaments, and some with gold-dust from the lost mines of the south. It also spoke of other jars filled with precious stones; of ancient gods; of arms and shields innumerable; while above all in value was the Golden Head of Montezuma!

These circumstantial details began to make the priest believe in a story to which at first he had attached but slight credence; still even supposing it to be all true, he did not see how to make use of his information, because, according to the plans, these riches were buried sixty feet deep on what was now private property, the owner of which was quite the last person in the world to allow excavations to be made on his land without very good reason. If he were taken into confidence, of course he would dig himself, and as he was a Liberal with no respect for the Church, he would take great care that the *padre* was no better for the find. Therefore that holy man had been constrained to keep his own counsel, until the day when he saw our friend hovering affectionately over the very spot.

When the latter understood the state of affairs, he was careful not to betray how absolutely ignorant of it all he had been, and after some little discussion he suggested that the best plan for securing the treasure would be to buy the land, and then give out that it was to be prospected for sulphur, in order to account for the extensive pit which would have to be dug. Of course, this scheme entailed letting one or

two others into the secret, but it would be to
their interest to keep it, while if the list were
true there was wealth enough for a hundred
people. The *padre* having assented to these
suggestions, his friend Don Anselmo began to
try to raise the necessary money for the purchase among his acquaintances. Finding that
though he could get a few private subscriptions,
treasure-hunting was not considered a sufficiently
steady business to induce any capitalist to em-
bark in it, he had to give up his idea in despair;
but nothing daunted, he soon formulated another.
He asked the people to whom he had applied
for the slight loan of $200,000, whether, if they
would not give him the money he required, they
would at least help him to dig on the land if he
got leave to do so without purchasing it? This
promised sport, and they willingly agreed. Don
Anselmo thereupon repaired to the owner of
the property, and told him that in the course of
some geological researches traces of sulphur
had been found on his ground, which naturally
would greatly increase its value. When, therefore, Don Anselmo proceeded kindly to offer to
excavate gratuitously himself, in the interests of
science, the gratitude of the owner knew no
bounds, and he gave leave for the entire estate
to be dug over if necessary!

The confederates therefore soon set to work,
the *padre's* share in the proceedings being to
tear backwards and forwards between the pit
and the village. telling his parishioners that the
hereticos were digging for sulphur, which, as it
belonged to the devil, would most assuredly
cause that gentleman to seize any of the faithful
who went near the sacrilegious party. This was
an ingenious and successful plan for keeping the
coast clear, for which the *padre* received much
credit. None of the workers being "to the
manner born," it took them a fortnight to sink
that sixty-foot shaft, and as they reached the
bottom the excitement became intense. The
plans said that at a depth of sixty feet would be
found a big boulder covered with hieroglyphics;
and sure enough, as they anxiously scraped away
loose soil, they saw deeply cut in the face of a
large rock the figure of an owl—the totem-mark
of Guatamoc.

But now began misfortunes. The owner, seeing the huge pit that had been dug without any
sulphur being discovered, came to the conclusion
that it was all a mare's nest; but as he had long
been contemplating the sale of his property, he
thought this was the best time to do so, as, of
course, the rumour of sulphur upon it would

help greatly in selling the land. Owing to this piece of financial genius, the ardent diggers were horrified, the morning after their great discovery, to learn that the estate had just been sold for a large sum to a man from whom they knew they might expect no mercy if he once discovered their secret. All that day they worked hard at driving a hole into the big stone, which was supposed to lead into the treasure-chamber. Late at night they put in a charge of dynamite which shattered the rock to fragments, but it also caused so much earth to fall in that another day was lost in clearing it all out again. As the last heap of rubbish was removed, the opening of a tunnel came into view, running straight into the hillside at right angles to the shaft. Curiously enough, the walls seemed to be fused, and they had evidently been subjected to great heat. For some ten paces the tunnel ran in on the level; then came a flight of steps leading upwards. On the third step was a copper spear-head, and at the top of the flight the adventurers were confronted by a solid-built wall, as hard as flint, and fused smooth as glass! It looked as though another week's work was before them. Their tools were blunted, and worst of all, their time expired that night. They knew that even could

they pick through the wall, it would take days
to remove the treasure, while long ere they
could do so the new owner would have heard
of the operations, and not only would they have
gone to prison, which would have been disagreeable, but every *onza* of the gold would
be promptly appropriated — a disaster too
terrible to contemplate!

So, after some consultation, they resolved to
abandon the work until such time as they could
make fresh arrangements with the new owner;
or, better still, find some one whose faith and
purse were proportionately large, to buy the
property on the strength of the thrilling addi-
tions they could now make to their former
shadowy " prospectus." Accordingly, all that
night and most of the next day they worked at
filling up the shaft again, throwing down it the
two trees which had served as landmarks; and
having finished this, they left the place, saying
that they had not been able to find any sulphur
— which, of all their explanations, appears to
have been the only true one. The next Sunday
the *padre* mentioned incidentally in the course
of his sermon that during their excavations the
hereticos had let out some of the *diablos* who
haunt underground regions, and that therefore

it would be well for his flock to avoid the disturbed spot. Needless to say that the said flock was very careful to keep near the fold ever afterwards. The new owner, a former member of the Government, and a most unscrupulous man, proved to be quite impracticable, so did various schemes for buying him out, and thus the matter rested, until, as a last resource, Don Anselmo went to Jack Jebb with the foregoing story.

The latter agreed to obtain permission to excavate, which he could the more readily do as his taste for curiosities was well known, and his request would fail therefore to lay him open to the suspicion which would have attended a similar demand from Don Anselmo. The application was successful; but, in spite of his satisfaction at this result, the Cuban seemed to be a little startled when he found that Jack proposed being accompanied on the expedition by an Englishman then visiting at his house. Still, all went well until the day previous to that fixed for the journey. Then a cablegram from England arrived, bringing news so disastrous to his guest that Jack at once postponed their share of the projected search. Not caring to venture alone, Don Anselmo agreed to wait until a more propitious season; but fate was against the recovery of the buried wealth, for a few weeks later Jack was obliged to return to England without having found another opportunity to join in the quest. When in a year's time he returned once more to Mexico, Don Anselmo had disappeared. No one had heard of his death, or of his having left the country, and to no man had he said farewell. But his place knew him no more, though whence he had departed in so strange and silent a fashion was a mystery to all.

It is possible that the Indian tribe had in some way discovered his knowledge of their dead chief's secret, and to ensure his safe keeping of the matter had quietly murdered him. Such things have been; and at all events he was gone, and the gold is still a *hidden* treasure — for the secret has been well kept. Probably it will never be divulged, for those who find the stores of gold and gems will scarcely bruit abroad the story of their success; but that a large portion of the countless wealth of Montezuma exists in the place described, one or two people will always believe.

A former treasure-hunt in Central America Jack himself has told in 'another place, and it need not be repeated here.[1]   But even Mr Robert Louis Stevenson has not imagined the veritable riches which in remote corners of the earth yet lie hid!

[1] "The Lost Secret of the Cocos Group." See 'Blackwood's Magazine' for January 1873.

CHAPTER XVIII.

FRESH FIELDS.

AMID a press of serious work, the next unprofitable affair in which Jack was concerned was a vigorous search for a non-existent mine. A Cuban of his acquaintance came to him one day with a long story about a gold-mine he had accidentally discovered on the hacienda of a mutual friend, and he gave so many circumstantial details that the matter seemed worth looking into, especially as the hacienda was considered one of the best in Mexico, and would therefore compensate for the day's journey to it, even if nothing further transpired. It was situated in the hot country; and when Jack and his companion and guide first caught sight of it, the former at least thought he had never seen anything so gorgeous as its fertile beauty. The old grey house was surrounded by acres of orange-trees, with every path through them lined with leafy bananas, while a clearing in front was overgrown with tall, sweet-scented flowers. Through the entire grounds wandered streams of clear water, giving a fresh appearance to the vegetation seldom seen in the tropics. From the flat roof of the hacienda there was a view for a painter to dream of — miles of rich land covered with sugar-cane, walled in by pine-clad hills; while far above them all towered the stately white cone of Popocatepetl.

The travellers arrived too late to do anything on the first day; and after the long, hot ride to the place, they found half an hour's communion with a cool creek, supper, and bed most refreshing. Next morning, however, they were up early in order to have time to examine the mine before the midday heat set in, when, according to a Mexican saying, " none but dogs and Englishmen go out." They went first to the place where the Cuban said he had made his discovery, searching carefully for the opening, while he explained at length his reasons for feeling sure that the mine was an old one which had been worked and then abandoned by the Spaniards, in accordance with their usual custom when they had taken out the richest of the ore. He talked so much and so graphically about his find, that Jack scarcely liked at first to point out the obvious fact that he seemed a little vague as to its locality, for the most minute search of the ground he indicated failed to show anything which by any stretch of imagination could be taken for a mine.

He appeared at last to awake to this fact himself, and began making investigations a little farther afield — with the same lack of result; until, late in the afternoon, hot, tired, and on the verge of sun-stroke, Jack declined to go another step, and added that he did not believe there had ever been any mine, as it is not a sort of thing you can easily mislay! The Cuban protested that he had seen it; but whether he was mad, or whether he was playing a bad practical joke from which he suffered equally with his victim, it is impossible to say. Jack inclined to the former opinion, which may be considered charitable of him, as he went back to Mexico in a very bad temper, with a scorpion in his portmanteau. Moreover, from being out in the sun all day he contracted a bad attack of fever; and besides, he must have been near some of the "poison ivy," which makes life a burden in the California foot-hills, for he was poisoned from head to foot. He was seriously ill for weeks; and after a long struggle to keep at work in spite of everything, he was at last obliged to give it up and go to Puebla to try the effect of the sulphur-springs for which the place is famed.

The springs bubble up into huge artificial baths, and as long as he could spend the morning reading his newspaper, with the tepid water up to his neck, the invalid was fairly comfortable; though the certainty of having to dry himself on a towel which would be small for a baby in arms was not inviting from any but a Mexican point of view. But the worst was, that the moment he left his harbour of refuge, the terrible irritation began again in full force. So at last he had to call in a local doctor, who scouted the idea of poison ivy, and suggested that haven for the destitute in medical science — rheumatic gout. Finding himself at fault there, he next inquired carefully into the ancestry — near and remote — of his patient, saying gravely that it was a sad oversight on the part of any man not to make himself fully acquainted

with the details of his great-grandmother's constitution.　After listening to the small amount
of information Jack was able to give him on the
point in question, he said that he had come to
the conclusion the invalid was suffering from
snake-bite!　He treasured this idea as an inspiration of genius, and was with difficulty weaned
from it, and induced to suggest some remedy
for an irritated skin.　It was only among first
causes that he lost himself, — with effects he was
at home; so he ordered bran-baths, which
proved to be so efficacious that the patient soon
began to take some interest in life again, and
prepared to enjoy wandering about the quaint
old streets and worn fortified walls of Puebla.

The manufactory of antiquities he found very
instructive: it is said that when one of the Astors
visited Mexico, Puebla was nearly ruined by the
strain on its resources.　But best of all in the
historical city is the curious old blue pottery of
distinctly oriental design, fragments of which
may still be found in back slums and out-of-the-
way places.　The story goes that, on settling
themselves at Puebla, the first monks who went
over from Spain soon discovered a similarity in
the clay to that used in their own country for
pottery.　They thereupon built works, and made

a large revenue from the manufacture of graceful and beautiful objects, few of which, alas! now remain; while the potteries themselves were pulled down and ruined a couple of hundred years ago.

Looking down upon Puebla from its solitary height is the extinct volcano of Malinché, formerly the headquarters of every bandit in the country. The tradition is, that their forces were at one time so strong that when at last the Government resolved upon their suppression, the outlaws lost over four hundred men in the struggle which took place before they were conquered; and this although their numbers were frequently thinned by private enterprise. For instance: the governor of a State was once robbed of $6000 not far from his own capital; and perfectly furious at the affront to his dignity, he turned out every trooper in the State bandit-shooting. For some days there was a regular battue, resulting in about two hundred malefactors being shot or hanged. All the same, the governor never saw his money again.

A Yankee drummer is supposed to be the only individual who ever proved a match for a whole party of bandits. He was in a coach which was "held up" in the usual way, when his fellow-passengers at once advocated unconditional surrender. But as luck would have it, the Yankee was travelling for the "Winchester Small Arms Company," with, of course, a full accoutrement. He grasped the situation with the inspiration of true genius, and, with the eye of a Stanley, saw his way to a magnificent advertisement. In an instant he was out and under the coach, his pocket full of cartridges, and his "sample" repeater in hand. Then he turned his shooting-iron loose, and emptied eight saddles before the astonished bandits could get out of range. This was the first introduction of repeating-rifles into Mexico, and it is superfluous to add that they sold well afterwards.

Before leaving Puebla, Jack found time to pay a visit to Cholula close by, where the wonderful artificial mound, whose origin is lost in the mists of antiquity, rears its lofty head. There are still a few who believe it to be a natural eminence, but the majority have accepted the dictum of the best authorities that each stone and each spadeful of earth have been piled up by human hands. The climb to the top is up so nicely graduated an incline, sheltered by such leafy trees, that, long though it is, it can scarcely be called very fatiguing.

Once on the summit, the view is magnificent. Popocatepetl, though miles away, looks near enough to touch; while on clear days it is possible to see a little way into the crater of the volcano. It is difficult to realise the labour involved, first in raising this great pyramid, and then in carrying up materials for building the stately church which crowns its topmost peak.

As soon as he felt really well again, Jack lost no time in getting back to work, especially as at the time his illness began he was engaged in an important piece of business — that of negotiating on behalf of his company for the acquisition of a large tract of mining property in the little-known State of Chiapas. As usual, there were several vendors, each with differing interests; and Mr Jebb found that all the tact, temper, and patience he could summon to his aid would certainly be required before the purchase was completed. Of course the inevitable preliminaries — the report of a mining expert, the haggling over price, and dispute as to details — were duly gone through before the mines changed hands.

Meanwhile Jack had to visit and inspect them several times. Now he was not given to grumbling over crumpled rose-leaves, and in his heart thought that a man who slept under a roof when the climate would admit of his reposing in the open was a singularly misguided person. Still, even he was constrained to admit that the journey to Chiapas was a little rough. The first day was spent in the lap of luxury on the railroad between Mexico and Vera Cruz; then, unless lucky enough to catch a Ward liner, came a day and night in a dirty, frequently unseaworthy boat from the latter place to Frontera. No beds were provided on these boats, and the night had to be spent on deck — no great hardship, but for the smell and uncleanliness, and worst of all, the mosquitoes. Except when once spending a happy day on the Mosquito coast, Jack had never encountered any of their species so hungry and pertinacious as these. But the worst was yet to come. To a night at Frontera — where the intense sticky heat made pyjamas feel like fur rugs for warmth, and where a perfect halo of mosquitoes turned the sufferer into a capital representation of a tortured medieval saint, in all but language — succeeded a day's journey in a smaller and a dirtier boat than the preceding one. This vessel was punted by Indians along a river which, shallow enough in the short dry season, was liable to become a raging torrent at very short notice during the rains. There being no sort of shelter, the fierce rays of the tropical sun worked their fiery will on the navigators of that river, while the mosquitoes, whose zeal never slackened, were ably seconded in their attack by a little black fly, whose vigour amply compensated for its size. The company has its own launches on the river now, and has besides improved the road to the mines, so probably there are a few alleviations to the trip. In those days there were none. Moreover, in the state of Chiapas even the rainy season is wild and irregular, quite refusing to conform to custom and confine itself to the proper time of year; so that not only is a drenching possible at almost any moment, but the roads are only to be called such by the courtesy of travellers. After leaving the boats (accompanied by various insects of affectionate disposition) came a long ride through marshland, where the mules frequently sank up to their knees in loose mud, and where progress, therefore, was apt to be a little slow. To this succeeded many leagues of arduous journeying over mountains, along the edge of precipices, through flooded rivers and rocky cañons, before the ride of forty miles was at last completed.

Even when, through much tribulation, Jack reached the mines, things were scarcely more comfortable. They had been worked little, if at all, for generations, and what had been considered a suitable headquarters in those days was now a hut through which the rain poured in torrents, and in whose walls were interesting gaps, where, it was impossible to help thinking, it would be very easy for a disaffected Indian to steal at dead of night and let out a little heretic life-blood with a knife. The one redeeming feature of the place was the fact that mosquitoes eschewed it, probably judging from its appearance that there would be nothing fit to eat within. But it must not be inferred from this that there was any lack of the animal creation. There were tarantulas and scorpions, snakes and jiggers; and worst of all was a little insect so minute that it was impossible to see it without a magnifying-glass, yet when it had worked its way under the skin, as it was in the habit of doing, it produced large irritable ulcers. Jack, after a week's attention from it, looked as though he were sickening for smallpox, and it was quite in vain that he tried all the usual preventives and remedies. It *liked* petroleum, and throve upon tobacco-juice; and the only relief to be obtained was by the heroic method of pouring pure spirit on the sores, which of course made them smart horribly, but allayed the irritation. These little *contretemps* did not, however, affect the value of the property, and as the sale proceeded to a satisfactory issue, no more need be said upon the subject.

Although he repeated this expedition several times, to his great regret Jack was never able to find time or opportunity to visit the ruins of Palenque — only three days' distance from the mines. Could he have gone straight there, it would have been easy enough; but to undertake the journey across country through jungle in which every step would have to be cut, and which in that climate would have grown up again before his return, was manifestly impossible. But it is not in Palenque alone that strange relics of a bygone civilisation are to be found, for even in the locality of the mines wonderful traces of a race which was beginning to decay before we emerged from barbarism could occasionally be encountered. For instance, Jack Jebb was shown an enormous metal bell, weighing several tons, which one would think could never have been conveyed over that marshy country by anything short of a railway, yet it could scarcely have been cast on the spot. But if not, where? He also saw the remains of what, generations ago, must have been a colossal statue hewn out of solid stone; but by whose hands and with what tools, history is silent.

The natives of the country are shy and wild, as is natural enough after the ages of slavery they have undergone. Indeed their present state is but little removed from it; for the owners of the vast estates on which they work also own the *tiendas,* or provision stores, where the Indians purchase the necessaries of life. They invariably run into debt at these places, the debt sometimes being even hereditary: so, as they are not allowed to leave the country until it is paid, there is very little chance of their ever being able to do so; while Chiapas is too far from the seat of Government for this state of things to be easily remedied. The people are said to hold in great veneration a huge snake of incalculable age, which they keep jealously hidden in some secret place. There is little doubt that something of the kind actually exists; and Jack, getting an inkling of its whereabouts, tried hard to penetrate the mystery. But as he was privately warned that he would certainly be murdered if he persisted in the search, he gave it up perforce, and strove to content himself with the few inanimate antiquities he was able to find — chiefly fragments of idols and arrow-heads.

There was a family likeness between all his visits to these mines, and it would be superfluous therefore to further describe them. But on this special journey he had travelled from Mexico to Vera Cruz with a perfect specimen of a British tourist, who was starting to explore Palenque with an eyeglass, and a gardenia in his button-hole. On his return a month afterwards, Jack met the same tourist, judging from his conversation, but, oh! how changed as to his outer man! He was neatly and lightly clad in a pair of old trousers and a pyjama jacket, while every portion of his person visible beyond and between these habiliments was clothed in a purple raiment of — bites! He had never got as far as Palenque either, and with much force of diction he expressed his intention of making no further effort to do so.

As for Jack, between the combined attack of fever and poison ivy from which he had but barely recovered when he left Mexico, and the blood-poisoning resulting from his late whole-sale consumption by insects of various sorts, he returned feeling considerably the worse for wear. A few days of good food, and such nursing as he would submit to, put him fairly right again; though eventually he had to take a sea-trip to New York before getting rid of the last traces of his misfortunes. There was a great accumulation of what his soul loathed — office work — waiting for him when he got back from the Chiapas trip, and, of course, it had to be steadily waded through before he could think of going away again, although he was anxious to visit once more the mines up in the mountains.

Between times he and his wife wandered over the city, down blind alleys, and through back streets, where in the unlikeliest places the most perfect curios were often to be found : gorgeous embroidered or brocaded vestments, sold by servants of the Church, who considered their mistress best honoured by the use of robes which were clean and bright and *new !* Sometimes the seekers after antiquities would run across lovely specimens of Venetian glass, or curiously jew-elled knives, or armour last used in raids against the Apaches; but most plentiful of all were idols — "ancient and modern." A quick eye soon learnt to detect the difference between those just dug up after a preliminary burial to "give them a tone," and those old images that once ruled the destinies of the people who believed in their power. There are few of the latter now to be bought, though it is not so much the law against their exportation which has affected the sale as the ubiquitous American tourist who visits Mexico in batches of a couple of hundred at a time, and buys everything that is shown to him at the price at which it is offered — a thing to sadden the heart of any collector.

CHAPTER XIX.

THE SIERRAS ONCE MORE.

BULL-FIGHTS have now been forbidden in the city of Mexico, but at the time of which this history treats, they gladdened the eyes of the population every Sunday. The bull-rings were always crowded, and the streets gay with the parti-coloured banderillas hawked about for sale by picturesque, dirty little Indians. If there was a stain or two of blood on the iron-tipped sticks, which looked so innocent in their frilled paper coverings, so much the better, for it proved that they had been actually used, and doubled their value. A good deal of sympathy is usually wasted on the principal actor in the weekly tragedy; but, as a matter of fact, a well-bred bull in good condition thoroughly enjoys a fight, while as soon as he begins to get "blown," nothing could be quicker or more painless than the death that awaits him. The best proof of this is, that should a matador ever fail to kill at the first stroke, he is promptly hissed out of the ring, lucky if a few benches do not follow him! The real cruelty is to the wretched horses. Animals are provided so old and worn out as to be under sentence of death in any case; but the lingering agony inflicted upon them in the bull-ring when, gored and torn, they are forced again and again upon the cruel horns, is a sight to turn a strong man sick to see.

Jack liked the preliminaries, the processions of gorgeously attired bull-fighters, the first skilfully evaded rush of the angry bull, the agility with which the men leapt over and over its back with their long jumping-poles, or rolled along the ground just beneath its horns; but he was always careful to leave directly the horses were brought in. It fell to his lot to escort a good many tourists first and last; because of course no properly constituted "Cook" would consent to leave Mexico without having seen the national pastime. It was amusing sometimes to see how they "took it." Some ladies threatened to write to the Society for the Prevention of Cruelty to Animals; some felt it their duty to faint; but one lady, with more *sang-froid* than the rest, leant over to her husband as the men planted the banderillas in the bull's neck, and asked placidly, "John, dear, does it hurt the poor *cow* to have that thing stuck in his *mane?*"

More amusing to the average foreigner than the actual fights are the bull-sports, in which that justly incensed animal takes an entirely involuntary part! About half-a-dozen men on horseback place themselves at intervals round a ring, and the same number of bulls come charging out at a given signal. It is then the duty of each man to catch a bull by the tail — no easy task, and one which calls forth some very pretty riding. Once caught, they all gallop furiously round the ring two or three times, the bull protesting vigorously meanwhile, when suddenly, while at full gallop, by a quick twist of the tail round the rider's foot, the animal is thrown over on its back; usually lying there for a few minutes with its legs in the air and a mingled expression of injured dignity, combined with inquiry as to how it was done, that is simply irresistible to the looker-on.

These, however, were diversions, and Jack was always too busy to afford himself very many, for he did not possess the happy faculty of forgetting business out of office hours. When an important negotiation was going on, or some obstinate ores refusing to be smelted, the subject was never out of his mind until he had conquered its difficulties, or had been vanquished by them — a much rarer event. At present he was anxious to get up to the mines, where he had spent his first years in Mexico, but which the press of other work had obliged him to rather neglect of late. Of course he received constant intelligence of their progress, and knew that they were now paying their own expenses — about as much as a self-respecting mine can be expected to do — but still, no amount of correspondence was equal to a personal inspection. He therefore strained every nerve to get through the arrears of work left by his Chiapas trip, and in a few months found himself fairly free to start for the sierras.

Their breezy heights seemed very refreshing after the heat of the tropics and the confinement of Mexico; besides, the natives were all glad to see him back, and anxious to know if the " people of the plains " were quite as black as they were painted. Altogether he soon slipped into the old routine, spending several weeks very congenially in going up and down monkey-poles, coddling furnaces, and assaying ores.

It was not that these joys began to pall, but because he had received several imperative messages from that arbitrary old gentleman, that Jack at last went off to pay a few days' visit to his friend the Cacique. The thirty-mile ride was worth taking for its own sake alone, for nothing more picturesque was ever imagined by poet or painted by artist than the narrow trail dipping steadily downward until, leaving the pine-crowned mountains behind, it wound through a tropical valley beside plashing brooks overhung by orange-trees and lined with ferns. On reaching the hacienda Jack found that, if possible, a warmer welcome than usual awaited him, the reason of which, and of his own summons, the old chief proceeded to explain over some very good Burgundy after dinner. It appeared that for the first time in his life he wanted advice as to how to deal with a criminal. Usually the rough-and-ready justice he dispensed was admitted by all but the culprit to be suited to the occasion, but this time every one was at fault, including himself. Had *he* been satisfied, it is

unlikely that he would have hesitated in defer-
ence to public opinion, as exemplified by his
peons.

The facts were as follows: there were two
Indians who lived close to each other, but at a
distance of several miles from the village. Each
man had his own adobe hut and little strip of
ground, whose cultivation provided him with
employment and food. Neither had any family
ties, so that, living in their isolated position, the
two men might have been expected to find com-
panionship in each other. So far from this being
the case, however, they were known to cherish a
mutual feud, and never to enter each other's
house. When, therefore, one of the enemies
suddenly disappeared and his blood-stained
clothes were found in his neighbour's hut, it
did not require a detective to arrive at the conclusion that murder had been done. In spite of
his passionate denials the accused was promptly
hauled off to gaol, there to await the sentence
of the Cacique; and as to what that would be
there was at first no doubt.

Oddly enough, considering the solitary life
he had led, the exact date of the missing man's
disappearance was known. He was negotiating
with an Indian in the village for the sale of a

sheep, and the day before his murder had made
an appointment for the following day, when the
bargain was to be concluded.   It was his failure
to keep this engagement which led to the discovery of the crime.   Now, so far all was plain
sailing; the difficulties were to come.   In the
first place, the most diligent search failed to
reveal the slightest trace of the body; and as
even in that part of the world a corpse is a
necessary detail of a trial for murder, this caused
a slight hitch in the proceedings.   Next, three
or four respectable *peons* came forward volun-
tarily and swore by all their gods that the
prisoner had been in their company the whole
of the time during which the crime could have
been committed, and that therefore it was impossible he could be implicated in it.   None of
these men were in any way related to the
accused, and there seemed to be no reason
why they should draw down the wrath of the
chief upon themselves by giving false evidence.
Still, their statements would probably not have
carried much weight had it not been for the
unaccountable absence of the body.   Some one
suggested that the missing man might have
gone away, leaving his clothes in his neighbour's
hut on purpose to cast suspicion of murder on

his enemy. But he could not have gone far without being seen; and besides, as mounted troops were out scouring the country in all directions, on the second day of the disappearance, they must have overtaken him, had this idea been correct.

Such was the state of affairs when Jack arrived at the hacienda, and the Cacique, between his conviction of the prisoner's guilt and his reluctance to proceed to extremes until the murdered man was found, was in a condition of mingled indecision and helplessness as novel as it was disagreeable to him. Next morning, together with his guest, he started early for the scene of the tragedy. Nothing in the hut had been touched, and on examining the clothes — left in a conspicuous place by the murderer — Jack quickly came to the conclusion that, judging from the position of the blood-stains, the victim's throat must have been cut. There was, however, no sign of any struggle having taken place, and outside the door the marks of many recent footprints had apparently obliterated the earlier tracks.

But Jack had not spent years in the Rockies for nothing; and presently, helped by the loose Indian sandals thrown among the other cloth-

ing, he managed to make out that the missing
man had walked alone from his own hut to the
one where he seemed to have met his death.
A few moments more of close scrutiny, and a
bare foot-mark *leaving* the house startled him
almost as much as his famous discovery did
Robinson Crusoe. Further search revealed here
and there faint tracks of a man who seemed to
have been running for his life; yet no trace
whatever of any pursuit followed in the tracks.
As the mystery deepened, Jack resolved to
make at least a vigorous attempt to solve it; so
he proposed that the Cacique should lend him
a couple of soldiers to carry anything he might
discover, and that he would then follow the
trail wherever it led. That potentate was only
too glad to accept the offer, and Jack with his
escort started off at a crawl, which soon became
a walk as the trail, at first nearly obliterated by
other marks, became plainer the farther they
went.

The rapid flight of the fugitive from the house
had soon changed into a quick trot, which never
varied for miles. He had made for the mountains, and over their rocky faces his footprints
were sometimes invisible; but Jack persevered,
and was invariably rewarded by finding the

trail again a little farther on. It was now quite obvious that no murder had been done, and the only other hypothesis to explain all the circumstances seemed to be that of insanity. Anyhow, the prisoner was innocent; for the minutest examination of the ground failed to discover the slightest trace of pursuing steps.

About mid-day the party halted to partake of the *tortillas* and *pulque* with which they had supplied themselves before starting; then, feeling refreshed and rested, they pushed on again. Jack soon began to see signs that at this stage the man of whom they were in search had begun to get fagged, and that therefore new developments might be expected. Sure enough, the trail presently stopped short, turned off abruptly to the right, going down a narrow zigzag path, and then broke off altogether at what looked at first like a thicket of ferns and overgrown weeds. A closer scrutiny showed that hidden behind the tangled bushes was the mouth of an old mine, and that though some one had certainly entered it recently, there were no traces of his having emerged. Therefore, dead or alive, the man was inside. And now came the unpleasant part of the business. The two soldiers had never been inside a mine in their lives, and their faces plainly showed that they would rather begin their researches on a more auspicious occasion than the present, when there seemed to be about an equal chance of finding either a corpse or a dangerous lunatic at the end of their investigations. Jack did not feel enthusiastic over the situation himself, but he prepared to explore the mine as far as possible, while his escort cleared away the underbrush from its mouth, so as to let in a little light — because, needless to say, not expecting this *dénofiment*, they had brought no candles. To add to the difficulties, Jack had not gone many paces before he found that the mine was full of water, so he had to return to the mouth and undress for swimming. When, on the second attempt, his body first touched the cold slimy water, in the almost total darkness of the mine, it must be confessed that his sensations were not cheerful. For one thing, there was scarcely room to swim, and he might at any moment be stunned by some overhanging rock, or stabbed by the man he was seeking, while at every stroke he half expected his hand to come in contact with the icy body of a corpse. Therefore it was almost a relief when his fears were partly realised, and suddenly, round a projecting point, he came upon a pair of glowing eyes looking fiercely into his. He remarked feebly, " Oh, you're there ! " Then he caught hold of one leg of the man, who was sitting up on a ledge, and after a breathless, silent struggle, managed to get him down into the water and swim back with him to the opening of the mine, the captive resisting furiously all the while. Once out in the daylight again, it was hard to say whether pursued or pursuer looked the maddest, as, torn, bruised, and exhausted with his exertions, Jack surveyed his forlorn-looking prize. The latter was evidently quite mad, and to the ravages of insanity in his face were added those of a five days' starvation ; yet he had strength for another desperate resistance before he seemed to take in the fact that it was hopeless, and suffered himself to be led away by the two soldiers, while Jack followed at his leisure.

It was late in the evening before the party reached the village, tired out by the long day's tramp, with its exciting climax. They were received with much joy by the villagers, who escorted them in a body to the Cacique. The latter had been so worried over the whole case that he was actually pleased to find that he had been wrong, and with copious thanks to Jack he sent at once to have the prisoner released, who, when he found himself free again, so over-whelmed his deliverer with gratitude for clearing him of the charge that Jack was fain to protest he should shortly wish he hadn't done so !

The lunatic never recovered his reason, so the cause of his sudden insanity and curious disposal of his clothing remained a mystery. But a narrow scratch on his throat, where he had evidently attempted to cut it, and then changed his mind, told the story of the blood-stains which so nearly cost a man's life.

If anything had been needed to increase the esteem in which Jack Jebb was held among the simple people of the sierras, his latest exploit would have supplied it. For although they could on occasion follow a plain trail themselves, with tracking as it is practised in the Rocky Mountains they were quite unfamiliar. Jack's achievement therefore seemed to them marvellous, while they also thought it passing strange that any white man should have taken so much trouble for one of their number.

In spite of the lavish hospitality heartily pressed upon him, Jack could not afford to linger long in the great hacienda of the Cacique, with its bare and lofty rooms, in and out of which a large variety of animals wandered at their pleasure. The visitor was often awakened in the morning by the cold soft nose of a doe thrust into his hand, or roused at night by the investigations of a huge hound which made him a special care. Still, all good things have an end (usually a speedy one), and in less than a week he was once more installed in " Poverty Row."

That "desirable residence" now concealed some of its original crudity under a luxuriant covering of roses, but the interior continued to justify its name. During Jack's long absence in Mexico a family of rats had installed themselves in his bedroom, and, grown arrogant by long occupation of the premises, they held noisy revels nightly, manifesting an open contempt for every missile the room contained. Then a few panes of glass were broken in the windows, and as the nearest store for the supply of that commodity was two days' ride over the mountains, naturally they had not been replaced. So that not only was there a strong current of the thin, keen Mexican air, which grows so chill when the sun has not risen to warm it, but there was a fine field of labour for enterprising insects. We have Scriptural authority for regarding the hornet as among this class; so it was perhaps not surprising that a few of them established a nest in a crevice of the wall near the broken glass, where they had a really commanding position for operations in the room. In a novel the sleeper would in these circumstances have " turned uneasily in his bed "; but Jack knew better than to do anything of the kind, for there was yet another animal, whose sole aim in life appeared to be getting itself overlaid. It was about the size of a ladybird, and as hard as a brickbat. It never bit, but contented itself with simply being there. Perhaps that was enough; for any sudden movement on the part of the persecuted occupant of the bed resulted in his feeling very much as though he were taking a playful roll over a pound of tin-tacks.

These, however, were trifles which interfered very little with Jack's enjoyment of the free unconventional existence which was to him the very breath of life. In a city, surrounded by all the luxuries — and bonds — of civilisation, he felt choked and restless; but at the first glimpse of his beloved mountains a great contentment always fell upon him. Unluckily he was now involved in a routine of office-work from which he could spare but little time, and which he would never have attempted to endure but that

it seemed to offer so good a chance of quickly
setting him free to follow his inclination to wander for the rest of his life. So, much as he
would have liked to stop and take his part in
the practical working of the mines, directly he
had done all for which his presence was necessary he felt obliged to start back to Mexico
again.

Little happened there of sufficient interest to
record; for the city being ruled by a strong
hand, no longer dared to play her earlier pranks,
and was quiet, respectable, and dull. A new
star at the Opera House or a ball at one of the
Legations formed her sedate excitements, and
for neither of these was Jack very likely to care.
So he worked steadily early and late, making
new combinations and planning fresh schemes
— when the monotony was disturbed slightly by
two events.

One of these was the advent of a little son,
and the other the acquisition of a new idol. Not
new in an opprobrious sense, for its pedigree
was unimpeachable, and Jack had long sighed
for it in vain. It was about two feet high, of
grey stone, tinged in places with pink, and its
complacent ugly face was where in a proper
anatomy its chest should have been. It had

been dug up in the excavations for the great
drainage works, amidst great excitement of the
native mind, and was recognised by the Indians
around as an ancient god of sacrifice said to have
been buried in that spot by their forefathers,
when the Spanish priests were sweeping the land
clear of its temples and its gods. With their
usual memory of tradition, the Indians could
point out the very spot on which a tall pole had
stood with this idol fixed upon its top, while
around the base was a grinning pile of skulls,
mounting ever higher and higher as fresh victims
were given to the silent, insatiable image.

There is seldom a chance nowadays of finding
any antiquity not hailing from Birmingham, and
naturally when Jack heard of this discovery and
its unquestioned history he was wild to possess
the idol. But it was in vain that he offered
bribes or promises; one of the native officials
had taken it, and refused on any terms to give
up anything so rare and interesting. Jack returned again and again to the siege, but with no
result. Judge then of his surprise when one day
an Indian appeared suddenly on the stair of the
house, bearing the idol on his back. No price
was asked for it, nor was any explanation given
of this sudden change of mind on the part of the

owner. The idol was simply put down and left. No reason was ever volunteered for this strange conduct, but in time Jack came to have his own opinion about the matter.

Meanwhile he was delighted with his new possession, set it upon a sort of throne in the corner of a room, and paid it about as much homage as even an idol could demand, for there were reasons for believing it to be the only god of slaughter still extant. A bygone chronicler has referred to the fact that when the Spaniards reached the city of its abode, they found the pole and the skulls, but of the idol there was no trace. Yet — it is not desired to encroach on Mr Anstey's preserves, but it is an absolute fact that from the day he became the owner of that placid-looking lump of stone, everything that Jack touched went wrong. One piece of business after another, which up to that date had been satisfactorily progressing, fell through and failed. Negotiations which he thought completed had to be commenced all over again, only after long suspense to be broken off finally. His own health gave way, three of his best and dearest friends died one after another, and the strange perversity of his affairs was such that he felt no surprise when, once having to raise

money on a reversion to which he was entitled,
the very day after he had sold his expectations
for a third of their value the holder died, and
Jack would have come in for the whole had the
signing of the deeds been delayed for twenty-
four hours. Of course it did not occur to him
to connect the idol with these mischances; but
it is a strange thing that when, broken in health
and fortunes, he went to London with his family,
the first night the Aztec god spent on foreign
soil was signalised by loud noises all over a
house hitherto warranted to be of the quietest
by its owners. Nor did the trouble stop here,
for every night, with other unpleasing mani-
festations, loud knockings took place at a particular door as long as the idol remained in the
house. So noisy were they that some people
could not sleep for the sounds, though others
heard nothing at all.

Nothing can be *proved* against a stone image,
but it seems within the bounds of imagination
that an unconscious figure looking down on cen-
turies of bloodshed should become in a manner
saturated with the malignant atmosphere around
it, and should give forth the spirit of its victims'
agony and curses. Whatever the cause might
be, the effects were as has been stated, and from

the day when he joyfully accepted it to that of his death three years later, the idol sat and smiled, while Jack struggled bravely, but went down — down !

One is glad to think that the Aztec deity also had its vicissitudes; for after a lady visiting the house which it graced with its presence had been kept awake three nights by the unearthly noises constantly going on in and about her bedroom, its owner decided that he must reluctantly make up his mind to part with it. To submit it to the indignity of sale was out of the question, so Jack offered to give it to one after another of his friends who had frequently admired its dubious charms. Rather to his surprise, none of them seemed to yearn for the joys of possession, although they had all laughed at the stories told of its proceedings.

For some time there appeared to be little chance of finding it a " comfortable home," although one gentleman offered to take it to his country-house and put it in the pig-killing shed, where it could have as much gore served up to it daily as it required. But this plan was put a stop to by the fact that the gentleman who made the offer was the husband of the lady who had vainly tried to sleep through the idol's nightly perambulations. It was not the little god she objected to so much as the loss of her natural rest, she was careful to explain; still she flatly refused to tolerate its presence on any premises over which she ruled. Finally it found a refuge with a lady and gentleman sufficiently enamoured of its appearance and antiquity to overlook its bad character and to risk the consequences of its wrath. They took it, and have so far stuck to it manfully in spite of the fact that from the date of its advent in their domestic circle their affairs have gone as crookedly as those of its former owner. But the end is not yet; and whether the malign influence exercised by the exiled god, the undoubted relic of the most bloody ritual the world has ever known, or the incredulity of his owners, will conquer at the last, remains yet to be seen.

CHAPTER XX.

CLOSING YEARS.

BEFORE the end of the strange sequence of misfortunes which began with the acquisition of the Aztec god of sacrifice came three years of comparatively stationary life in Mexico, varied only by occasional visits on business to the mines, and on pleasure to some of the great haciendas. One of the latter, whither Jack had a standing invitation which he frequently availed himself of, was a perfect *beau idéal* of a haunted house. With its vaulted and gloomy stone corridors, its secret stairways, and its deserted wing where endless echoes of the past seemed to resound with every footfall, the huge fortified building told in every part of the sad and stern scenes it had witnessed in bygone days. Outside, the busy

stir of farm life and the lowing of thousands of
stock went far to counteract the gloom of the
house, while a little farther on was a large reed-
bordered lake, on whose sunny waters it was
difficult to feel even the shadow of care. Many
a long, lazy summer day sped past like a dream
as, punted slowly along by Indians, Jack, with a
few friends, lounged idly in the little skiffs on
the lake, shooting duck whenever they could get
near enough, but for the most part doing nothing
at all, and enjoying the operation. The birds
were very wild, which was not surprising, as two
or three times during the season they were
driven in all around the shores, and then every
gun on the estate took part in a regular battue,
killing thousands within a couple of hours. Still,
an unwary bird sometimes fell to the gun of a
patient sportsman, and if "bags" were small,
the manner of trying for them on the still bosom
of the lake was sufficient pleasure in itself. The
restful peace of a few days like these always went
far to compensate Jack for the city worries of
stocks, shares, and negotiations which his soul
loathed; and whenever, in the rush of work, he
could spare himself a holiday, it was safe to
predict that it would be spent out of doors in
company with a gun.

He once made one of a party going for a week's picnic to the broad waters of Lake Patz-cuaro, a day's railway journey from Mexico. They put up at the little hotel, which, like all those in outlying districts of the country, was a cross between a barrack and a workhouse, only probably not so clean as the former, and less comfortable than the latter. Jack was accommodated in a bedroom that to his great surprise contained a piano in addition to the usual furniture of a camp-bed and a washhand-stand about the size of an ink-pot. So of course a concert was held nightly as soon as the mosquitoes began to make life unsupportable on the lake. At first all went well, although a few strings were broken, and the ancient instrument was wofully out of tune: still, by dint of absolute physical force some stray airs could be evolved. On the last night, however, of the visitors' stay the piano refused to produce anything but groans, and it was not till well on the way back to Mexico that Jack remembered a very probable reason for its melancholy. He had shot a gaily plumaged bird the preceding day, intending to get it stuffed, and on returning to the hotel had put it inside the piano, as the only place in the establishment safe from the investigations of the half-wild curs infesting every Mexican village. He had then proceeded to carefully forget all about it, and there the bird still remained, doubtless greatly to the discomfort of the next wayfarer who occupied that bedroom. There are no drains in Mexico, so no one could suppose any peculiarity in the atmosphere to arise from those trials of civilisation; but one wonders whether the victim of Jack's forgetfulness had the boards up in search of dead rats, or held his nose and suffered in silence.

It is near Patzcuaro that the famous picture of the Black Virgin, supposed to be by Murillo, hangs in a little village church, so jealously guarded that but few strangers have ever seen it. By assiduous cultivation of the *padre* and gifts to the church, Jack managed to get a sight of the strange, weird painting; but when he came out, the edifice was surrounded by an angry throng of excited Indians, whom the priest himself found difficulty in keeping in check until Jack reached his boat. Of course the entire tribe believe firmly in the authenticity of the picture, and they are convinced that the whole world is in league to rob them of their treasure.

Between work and play the months slipped imperceptibly past, until there came a time when

Jack began to think it would be well for him to go home, and if not to settle down permanently, at least to spend a year or two in looking after his own interests in London. The practical working of the company he represented was established; he had amassed a great many shares, which were expected to pay a large dividend in the near future, so that his prospects seemed in a measure assured. Moreover, he was now well on in the forties, and long years of " roughing it " were beginning to tell on a constitution which had once been adamantine. Altogether, if he were ever to leave off work, the time appeared to have come for him to do so; and some English friends being about to return, the opportunity of pleasant company on the voyage home was seized, and Jack began to get his affairs in order. Before starting, however, he had to pay a final visit to the mines, and, accompanied by the lady and gentleman who were to share the journey home, he went first to the little town in the sierras. His friends were not so much impressed by its law-abiding orderliness as they might have been if a couple of murders and a free fight had not occurred on the first night of their stay. But *contretemps* will happen, and as a rule there was less spontaneous shooting in this Indian village than in many a more pretentious place on the Texan border. Knives, of course, often came into play, but as every Indian carries one, his companions know what to expect if they become quarrelsome.

A brief inspection of the mines occupied but a few days, and the party were soon on their way back to Mexico, where they arrived tired out by a sixty-mile ride, completed by twelve hours in a lumbering coach, over stony surfaces which it would be misleading to call roads.

After a short rest Jack had to start again for a farewell visit to Chiapas; and his friend volunteering to go with him, the two men embarked for that animal kingdom, leaving their respective wives to pack up their mutual belongings and join them later on. The arrangement was that the latter should go down to Vera Cruz, taking the luggage with them, and there get on board an American liner which called at Frontera two days after leaving Vera Cruz. Their lords would by that time have completed their journey and be waiting at Frontera for the arrival of the ship containing their wives and — almost equally valuable — a bath and a change of clothes. For Chiapas is not a country where it is possible to travel with much personal luggage, while the entire State probably does not boast a single bath. But the plan did not work smoothly. When the ship got to Frontera, anchoring as usual about a mile from shore, clean clothes and cool drinks were prepared for the travellers, who were expected to come out with the agent in the tug, which soon hove in sight. But to the surprise of everybody, that gentleman proved to be quite alone, and in response to the questions with which he was besieged directly he reached the ship's deck, he said that there were no Englishmen in Frontera answering to the given description. He added, moreover, that he had never seen Mr Jebb in his life, and therefore could not tell if he had passed through the town. Knowing that statement at least to be a lie, nobody knew exactly how much to believe of the rest of the agent's assertions; and as the hours went by with still no sign of the missing men, the anxiety of their wives was shared by every one on board. The only explanation seemed to be that they might have been detained on the journey from the mines; but that was very unlikely, as they knew the exact date of the ship's arrival, and would certainly allow themselves plenty of time to catch her.

When, after waiting till the last moment with

no result, the ship once more put to sea, the feelings of two at least of the passengers may be better imagined than described. But to their great relief, at the next port, twenty-four hours farther on, came a telegram from the wanderers, dating from Vera Cruz, and saying that as they had missed this ship through reasons which should be explained later, they intended taking the next one. Meanwhile their wives were to proceed to New York, and there await their arrival. This communication was, of course, highly satisfactory in the sense of proving the travellers' safety; otherwise it simply deepened the mystery, because, in order to have reached Vera Cruz in the time, they must have left Frontera before the ship was due there, while their going back to Vera Cruz at all was inexplicable, as, besides being a detestable journey, it was twenty-four hours out of their way. Conjectures were, however, idle, and there was nothing for it but to wait with what patience could be summoned until reaching New York a week later, where an explanatory letter would probably be found. But the more the two ladies thought over the instructions to themselves contained in the cablegram they had received, the less did they feel inclined to comply with them. To begin with, it would be necessary for them to spend at least ten days alone in New York before they could hope to be rejoined by their missing spouses. Moreover, judging from the tale of the agent, they felt a strong conviction that the travellers had failed to time their journey to Frontera properly, in which case an object-lesson on the virtue of punctuality might be a good thing to administer. They, therefore, replied briefly that to wait in New York would entail needless expense, and so they had decided to go straight on to London, whither their husbands could follow later. This message appeared to act like the proverbial " last straw " upon men who proved to be more sinned against than sinning, and it brought forth a prompt response, to the effect that, instead of going on by sea, they would take train to New York, thereby reaching that city almost as soon as their wives.

This was accordingly done, and a few hours after their own arrival, the two ladies were startled by the apparition of a pair of unshaven, dusty objects, clad in grey flannel shirts and very inadequate suits of slops — they were both large men, and the average Mexican is small! Appropriate language in which to recount their wrongs frequently failed the travellers, but the gist of the story was as follows: Anxious not to run the slightest risk of missing the ship, they had arrived at Frontera after a long and arduous journey the day before she was expected, and settled themselves down there to wait, fortified through the long hot hours by visions of the delicious breeze there would be on deck, and of the delights of once more, clean and well-clad, sitting down to a comfortable meal. They had taken only old clothes with them to Chiapas, and these had been left at the mines; so that by the time they reached Frontera, they possessed literally only what they stood up in, and a sack of fern and orchid roots.

Still, had all gone well, that would not have mattered; but in an evil hour they went off to call on the Mexican agent of the American liner they were to meet. To their absolute horror, he told them that, this being the " norther " season, the ship would probably not call at the port this voyage, as, whenever there were any indications of one of these dangerous hurricanes blowing up, ships always kept well out to sea. He added that there was every sign of a " norther " coming on that night — indeed the approach of one had been telegraphed — and that therefore the expected vessel would steam straight out from Vera Cruz to Progreso. But he went on to say that if the two gentlemen started at once in one of his boats for Vera Cruz, they would probably be able to catch the liner before she left that port.

Now Jack knew perfectly that the first part of this story was true, and as to the indication of an impending " norther " he preferred to take the opinion of a native rather than his own; therefore in a very short time he and his friend were seated in one of the miserable tubs called boats in those parts, making the best of their way back to Vera Cruz. The weather kept perfectly clear all night, and as they sat bolt upright, enduring every species of discomfort, they were beginning to wish they had risked it and waited — when to their horror, about midway between Frontera and Vera Cruz, they made out their ship steaming gaily to the port they had left! It was impossible to make her see or to catch her up, and they saw too late that the agent had " sold " them for the sake of the $40 he received for their passage-money in his own boat! There was no redress, — nothing for it but to go on to Vera Cruz, as they sadly watched the ship containing all their clean shirts pass away out of sight! Even their thirst for the blood of that agent, though great, was not sufficient to take them voluntarily back to the place they had just quitted, although, had they then known that he intended to disclaim having ever seen them, when he was interrogated by their anxious wives, they might have sacrificed all things to embruing themselves in his gore! On reaching Vera Cruz, and receiving the reply to their cablegram, they went straight up to the city of Mexico, and after investing in ready-made clothes, which, if ugly, were at least clean, they embarked at once on the weary, dusty journey between Mexico and New York — arriving there a week later looking considerably the worse for wear. They were, besides, consumed with righteous indignation about the action of their wives, which had rendered this hurried pursuit necessary, if they wished to accompany them across the "pond." But their appearance, being chiefly a matter of clothes, was soon altered for the better, once they came into possession of their respective portmanteaux; and a few days more saw the reunited party, with their past woes softened by distance, and their misunderstandings cleared up, on an Atlantic liner bound for Liverpool.

Jack Jebb, with his family, took a house in London, intending to settle down there for the two years or so which he expected to elapse before his pecuniary affairs were in sufficient order to admit of his buying the long-wished-for steam-yacht, and beginning his wanderings afresh. But that elusive vessel soon proved to be as far off as ever; for whether it was the vengeance of the expatriated idol (who looked singularly out of place in a London drawing-room), or simply the evil star under whose influence he appeared to have been born, Jack's lifelong ill-luck still pursued him. The shares failed to keep their promises of speedy dividends; one or two small ventures of his own fell through; an expected legacy came to nothing; and the financial outlook grew to be as dreary as that into the London fog, with which he had been unfamiliar for many years. Had he been alone in the world all these things would have touched Mr Jebb but lightly, for with a gun and a few cartridges he could always provide himself with most of the necessaries of life, in the distant lands where he had spent so much of his lifetime. But now there were others dependent upon him, and for their sakes he grew depressed as he thought of the small return in kind that he had got out of an exceptionally hard-working career. He had, of course, never relied entirely upon what he could make, but, like most men who have lived much in the wilds, he knew no medium between "roughing it" in a way no English day-labourer would do, or, on the other hand, luxuriating in every product of an over-cultured age. He would live for months upon salt pork without a murmur, but when he had truffles he required them to be fresh. Altogether, it took but a few months of an English winter and a restricted income combined to make him feel like a caged animal, willing to sacrifice almost anything for the fresh breezes of the sierras. Therefore, when some new business offered, which, in spite of its being of a slightly visionary nature, promised, as usual, great things, he turned his back on London with much joy, and, together with his wife and the originator of the brilliant idea that was to make all their fortunes, he once more retraced his steps to the sunny land he had so lately left in order to "settle down."

After a short delay, first in New York and then in the city of Mexico, Jack, together with his captive inventor, went on to some rather inaccessible mines — for, of course, their business was connected with mining — where the former threw himself with increased energy into the work from the fact of his year's abstinence from the delights of monkey-poles and refractory ores. To his great surprise, however, he soon found that he had become physically incapable of supporting fatigues which hitherto he had taken as a matter of course. But he felt that this was his last chance — that everything depended upon this final throw of the die, and he would neither allow himself to complain or to shirk any particle of labour which might promote the success of the scheme. Consequently his ill symptoms increased as they were neglected, and when occasion arose for him to go back to Mexico to see about some consignments that had failed to arrive at the mines, it was with difficulty that he performed the intervening two days' journey on muleback.

The day after his arrival he consulted a doctor, expecting to be told merely that he had a worse attack of malaria than usual. But matters were far more serious. He was warned that he was suffering from a complication of diseases always difficult to deal with, but which the altitude of Mexico was speedily rendering absolutely dangerous, and it was added that if he valued his life he must journey to a lower level without delay. This advice was sufficiently startling to have sent most people helter-skelter out of the country. Not so Jack Jebb: having made up his mind that it was his duty to do all that lay in his power towards the satisfactory conclusion of the business in hand, no entreaties or persuasions could move him from the position he had taken up. The most that he would consent to do in his own physical interests was to spend a fortnight in the hot lands near sea-level, before returning to the mines. Probably he would not have conceded so much, had it not been that, at the same time, he could direct the making of some new implements required in the work. Another month was expected to decide the fate of the venture, and for that period he was resolved that no weakness should prevent his doing his share towards its success.

At the end of a fortnight passed under the shadow of the great white mountain of Orizaba, he had recovered enough strength to give rise to some' hope that the severity of the medical sentence had been exaggerated, and he went off to the mines once more, feeling better, and with a dogged determination to win the game. But in neither sense was he to do so; for this time he was fighting not only against his own persistent ill-luck, but against that powerful enemy who prevails always at the last.

The beginning of the end was that, to the surprise of every one concerned, when put to practical tests the great scheme collapsed utterly, giving no hope of better things without the expenditure of more time and money than Jack had left to bestow. So that it was with health and spirits brought down to a yet lower ebb than heretofore by the burden of a great disappointment, that he sadly said his last " Goodbye " to the country which for many years had been his home.

On the voyage to New York he grew gradually worse; but proceeding to spend a few days on Long Island with an old friend who was also an eminent medical man, he was there temporarily patched up for the further journey to England. His host owned a small yacht; and stretched full length on deck in the hot autumn weather, while faint breezes stirred the white sails as they moved lazily over the sleepy sea, Jack almost forgot in the content of the present the disappointment of the past and the uncertainties of the future. For to him it was yet uncertain — though his friends knew that the sword above his head must surely fall ere long; and feeling that it must be for the last time, it was with aching hearts that they sailed and sailed.

Well, at length he got back to the house in London, which he had left with such bright hopes, and soon he too knew that his work was done, and that there was nothing left to him but to wait. At the age of fifty, with the frame of an athlete, he was worn out by the privations and perils in which his life had been passed. For six weary months he endured, with never a murmur, a confinement which, to a man of his habits and still active mind, must have meant torture, and no Indian ever bore pain with a more silent fortitude, as day by day he drew nearer to the peace he longed for and the rest he had earned. When, on the 18th of March 1893, he breathed his last, besides those to whom his loss was irreparable, he left a void in many lives; for a nature so loyal, so rich in brave and generous instincts, in self-forgetfulness and truth, could not fail to make more than a passing impression upon all with whom it came into close contact.

Perhaps, from a material point of view, Jack Jebb's life was a failure, in that, having set himself to replace the fortune he had lost, he never succeeded in doing so. Still there are failures more noble than success; for there had been times in his checkered career when, by some slight advantage taken or some illegitimate power used, he might have won all his aims. But no mean thought ever touched him who, through all his years,

> " Bore without abuse
> The grand old name of gentleman."

THE END.

AN INLAND VOYAGE.

By ROBERT LOUIS STEVENSON.

With Frontispiece Illustration by Walter Crane.

16mo. Cloth. Price, $1.00. Paper covers, 50 cents.

"Since Robert Louis Stevenson wrote his delightful 'Travels with a Donkey in the Cevennes,' English and American readers have been waiting in anxious expectancy for some second work from his pen. That volume was so full of light and air, so utterly unconventional, and combined in so natural and charming a manner descriptions of strange people and strange scenes with bits of reflection and sentiment, that everybody read it with enjoyment and turned its last lea with regret. And now, in 'An Inland Voyage,' comes its fitting companion just as fresh and bright, and marked in even a higher degree by the same qualities which gave its predecessor so wide a popularity." — *Boston Transcript*

"The weary wight who would get to himself an hour of harmless pleasure cannot do better than to go on 'An Inland Voyage' with Robert Louis Stevenson The voyage is through the canals and rivers at the Netherlands, and is made in canoes. The chronicler of this pleasant journey tells the story of the expedition with exquisite grace and humor. The slightest detail affords matter for enticing comment. All the little adventures of ordinary travel are interpreted with the imagination of the artist. A bit of landscape or color is sketched in a sentence or two. And in all this is conveyed a graphic impression of the country and its inhabitants. One does not often meet with a book more thoroughly charming from the literary point of view, with such attractiveness and freshness of style, or with so piquant a flavor of individuality." — *Philadelphia Item.*

"He has an uncommonly vivid fancy, and the faculty of producing odd contrasts and securing striking effects by unexpected arrangements of familiar things. He is also a keen observer, and he has a piquant and vivid style. In this charming little volume he records a journey in a canoe through one of the oldest and most attractive portions of the continent, starting from Antwerp. The peculiarities of a very striking local life are reproduced by many quiet touches which leave a delightful impression of freshness upon the mind of the reader. Altogether this volume must be regarded as one of the most readable of the season." — *Christian Union.*

Sold by all Booksellers. Mailed, postpaid, by the publishers,

ROBERTS BROTHERS,

BOSTON, MASS.

POOR FOLK.

A Novel.

Translated from the Russian of FEDOR DOSTOIEVSKY, by LENA MILMAN, with decorative titlepage and a critical introduction by GEORGE MOORE. American Copyright edition.

16mo. Cloth. $1.00.

A capable critic writes : "One of the most beautiful, touching stories I have read. The character of the old clerk is a masterpiece, a kind of Russian Charles Lamb. He reminds me, too, of Anatole France's 'Sylvestre Bonnard,' but it is a more poignant, moving figure. How wonderfully, too, the sad little strokes of humor are blended into the pathos in his characterization, and how fascinating all the naïve self-revelations of his poverty become, — all his many ups and downs and hopes and fears. His unsuccessful visit to the money-lender, his despair at the office, unexpectedly ending in a sudden burst of good fortune, the final despairing cry of his love for Varvara, — these hold one breathless. One can hardly read them without tears. . . . But there is no need to say all that could be said about the book. It is enough to say that it is over powerful and beautiful."

We are glad to welcome a good translation of the Russian Dostoievsky's story "Poor Folk," Englished by Lena Milman. It is a tale of unrequited love, conducted in the form of letters written between a poor clerk and his girl cousin whom he devotedly loves, and who finally leaves him to marry a man not admirable in character who, the reader feels, will not make her happy. The pathos of the book centres in the clerk, Makar's, unselfish affection and his heart-break at being left lonesome by his charming kinswoman whose epistles have been his one solace. In the conductment of the story, realistic sketches of middle class Russian life are given, heightening the effect of the denoument. George Moore writes a sparkling introduction to the book. — *Hartford Courant.*

Dostoievsky is a great artist. "Poor Folk" is a great novel. — *Boston Advertiser.*

It is a most beautiful and touching story, and will linger in the mind long after the book is closed. The pathos is blended with touching bits of humor, that are even pathetic in themselves. — *Boston Times.*

Notwithstanding that "Poor Folk" is told in that most exasperating and entirely unreal style — by letters — it is complete in sequence, and the interest does not flag as the various phases in the sordid life of the two characters are developed. The theme is intensely pathetic and truly human, while its treatment is exceedingly artistic. The translator, Lena Milman, seems to have well preserved the spirit of the original — *Cambridge Tribune.*

ROBERTS BROTHERS, PUBLISHERS,
BOSTON, MASS.

KEYNOTES.

A Volume of Stories.

By George Egerton.   With titlepage by Aubrey Beardsley.   16mo.   Cloth.   Price, $1.00.

Not since "The Story of an African Farm" was written has any woman delivered herself of so strong, so forcible a book. — *Queen.*

Knotty questions in sex problems are dealt with in these brief sketches. They are treated boldly, fearlessly, perhaps we may say forcefully, with a deep plunge into the realities of life. The colors are laid in masses on the canvas, while passions, temperaments, and sudden, subtle analyses take form under the quick, sharp stroke. Though they contain a vein of coarseness and touch slightly upon tabooed subjects, they evidence power and thought. — *Public Opinion.*

Indeed, we do not hesitate to say that "Keynotes" is the strongest volume of short stories that the year has produced. Further, we would wager a good deal, were it necessary, that George Egerton is a nom-de-plume, and of a woman, too. Why is it that so many women hide beneath a man's name when they enter the field of authorship? And in this case it seems doubly foolish, the work is so intensely strong. . . .

The chief characters of these stories are women, and women drawn as only a woman can draw word-pictures of her own sex. The subtlety of analysis is wonderful, direct in its effectiveness, unerring in its truth, and stirring in its revealing power. Truly, no one but a woman could thus throw the light of revelation upon her own sex. Man does not understand woman as does the author of "Keynotes."

The vitality of the stories, too, is remarkable. Life, very real life, is pictured ; life full of joys and sorrows, happinesses and heartbreaks, courage and self-sacrifice ; of self-abnegation, of struggle, of victory. The characters are intense, yet not overdrawn ; the experiences are dramatic, in one sense or another, and yet are never hyper-emotional. And all is told with a power of concentration that is simply astonishing. A sentence does duty for a chapter, a paragraph for a picture of years of experience.

Indeed, for vigor, originality, forcefulness of expression, and completeness of character presentation, "Keynotes" surpasses any recent volume of short fiction that we can recall. — *Times*, Boston.

It brings a new quality and a striking new force into the literature of the hour. — *The Speaker.*

The mind that conceived "Keynotes" is so strong and original that one will look with deep interest for the successors of this first book, at once powerful and appealingly feminine. — *Irish Independent.*

Sold by all booksellers. Mailed, post-paid, on receipt of price by the Publishers,

ROBERTS BROTHERS, Boston, Mass.

THE KEYNOTE SERIES.

KEYNOTES. A Volume of Stories. By GEORGE EGERTON. With titlepage by AUBREY BEARDSLEY. 16mo. Cloth. Price, $1.00.

THE DANCING FAUN. A Novel. By FLORENCE FARR. With titlepage by AUBREY BEARDSLEY. American copyright edition. 16mo. Cloth. Price, $1.00.

POOR FOLK. A Novel. Translated from the Russian of FEDOR DOSTOIEVSKY. By LENA MILMAN. With a decorative titlepage and a critical introduction by GEORGE MOORE. 16mo. Cloth. Price, $1.00.

A CHILD OF THE AGE. A Novel. By FRANCIS ADAMS. With titlepage by AUBREY BEARDSLEY. 16mo. Cloth. Price. $1.00.

THE GREAT GOD PAN AND THE INMOST LIGHT. By ARTHUR MACHEN. 16mo. Cloth. Price, $1.00.

DISCORDS. A Volume of Stories. By GEORGE EGERTON. 16mo. Cloth. Price, $1.00.

PRINCE ZALESKI. By M. P. SHIEL. 16mo. Cloth. Price, $1.00.

THE WOMAN WHO DID. By GRANT ALLEN. 16mo. Cloth. Price, $1.00.

Sold by all Booksellers. Mailed, postpaid, on receipt of price, by the Publishers,

ROBERTS BROTHERS, BOSTON.

BOOKS OF TRAVEL.

"It is a very good office one man does another, when he tells him the manner of his being pleased." — SIR RICHARD STEELE.

THE SILVERADO SQUATTERS. By ROBERT LOUIS STEVENSON. With a frontispiece. 16mo. $1.00.

"The interest of the book centred in the graphic style and keen observation of the author. He has the power of describing places and characters with such vividness that you seem to have made personal acquaintance with both. . . . Mr. Stevenson's racy narrative brings many phases of life upon the western coast before one with striking power and captivating grace." — *N. Y. World.*

SINNERS AND SAINTS. A Tour across the States and around them, with Three Months among the Mormons. By PHIL. ROBINSON, author of "Under the Sun." 16mo. $1.50.

"Although he has won a reputation as a humorist, Mr. Robinson is one of the most faithful of descriptive writers, and his pictures of life in the United States, as seen through the eyes of the cosmopolitan Englishman, may be accepted as trustworthy and instructive. His humor is of the sort that never wearies, for it is never extravagant or forced."

OUR AUTUMN HOLIDAY ON FRENCH RIVERS. By J. L. MOLLOY. 16mo. $1.25.

"A quite fascinating book for idle summer days. Mr. Molloy has the true gift of narrating. He is a charming chronicler of the voyage of 'The Marie' on the tumultuous Seine, and on the solemn, mighty Loire." — *Advertiser.*

BITS OF TRAVEL. By H. H. Square 18mo. $1.25.

"This little book, by Mrs. Hunt, is a series of rare pictures of life in Germany, Italy, and Venice. Every one is in itself a gem." — *Boston Courier.*

BITS OF TRAVEL AT HOME. By H. H. A new enlarged edition. Square 18mo. $1.50.

"The descriptions of American scenery in this volume indicate the imagination of a poet, the eye of an acute observer of Nature, the hand of an artist, and the heart of a woman." — *N. Y. Tribune.*

A NILE JOURNAL. By THOMAS G. APPLETON. 12mo. $2.25.

"It gives a vivid photograph of that wonderful East for whose shores we all have a reverent longing." — *Phila. Ledger.*

Our publications are sold by all booksellers. Mailed, postpaid, on receipt of the advertised price.

ROBERTS BROTHERS, BOSTON.

BOOKS OF TRAVEL.

BOOKS OF TRAVEL.

"It is a very good office one man does another, when he tells him the manner of his being pleased." — SIR RICHARD STEELE.

LETTERS HOME. From Colorado, Utah, and California. By CAROLINE H. DALL. 12 mo. $1.50.

" There is a freshness about her Diary that is not often met with in books of this sort, and a happy regard for the minor details which give color and character to descriptions of strange life and scenery," says the N. Y. Tribune.

SEVEN SPANISH CITIES, and The Way to Them. By E. E. HALE. 16mo. $1.25.

" Mr. Hale makes Spain more attractive and more amusing than any other traveller has done." — *Boston Advertiser.*

GONE TO TEXAS ; or, The Wonderful Adventures of a Pullman. By E. E. HALE. 16mo. $1.00.

" There are few books of travel which combine, in a romance of true love, so many touches of the real life of many people, in glimpses of happy homes, in pictures of scenery and sunset, as the beautiful panorama unrolled before us from the windows of this Pullman car."

AN INLAND VOYAGE. By ROBERT LOUIS STEVENSON. 16mo. $1.00. Paper covers, 50 cents.

" Those who have read Mr. Stevenson's delightful ' Travels with a Donkey,' in which he told the story of a unique trip among the mountains of Southern France, will gladly welcome this bright account of a canoe voyage through the canals of Belgium, on the Sambre, and down the Oise. Unlike Captain Macgregor, of ' Rob Roy ' fame, Mr. Stevenson does not make canoeing itself his main theme, but delights in charming bits of description that, in their close attention to picturesque detail, remind one of the work of a skilled ' genre ' painter." — *Good Literature.*

TRAVELS WITH A DONKEY IN THE CÉVENNES By ROBERT LOUIS STEVENSON. With Frontispiece illustration by Walter Crane. 16mo. $1.00. Paper covers, 50 cents

" Charming, full of grace and humor and freshness, — such refined humor it is, too, and so evidently the work of a gentleman. What a happy knack he has of giving the taste of a landscape, or any out-door impression, in ten words ! "

Our publications are sold by all booksellers. Mailed, postpaid, on receipt of the advertised price.

ROBERTS BROTHERS, BOSTON.

TREASURE ISLAND:

A Story of the Spanish Main.

BY ROBERT LOUIS STEVENSON.

WITH ILLUSTRATIONS BY F. T. MERRILL.

16mo. Cloth, $1.00; paper covers, 50 cents.

"Buried treasure is one of the very foundations of romance. . . . This is the theory on which Mr. Stevenson has written 'Treasure Island.' Primarily it is a book for boys, with a boy-hero and a string of wonderful adventures. But it is a book for boys which will be delightful to all grown men who have the sentiment of treasure-hunting and are touched with the true spirit of the Spanish Main. Like all Mr Stevenson's good work, it is touched with genius. It is written — in that crisp, choice, nervous English of which he has the secret — with such a union of measure and force as to be in its way a masterpiece of narrative. It is rich in excellent characterization, in an abundant invention, in a certain grim romance, in a vein of what must, for want of a better word, be described as melodrama, which is both thrilling and peculiar. It is the work of one who knows all there is to be known about 'Robinson Crusoe,' and to whom Dumas is something more than a great *amuseur;* and it is in some ways the best thing he has produced." — *London Saturday Review.*

"His story is skilfully constructed, and related with untiring vivacity and genuine dramatic power. It is calculated to fascinate the old boy as well as the young, the reader of Smollett and Dr. Moore and Marryatt as well as the admirer of the dexterous ingenuity of Poe. It deals with a mysterious island, a buried treasure, the bold buccaneer, and all the stirring incidents of a merry life on the Main. . . We can only add that we shall be surprised if 'Treasure Island' does not satisfy the most exacting lover of perilous adventures and thrilling situations." — *London Academy.*

"Any one who has read 'The New Arabian Nights' will recognize at once Mr. Stevenson's qualifications for telling a good buccaneer story. Mr. Stevenson's genius is not wholly unlike that of Poe, but it is Poe strongly impregnated with Marryatt. Yet we doubt if either of those writers ever succeeded in making a reader identify himself with the supposed narrator of a story, as he cannot fail to do in the present case. As we follow the narrative of the boy Jim Hawkins we hold our breath in his dangers, and breathe again at his escapes." — *London Athenæum.*

Sold by all Booksellers. Mailed, postpaid, by the publishers,

ROBERTS BROTHERS,

BOSTON, MASS.

TRAVELS WITH A DONKEY
IN THE CÉVENNES.

By ROBERT LOUIS STEVENSON.

With Frontispiece Illustration by WALTER CRANE. 16mo.
Paper covers, 50 cents; cloth, $1.00.

"This is one of the brightest books of travel that has recently come to our notice. The author, Robert Louis Stevenson, sees every thing with the eye of a philosopher, and is disposed to see the bright rather than the dark side of what passes under his observation. He has a steady flow of humor that is as apparrently spontaneous as a mountain brook, and he views a landscape or a human figure, not only as a tourist seeking subjects for a book, but as an artist to whom the slightest line or tint conveys a definite impression." — *Boston Courier*.

"A very agreeable companion for a summer excursion is brought to our side without ceremony in this lively reprint of a journal of travel in the interior of France. For all locomotive or four-horse stage coach, the writer had chartered a little she-ass, not much bigger than a dog, whom he christened 'Modestine,' and whose fascinating qualities soon proved that she was every way worthy of the name. Mounted on this virtuous beast, with an inordinate supply of luggage slung over her patient back in a sheepskin bag, the larder well provided with cakes of chocolate and tins of Bologna sausage, cold mutton and the potent wine of Beaujolais, the light-hearted traveller took his way to the mountains of Southern France. He has no more story to tell than had the 'weary knife-grinder,' but he jots down the little odds and ends of his journey in an off-hand, garrulous tone which sounds as pleasantly as the careless talk of a cheerful companion in a country ramble. The reader must not look for nuggets of gold in these slight pages, but the sparkling sands which they shape into bright forms are both attractive and amusing." — *N. Y. Tribune*.

"'Travels with a Donkey' is charming, full of grace, and humor, and freshness: such refined humor it all is, too, and so evidently the work of a gentleman. I am half in love with him, and much inclined to think that a ramble anywhere with such a companion must be worth taking. What a happy knack he has of giving the taste of a landscape or any out-door impression in ten words!"

Sold by all Booksellers. Mailed, postpaid, by the Publishers,

ROBERTS BROTHERS, BOSTON.